LEE
R. N. ARCADIA

ISBN: 979-8-9999849-2-0 (Paperback)

First Edition.

Published by Obsidian Odyssey

Cover and Formatting: Colby Bettley at 3Crows Author Services.

Editing and Proofreading: Amy and E.M. Lee

Beta Readers: Chloe, Adriana, Ashley, Jo, & Amy

Printed in the United States of America.

For those who like taboo and dark, this one is for you.
Always remember that your trauma doesn't own you.
You own you.

Author Note

Hello *Preylings!*

A few things first.

This is a standalone. A project carefully crafted from my love of Edgar Allan Poe, the daddy of spook; one of the originals, anyway. The characters, places, and references are symbolic with their names and anagrams in relation to Poe. I wanted to switch it up, *like always.*

In this book, there's a combination of themes from various E.A.P.'s works. (ˉ ω ˉ)

As homage to the man himself, "Lee" is twisted and uncomfy in the trauma and situations. There are taboo themes that are listed below. *Feel free to skip if you don't want any spoilers.*

18+ due to the mature and dark content this book contains.

Content within the pages ahead: Death of family members, death of parents (off-page, flashbacks, and mentioned), SA (flashbacks), suicide (mentioned/remembered), suicidal ideation, murder, potentially disturbing scenes with dead bodies in relation to funeral directing/death, voyeurism, breeding, exhibitionism, multiple sex partners of multiple genders, stalking, obsession, familial abuse, torture, struggles with mental health, amnesia, panic attacks/anxiety, depression, death aftermath, sibling sexual relations/incest (off page, on page, flashbacks, and mentioned, sometimes unknowingly).

If I forgot any content themes, it was not my intention. Please read with caution.

There aren't many in the pages ahead, but all *the 'quotes in here'* are quotes from Edgar Allan Poe himself, to whom this story is inspired. *'It was now midnight, and my task was drawing to a close.'*

"They who dream by day are cognizant of many
things which escape those who dream only by night. In
their gray visions they obtain glimpses of eternity, and
thrill, in awakening, to find that they have been upon
the verge of the great secret. In snatches, they learn
something of the wisdom which is of good, and more
of the mere knowledge which is of evil."

—EDGAR ALLAN POE

*In the night they come,
With all dark things undone.*

*There are things I wish not to be true,
Lost because of you.*

*My memories were abandoned to time,
With feet lost wandering, wondering what is,
Mine, mine, mine.*

*Can you see your reflection?
The face which breaks,
From me, all you do is take and take.*

*Lies and death,
I will leave until my last breath.*

*Damned until the end,
There is nothing to amend.*

*Can you see our reflections?
It isn't me.
Familial love isn't protection,
It's an infection.*

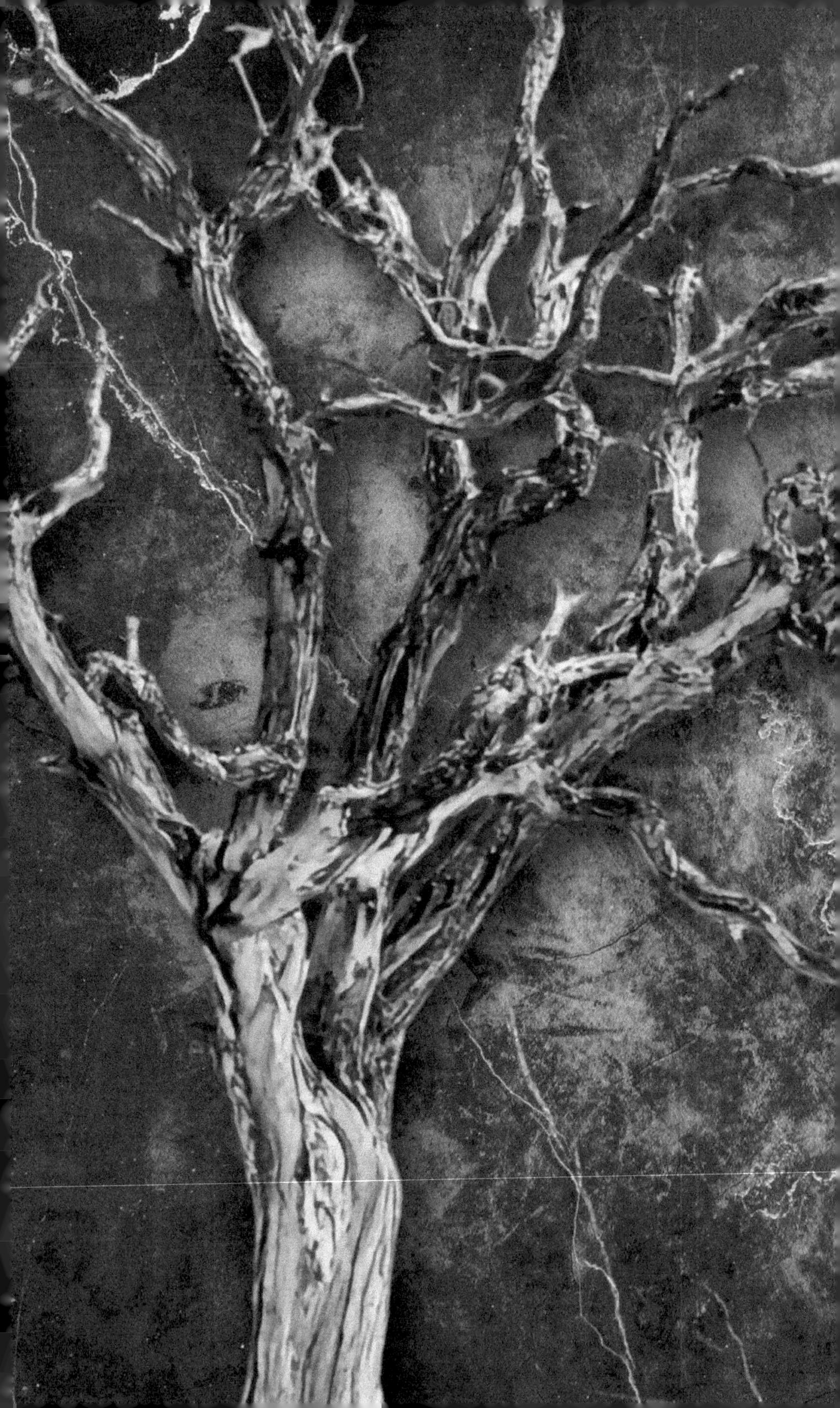

All that's left of me now,
Drifting and asking how.
Your dreams I leave behind,
For they are not mine.

This is me.
The foundation of what will no longer be.
For the crack in the family tree,
Leads to the fall of the House of Lee.

E.G. Poa

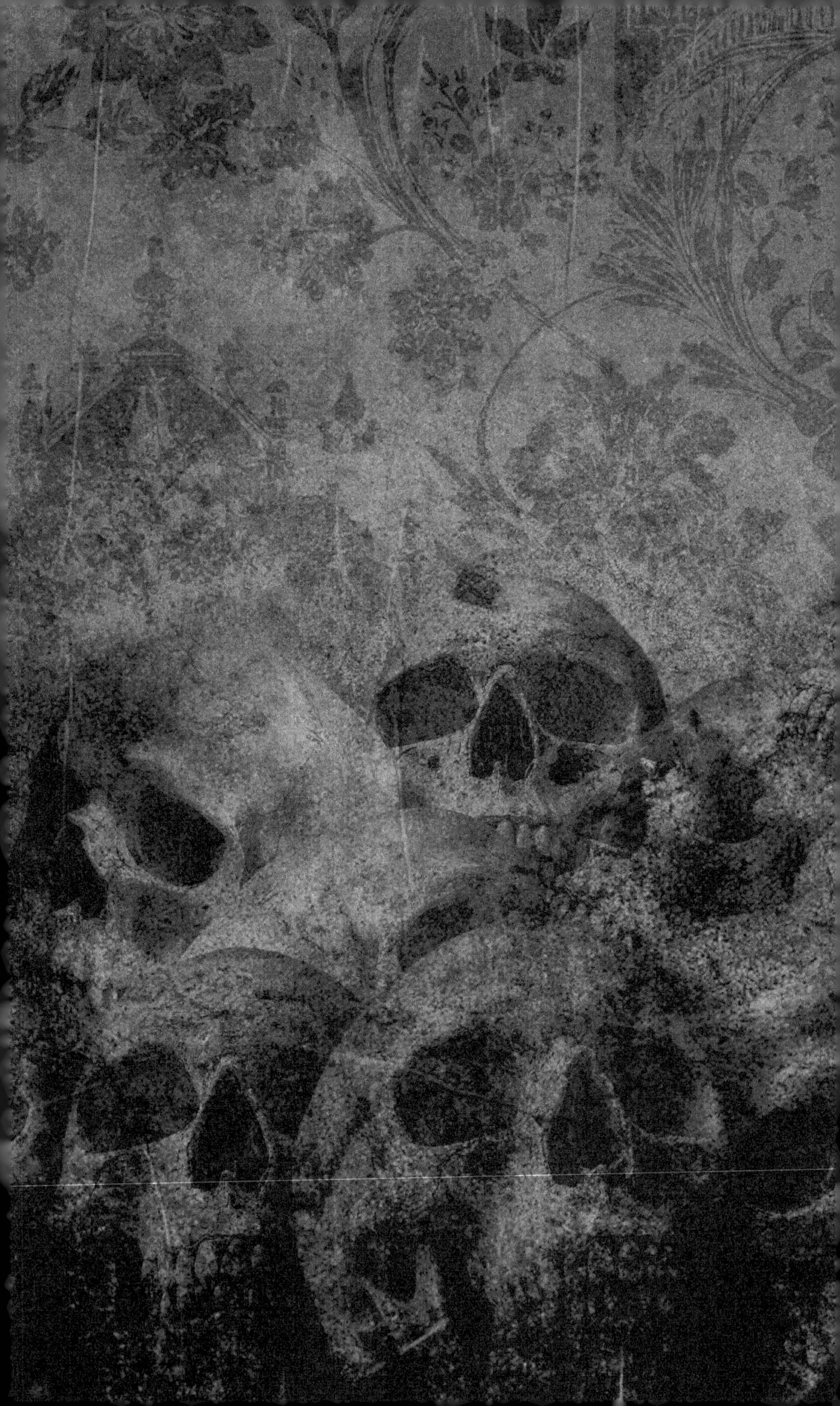

PART ONE

THE END

The wind tugged at my back, as if to tell me, *"Don't do it."*

Threatening clouds swirled above, and I dared to peek over the cliff's edge.

It's so far down.

"I'll die," I whispered in knowing, but the presence at my back loomed. A reminder of who would always be waiting in the dark.

All the memories and problems that led me to that point lingered there with me.

If only I hadn't been born, I wouldn't have to endure.

I should have died in my mother's womb.

My family had fallen.

A suicide, a murder—amongst the other skeletons on my family's tree littered our closets; so much so, that we were entombed in our mausoleum of a house.

There were experiences that no child should have gone through. Yet, there I was, another body in the grand scheme of time, although my body didn't feel like mine anymore.

I'm still a child.

My eyes filled, as so many emotions swirled. Regret,

sadness, shame, and isolation. Death awaited me down in the waters below.

The dark was all I knew; all I'd *ever* known.

It didn't matter if it came from my family or the person at my back. The one who spent every waking moment making sure I was tormented and possessed.

"I don't want to do this," my lip quivered. My throat felt as if it would close up at any moment.

For a slight pause, there was silence, and all the comfort I had was in the caress of the wind, blowing my white dress around.

"You refused *our* legacy. We cannot coexist, so I'll erase *you.*"

I released a cracked cry, begging, *"Please."*

"You don't love me. Not as you're supposed to."

"But it's wrong!" I half-turned to the side in protest, but it was of no use. I was trapped in an unforgiving embrace.

An arm wrapped tighter around my stomach, and before I knew it, my head was forced forward. A cheek rested against mine.

All that existed before me was the endless sea beyond.

"It's too late. You've disappointed me for the *last* time."

"I didn't mean to—," I began. A single finger was held to my lips to silence me.

"The time has ended for your excuses."

Wracked in sobs, unsteady tremors traveled throughout my body.

"Step forward before I make you."

Protesting, I shook my head as I tried to grab onto the hand that held me tight.

The edge gradually came closer to the tips of my toes.

My end.

But first, one last promise seeped from their lips.

"I found you in this life, and I will find you in the next. You will never escape me. This is the only way. Whether you believe it or not, I

I didn't want my last words to be a lie.

"I thought not," he sneered.

With my vision clouded, I'm unsure of the next few seconds.

Except for the free-falling. The weightlessness of being airborne as wind rushed past me.

That was all I remembered.

Did I truly fall, or was I pushed?

I suppose it didn't matter in the end, because I crashed into the sea, and it consumed me.

CHAPTER 1

"WHO IS ANABEL LEE?"

There's a haziness when my eyes flutter open, as I try to adjust to the light. Coming to my senses, *back to life*, it feels like awakening from a dream. Am I even real?

Once my eyes adjust, I notice the window with an endless supply of trees. I wiggle my limbs and find in horror that my arms are strapped to the chair beneath me.

Wide-eyed, I stare down at myself to find I'm clothed in only a hospital gown. Clenching my jaw between shuttered breaths, I try to ignore the fear coiling up my spine like a serpent rearing to strike at any moment.

From my periphery, I notice a weathered couch on my right. The ivory leather is riddled with cracks and ripples. On my left, a white oak coffee table remains chipped and barren. Even the walls holding me hostage are blinding white against scorching red fear building behind my eyes. I'm on an upper level in whatever place I'm in.

While attempting to force my mind and body into a state of cohesion, my sole attention quickly turns to the white bracelet fastened around my wrist. It's black letting, a slew of information, but only one piece stands out at the moment. My name.

Anabel Lee.

"Where am I?" I rasp aloud, not knowing, well, *anything.* My throat is beyond dry, and my head throbs. The overwhelming lack of color, swallowing the room, has my eyes burning, blinking rapidly for a taste of relief.

With the need to find a strand of hope, I glance down at the bracelet once again.

At least I know my name.

I lean my head back as far as I can manage, trying to get a glimpse of absolutely anything that could offer more answers than questions. But as I strain my neck to its limit, dizziness takes over, rendering my efforts futile.

Adjusting my position once again, the room spins as my body figures itself out. My stomach is heavily laden with nausea, as a groan slips from my parched lips. I squeeze my eyes shut, but not even the black I find with them closed can blind the sickness that holds my body hostage.

Time drags, though I have no way of knowing how long, until finally the dizzy spell passes.

Slicing through the stale silence of the room, a gentle knock echoes from behind me.

"Good morning," an unfamiliar voice hums, accompanied by the creak of a door's hinges and the pattering of footsteps.

I angle my head to the side, but all I can see is the fucking table. The person behind me releases a sudden gasp, which is followed by an urgent shout. "Quick, get a nurse!"

Somehow, I'm even more confused than I was when I woke up. I try blinking my eyes a few more times, willing myself to wake up from this bizarre dream. Instead of opening my eyes to a scene that makes sense to me, I find a middle-aged male staring back at me. His white coat churns my stomach yet again. Shining a light into my already sensitive eyes, the man peers down at me in shock.

"Well, I'll be damned," he says when a nurse scrambles in with a cart of medical supplies and equipment. There's a short pause before the male continues, "Check her vitals for me, please."

I hear shuffling, along with a rushed, "Yes, sir."

As the nurse pokes and prods, the doctor leans in closer, "Anabel, can you hear me?"

I nod my head slightly, willing my nerves to steady and nausea to dissipate.

Even if I were clear-headed enough to answer the man's weird questions, I wouldn't be able to. Right now, my mouth is too dry to even consider speaking.

"Good. Do you know where you are, or how you got here?"

I shake my head, *no*.

"Hmm." The man studies me further, as if I'm a strange test subject he can't wait to dissect.

The nurse wanders to the other side of me, a female in— you guessed it—*white* scrubs. Of-fucking-course.

"Nurse Marigold is going to check your blood pressure and then draw blood for a full work-up," he says, his voice too technical to be caring.

I watch as the lady puts a cuff around my upper arm. "This may feel a little tight," she informs me, "but I promise it will be over before you know it!" She pulls at some sort of medical device draped behind her neck and down her shoulders. It must be a listening device, because she places two connecting pieces of the cord against her ears. A shiver runs down the length of my arm as the final piece—a cold metal of sorts—is placed on my skin, directly below the cuff. After a click, the cuff begins to tighten. I wince, bracing for discomfort to morph into pain, but luckily it passes instead. While I watch her, I notice a strange mark on my wrist. Nausea forgotten, I begin to wonder.

What the hell kind of scar is that?

It has jagged, uneven lines, and echoes of an event I can't recall. Although it's mostly blended into my skin, the longer I stare, the clearer it gets. My eyes drag to my other wrist, where I find more of the same.

How the hell did I get these?

"Anabel," I hear, pulling my focus away from my marks.

I blink, looking up at the first man; the one in the white coat. There's a name tag I didn't notice before. It reads: *Dr. Lipton.*

"Let's take things slowly. That okay, Ms. Lee?"

Shaking off the eerie feeling of my name—one I don't even remember, I force myself to speak. At first, not a single word comes out. I make every effort to coat my throat with what little saliva I can before trying once more. This time, a raspy voice creaks out, "Can you tell me what's going on, please?"

He slouches in relief. Of what? I'm unsure. "Oh, Ms. Lee, you must be parched," he hushes me. "I'll get you some water."

He begins to leave but looks over his shoulder with a puzzled look. "Are you sure you don't remember anything?"

I shake my head again, wishing I had more information to give him. Honestly, I wish I had more info for my own damnself. Yet, here I am with nothing but a name. With a perplexed look, he shrugs, leaving the room to likely—hopefully—grab water, while the nurse draws my blood.

"Your blood pressure is slightly high. Nothing to be too concerned by, but try to take a few deep breaths for me," she says gently in a soothing voice. "That's it, sweetie. Now you're going to feel a little pinch, but it will be over before you know it."

Every muscle tenses as she rests the needle against a highway of blue lines clearly visible beneath my pale skin. "One more deep breath," she coaxes before pressing in. Just as she said I would, I feel a quick pinch and watch in sick fascination as my blood flows through clear tubing and into an attached container. A container labeled: A. Lee.

Dr. Lipton returns with a decanter and a cup for me, just as the nurse sets a bandage in place. The condensation has my mouth watering.

Finally, he hands me a full cup and I guzzle it down, nearly choking in the process.

"Easy. You've been through quite the ordeal." He refills the cup, and I reluctantly drink it more slowly this time.

"Let's start with a summary of why you are here," he pauses to gauge my response. I nod for him to continue. "There was an accident. You sustained a brain injury, causing your brain to swell, and it took you a long time to recover. You are in this facility because you fell into a comatose state from the injury. It appears you may be experiencing some amnesia."

"Amnesia?" I ask.

"Memory loss."

Staring at nothing in particular, I try to take in his words.

"An accident?"

He inclines his head to my question.

"The exact reasoning isn't important at this stage of recovery. Even though you're healing physically, parts of you may feel lost to time. And perhaps you'll get back your memories, but for now, it's a miracle you're even responding. When you finally came out of the coma, you were catatonic. It's been a year since you woke up, and not a word was spoken until today. For your safety, you were restrained due to frequent outbursts."

At least that explains the restraints. My wrist scars probably came from whatever *accident* I experienced.

"How old am I anyway?"

He glances out the window, as if he's searching for the unknown amidst the trees. "You'll be seventeen in a few months."

"Okay… What season is it?" I ask, taking his words as truth.

I am lost to time. My whole life is nothing but blankness. Not sure if it's a good or bad thing.

"It's currently Fall," he says, then asks more basic questions to determine where my mind is, apparently. I'd like to know that myself.

The arm restraints are removed as he finishes up. Nurse Marigold helps me shuffle from the chair to the hospital bed. My legs seem to forget how to work properly, and I start to fall. Luckily, the doctor finds my side in time and helps me the rest of the way.

Once I sink into the lumpy mattress, I barely notice Dr. Lipton is still standing by my side. I'm spent. My mind is completely blank.

"We'll have to do some more tests later, but the good news is that you're awake *and* aware."

I give him a slight nod, failing to keep my eyes open. "What happens after this?" I ask, sounding so small, weak.

"We do rehabilitation and therapy. Your speech doesn't seem to be affected, which is good, but we'll have to investigate to see if there are any other areas for concern."

"And after that? Do I have somewhere to go?"

Who is Anabel Lee?

Does she even have a place to call home?

He forces back an obvious grimace. With a much softer tone, he reluctantly replies, "I'm sorry, but after you are cleared from this facility, you'll be sent to a children's home. Unfortunately, we have no choice. When you come of age, that changes. Then, the world is your oyster—or so they say anyway. But for now…"

Dr. Lipton offers a smile, trying to ease the harsh reality that I have no home or family.

I'm alone.

Yet strangely, I don't feel so alone. It feels safe in the bed with the nurse and doctor taking care of me. I didn't have to think or know things—*yet*.

"Thank you," I tell them both as they smile politely and leave.

The light outside is fading to gray, and I seem to have regained a small bout of energy. I feel as if I have been awake and busy for a long time, so I settle in for a dreamless sleep.

If my healing, blank-slated mind could dream, what would I see? Would I even want such memories that should remain forgotten?

The past may be blank, but the future holds endless possibilities.

Just who will I become?

CHAPTER 2

"IT'S ME AND THE TREES"

ANA — *AGE 17*

I celebrate my seventeenth birthday in the facility. Nurse Marigold is kind enough to bring me a chocolate cupcake with a candle.

"Make a wish!"

I consider my options for a moment before I blow out the candle.

Let me remember.

A wish that fills my entire being, consuming my mind. Entangled in the breath I force from my lungs, it snuffs the flame yet lingers in the air. Time stalls. The noise around me becomes muffled into silence before a dull ringing takes over. Suddenly, for the first time, I feel as if something is *wrong*. I have no idea *what*, but I get the sense of dread.

Before I'm able to process the moment, time itself freezes. I see something. A flash so quick I almost miss it. Someone. Me?

It *is* me. At least a slightly aged ghost of who I am. My figure has her gaze fixed on the edge of the cliff.

Why am I seeing myself?

Remembering a grounding exercise I was taught in my one-of-many therapy sessions, I count my deep, steady breaths.

When the ringing fades, along with the vision, I open my eyes. Time returns as if it never left, along with praise and cheers from the nursing staff at the entrance of my room. Even Dr. Lipton appears joyful, a rare grin across his face.

Where did the previous terror come from? And where did it go?

Trying to ignore what I don't understand, I take the candle out and dig in. Rich chocolate fills me with warmth, as I sigh in delight.

A few more birthday wishes are exchanged before I find solitude in my room once again. Although I'm considered alone to others, I don't feel that way. I don't feel much of anything.

I wander over to the familiar window that's become my safe viewing point.

Everything else fades. It's just me and the trees.

The fall foliage creates something beautiful and hopeful.

The past few months leading up to this day droned on with therapy after therapy. *And then more therapy.* Plus endless tests. I couldn't be released until I received a clean bill of health.

Housing arrangements were made, according to Dr. Lipton. In a few days, I'll be shipped off to my new home until I turn eighteen.

A lot can happen in a year.

My mind drifts away, thinking back to the image of me on the cliff. Was that how I came to be this shell I am today? Or maybe it's a convoluted future of some sort?

I'm missing a part of myself, and therapy can't fix that. It can heal my mind and process this *new* life, but nothing can be done about the past until I remember something.

What will I uncover if I do discover my lost memories? Do I even want to know?

The truth can't be good if it resulted in my abandonment. My isolation.

I stare into the forest beyond the window from my top-floor room. I still have yet to step outside since waking up. Any time I considered venturing outside, it felt too open and vulnerable. I couldn't explain *why,* but it was unnerving enough to keep myself safe behind glass—*my familiar sanctuary.*

With a new home in my near future, I'll have to push through this uncomfortable feeling of being outdoors.

Leaning my head against the glass, my breath fogs the windows as I trace abstract shapes with my finger.

The future holds so much uncertainty, but so does the past. My mind is a void of its own. Surely, my brain is protecting me from something. The least I can do is keep my mind open and clear, regardless of how fate led me to this point.

Memories from before don't have to necessarily matter to me now. The fact is: I have no real home or family to return to.

I'm alive; *I'm here.*

For whatever reason, I survived, and I will continue to do so.

Another year lies ahead of me. Then, I'll see where my feet carry my heavily laden spirit.

So many endless possibilities, and that's the beauty of it, isn't it?

The mysteries of life; the unknown. It has a sense of ambience if the nervousness of it all can be bypassed.

I can figure out who I want to be and where to go.

It's my freedom, and what I need—I can't explain how I know, but I certainly *feel* awaiting freedom down to my bones.

My only hope is that this new place will be better than wherever I came from.

CHAPTER 3

"THE DOMAIN OF ARNHEIM"

ANA

The Domain of Arnheim. My home and place of learning for the next year. Standing outside the strange-looking structure, there's a sense of unease, as with all new beginnings, I suppose.

Yet, the building's unique architecture has piqued my curiosity. Gazing at the monolith in front of me, I find myself engrossed in the artfully done structure. I'm fascinated by the towering walls and arched roofs. The ethereal statues are placed symmetrically throughout the property. The pale-stoned exterior gave way to the dark contrast, revealing how it withstood time and weather. Centuries, at least, I suspect.

Two women in stark black stand at the oversized wooden doors adorned with giant, angel-shaped iron knockers.

Is this a place of worship?

I step forward, holding nothing, as I own nothing.

The woman on the right is wearing a thick, ivory fur coat, looking more authoritative—is one way to put it, with how upturned her nose is.

At her left, a lady smiles warmly. "You must be Anabel. Welcome to Arnheim! This is our headmistress, *Lenore.*"

I nod my head in acknowledgment and offer an uneasy smile. Lenore's dark eyes take me in, though she remains silent. A woman of fewer words, perhaps. The friendly lady to Lenore's left continues, clearing her throat, "I am Helen, and I'll be showing you around today."

I move up the steps until Lenore steps in front of me. Her face is so passive, I can't tell if she's cruel or if her face is simply reflecting an unpleasantness within.

"Clothes are provided for you," she says flatly. "If the measurements are off, please refer to Helen."

Nodding once more, I feel my pulse give rise to worry.

Does this woman not like children? Not like *me?*

After giving me a last once-over, Lenore turns abruptly to leave. "Welcome to Arnheim," she calls over her shoulder; the greeting is nowhere near as welcoming as Helen's.

I make my way slowly toward Helen while Lenore disappears around the building.

"Don't mind the headmistress. She's like that with everyone and hardly smiles either. Don't take it personally."

Saying nothing in return, I follow her through the heavy doors down a long-vaulted hallway.

"The campus is relatively simple; on the left side are the girls' dormitories," she indicates as we move further, walking past hallways and a large, scenic courtyard in the middle. There are blossoming trees and similar weathered statues. A stone pathway curves from two entry points closest to where Helen and I stood. "The right side is for all the boys. Straight ahead are the classrooms, library, study area, gardens, and the dining hall."

We pause at the edge of the courtyard on the stone pathway. Taking it all in, I appreciate the scenery and the fact that the tree in the corner looks like a good place to read a book.

There are also a couple of children wearing black, chatting in the far distance near another angel statue.

There are no doors anywhere, except down the hallways. I find the openness interesting, yet charming all the same. The building is open and in harmony with nature, especially the open courtyard, which is somehow more appealing than venturing into a forest.

"Let me show you to your room and let you settle in. I am aware you don't have many, if any, belongings; so, I left you with some things I think you'll find useful for your stay here—hope that's alright."

Unsure what things she's talking about, I still offer her a warmer smile than earlier, as a sign of thanks. I relax my shoulders more and trail slightly behind Helen.

Thankfully, she's comfortable with doing the talking as we backtrack toward the front entry.

"It gets busier here during the late summer through the following spring. Since you're here in March, we'll need to assess your educational skills to determine where to place you for the upcoming fall. The time between now and this summer will be used to try to catch you up to your required age level, but first, you'll have a week to settle into your new home. So, no rush."

I say nothing as she pauses two hallways down from the front entry, before continuing left. "There are a few other children here of various ages. We serve those without homes or who are more troubled than others. For behavioral issues, when all other schools fail, we do not."

I definitely don't want to know what that means.

She leads me to the end of the long corridor, humming unknown tunes.

"Outside of classes," she starts after a few moments of silence, "you have free rein. If you require anything, I'm easy to find, but you may also ask any of the staff. Some may appear intimidating, but they're here to help."

Stopping at the end of the hallway, she gestures to the left-hand door. "This room is yours."

She opens the singular wooden door, revealing a massive room—fit for someone who isn't *homeless.* My mouth falls as I take in the four-poster bed, vanity, and dresser near it. A door off to the side leads to a bathroom. There's a lounging area with two dark brown sofas and a table with a fireplace. A shelf stands in the corner with a study desk next to it. Two towering windows are on two of the walls, one near the bed and one by the lounging area near the fireplace.

Helen catches me looking around in wonder, "Impressive, isn't it?"

I catch her friendly demeanor and nod in agreement.

"I hope you warm up to the place and the people you meet. It's lovely to have you. You missed breakfast, which is at eight in the morning. Lunch is served between twelve and one, while dinner is at five-thirty in the evening. I will let you settle in."

She strides towards the door, pausing at the entry.

"Before I forget, there's a strict rule of no boys in the girls' dormitories. Same for girls in their rooms. If you're caught, there are punishments in place. You can be friendly or romantic, but this isn't the place for love. Love in youth never lasts, but you seem quiet and withdrawn anyway. Your next year should be quick enough if you focus on your studies and work hard."

I meet her gaze and take a deep breath. "Thank you," is all I manage to get out.

Love is not something I intend for. For how could anyone love an empty vessel?

Helen relaxes visibly. "You are welcome, my dear. Take in the sights and get used to the surroundings for the next week. I can tell that you'll be just fine here, Anabel."

She leaves without another word, closing the door behind her.

Although it's late morning, exhaustion is hitting me.

All the furniture is ebony, except the bed, which is covered in deep maroon blankets. I smooth my hands over the abstract pattern on the spread as I sink onto the edge of the mattress. The ceiling seems to stretch even higher as I flop backward. It isn't long before my mind empties, and I drift off.

It's dark when I wake abruptly to a knock at the door. Rubbing my eyes, I answer it to find Helen with a plate of food.

"Just waking up? You must've been tired from your journey. Here, let me help. I'll show you how to set the fire and light the candlesticks, since it gets drafty in the building at night."

In my sleepy state, I miss how much brighter the room becomes as she moves past me, setting the tray of food on the table and lighting the sconces on the wall that I failed to notice earlier.

"Just so you know, matches are brought daily, and there's always wood provided from the housing staff. There's a poker and an igniter here for you. If you ever need help, ask away. We replenish supplies, but we don't do *everything;* only the necessities. Makes sense, right?"

"Yes," I manage to say, yawning.

She ignites the fireplace, and a steady flame begins as I sit on the sofa.

"There's no electricity in the dormitories, but there is in the rest of the building. Can't let the books and supplies catch fire, now, can we?" She chuckles to herself at her own joke, but I'm not awake enough to make sense of *anything.*

"Anyway, I wanted to make sure you were fed before the

kitchens closed. After you finish, just leave it outside your door, and someone will get it later. Enjoy!"

I begin to wonder if she's more animated in the evening than in the morning, as she shuts the door behind her.

Sighing, I look at the tray, lifting each lid to reveal all the food groups. A small chocolate dessert—*which will be my favorite*—chicken, potatoes, green vegetables, and a roll. There's also a decanter filled with water and a glass.

My rumbling stomach answers to the sight of the feast in front of me as I breathe in the smell of such delicacies. As someone without much, I'm grateful for what I have in front of me.

It doesn't take me long to finish my food, plus the water, and crawl under the covers to sleep, not caring to change clothes.

I may have slept all afternoon, but I'm still exhausted. Going outside of my new room isn't in the cards for me today—maybe tomorrow...*or the day after.*

CHAPTER 4

"SMALL STEPS ARE MY ONLY STEPS"

ANA

I spend most of the first week in my room, minus dinnertime. Initially, just finding the kitchen and dining hall was nearly too much for me; so, instead of exploring the place, I went to bed immediately after eating.

Helen didn't give me the full tour, only the need-to-know places. At least it was easy enough to find the library. I didn't talk to anyone, and just as I preferred, no one bothered with me either—not that I have much to say anyway. Even if I did, there aren't a lot of children in Arnheim, mostly just staff.

Apparently, I'm in a depression; hence, my sleep-only schedule. Maybe my mind can't process all that's going on. The big life changes are just too much for me to handle—*I'm still uncertain about that.*

Not until the weekend do I even dare to go into my drawers, bathe, or venture outside.

God, help me.

I wander to the library for an easy read before venturing to the courtyard for that spot under the tree to sit. The sun is out—a cure for my depression, perhaps.

There are a couple of children around my age on the opposite side of the courtyard, reading against the large angel statue under the shade of another lone tree. The children look serene as their eyes are glued to the pages in their hands. I don't look at them directly, and thankfully, no one disturbs me as I open the book I borrowed. It was located on a shelf of recommended fiction, so I swiped it at random. A book is just the distraction I need from whatever my life is.

The doctors have said my brain is *fine* in a technical sense. I can understand language, read, and write. My senses are still intact, yet all that's missing are my memories.

I'm not too worried about those yet.

To my surprise, I'm able to get lost in the fantasy book until I hear the dinner bell. Marking my page with a random wildflower, I leave my cozy spot and head to the dining hall. I wonder what's for dinner as I browse, picking up some chicken and green beans with a roll and corn.

While I sit off by myself and eat, a slow smile creeps upon my face at the realization that I spent hours outside *in the sun.*

I haven't gone outside willingly in months. Small steps are my only steps, and that's okay. More than okay. Feeling proud of myself, I finish dinner and dare to fall into a routine of reading in the courtyard again the following day, and until my summer catch-up classes begin.

The first week of catch-up classes involves me simply adjusting.

The second week comes around, and so does the studying and homework.

I have four professors.

An older man who looks like Einstein teaches math and

science. Then there's a middle-aged lady with blonde hair who teaches history and language. Her glasses overtake her face, and when she faces me head-on, she looks like a bug magnified. Strangely, the young woman who teaches *arts and hobbies* looks the most normal, wearing all black with long brown hair. *An odd thing to be required for a class, but whatever.* The final professor is a middle-aged male who teaches life skills. He looks like he's seen some things in life with the wisdom he speaks. Well, until I find out the truth of it. I quickly realize that the life skills class is aimed toward the female gender. At least there are a couple of varying students in each class, so I don't have to suffer alone.

Everything goes by in a blur because of my busy schedule.

Wake up. Eat. Class. Class. Lunch. Study. Class. Class. Dinner. Sleep.

Rinse and repeat.

The days I look forward to are Sundays, since those are free days. Saturdays are half days for students struggling in certain areas. Unfortunately for me, mine is math.

My first month came and went without a hitch, a mundane routine. Once I pass math, my Saturdays are free. The month of May flies by, and it's finally summer.

Thank goodness!

It's my last year until the rest of my life officially begins, and into the real world I go.

The thought of that is unnerving, as I try to find a way for myself without memories from before. At least I have school to keep my mind distracted.

The break between summer and the fall school year can't come fast enough.

It's during the last month of summer catch-up classes that someone new enters.

A dark, quiet storm rolls through Arnheim. A storm with sad eyes and dark ash brown hair hiding him away from the world, too.

A storm calling to the one that lives within me, too.

CHAPTER 5

"SAD EYES"

ANA

I don't speak to the mystery guy for at least a week, and neither does anyone else. He only comes out for mealtimes, and I suppose, like me, he needs to adjust. My curiosity brews on what his story is or how he came to be at Arnheim.

When Saturday rolls around, I attempt to fly a homemade kite as a project for class. I was able to build it *in* class days prior, yet for full credit, it needs to fly, too. Thankfully, there's enough wind today, so it's the perfect time to test it out.

I take the kite I made in class outside on the grounds, some distance away from the building, to a grassy hill near a lone willow tree.

Okay, this is easy; fly the damn kite, Ana!

I steady the kite's basic diamond shape and release it, slowly letting the twine unravel.

Excitement flows through me like rushing water, as the silly kite begins to lift like it's supposed to.

Higher and higher the kite soars, until a gust of wind blows the stupid thing right into a damn tree.

Cursing to myself, I try to save it.

Can I even climb the tree?

I try to tug on the twine hanging down, but the kite begins to tear.

"You stupid shit, come on!" Grunting and groaning, I hope no one sees me trying and failing to jump up and grab for it.

After many useless attempts and lightly bashing my forehead against the tree while trying to think, I get the feeling that I'm no longer alone in my misery. My head tilts to the side, my nervous system taking over at finally seeing the mysterious boy staring at me.

"Do you need some help?" He inquires after a long moment of our eyes boring into one another. Chills travel down my spine at the sound of his deep yet sweet voice.

"It'll break," is all I whisper as I take a step back and glare up at the tree and my kite. I feel him move closer until he's looking up with me.

"They have the materials to make another. I'll help you."

Flattered over his offer, I sigh and yank the kite down as pieces of it splinter and tear, falling.

"Okay," I tell him as we bend over in unison to gather up the broken pieces. Somehow, I put that symbolism of the kite shattered on the ground, relating it to my life. Me and the kite —we're both broken.

The two of us walk in comfortable silence to the workshop next to the greenhouse. It is attached to the main property on the backside of Arnheim. I lead the way, since I'm unsure how familiar he is with the place.

Once we're there, I set the torn pieces of the pesky kite in one of the cans and search for materials to begin again. Building things is not my strong suit, and I dread redoing it even if it is simple enough.

I thoroughly enjoy science and learning about anatomy but not building a damn kite.

"I'm not the best at building things; that broken kite took

me more than a day," I say to him as he moves about looking for other materials.

This guy must be the quiet, brooding type. *Lovely.*

I say nothing as he takes charge, and I watch him in wonder.

Unsure of what he grabs, it takes him not even an hour to replicate the damned thing—but better, *of course.*

"What did you…"

He turns to the side, indicating his head to follow him back outside.

The afternoon sun warms my skin as he leads me to another spot *without* a tree nearby.

Watching the scene unfold before me, he tells me to hold the string tight. Nodding in agreement, the kite takes off without a hitch, and my mouth falls open.

Mystery Guy made a bigger and better kite, because, *of course,* he's good with his hands. Unlike me.

Wonder what else he's good at? Or with?

A laugh escapes from me as the kite soars around with the wind.

I catch him standing next to me in my periphery; I dare to peek to the side and spot a slight curvature of his lips. A small smile, but not quite.

This guy's hard to read.

"Thank you," I say quietly enough, but I know he hears me.

His sad blue eyes meet mine. "You're welcome."

We stand there for a while, saying nothing else. Somehow, the silence doesn't bother me, and he doesn't seem to mind either. I also get the sense that he's slow to warm up.

"Want to have a go? You created it, after all," I say, passing the string to him.

He doesn't answer, but he takes it wordlessly. Just briefly, I see something light up those eyes before it disappears just as quickly. Maybe it's the rays from the sun beaming down on him or the angle I'm seeing him. Regardless, he's certainly handsome to gaze upon with how his dark hair falls in his face, creating a brooding work of art. I take time to admire the view with his broad shoulders and clean-shaven face. He towers over me like a protective cloak.

I close my eyes briefly, enjoying the breeze and the late afternoon sun. The silence of the moment, along with sharing it with this mysterious stranger beside me, is somehow blissful. At least we can relate to *that;* we remain like this until I think I hear the dinner bell.

My eyes open and drift to find sad ones looking back. I wonder what he's thinking, and if he's actually sad or if it's the energy I'm picking up on. Maybe I'm also projecting, and I'm really the one who's sad.

Am I strange to him? Is there a lot on his mind? Or is there nothing in his mind, like me?

"Come join me for dinner?" I offer as he looks from the kite to me before reeling it back in.

"Okay," he agrees quietly.

Happy with the answer, we make our way to the classroom, store the kite, and head to the dining hall.

He sits directly across from me as we add poultry and salad greens to our plates with steamed potatoes and a piece of apple pie.

Once he meets my gaze, I offer him a small smile before digging in. I'm unsure if he smiles back, but somehow, I'm grateful for his company.

There's more to this stranger than his quiet company, but it settles me. He doesn't need to say as many words to make me feel like I found an unexpected friend in this place.

CHAPTER 6

"IT'S NICE TO NOT FEEL ALONE"

ANA

The heat of the summer has me sweating bullets as I take my summer exams. Studying and reading have been all I've known this season. Catching up with life and *normal* people feels like such a chore.

A silver lining during the last month was a certain sad boy's company.

Atticus is his name.

I place my pencil down at the end of the testing hour, and a small smile draws up, as I think of how we began the initial conversation.

During the past few weeks, the mysterious boy accompanied me at mealtimes and, only recently, for quiet reading times in the library. Most of our time was spent in silence, but it didn't bother me until two weeks in.

We were eating some beef stew with potatoes and vegetables when I sighed heavily and stared at him.

It didn't take him long to meet my gaze, tilting his head in acknowledgment.

"I don't know your name."

I waited a long moment, and his eyes appeared lighter. I was slowly starting to read him better on his body language when he was relaxed or thinking.

He wasn't much of a talker for one, but I could tell by how relaxed he was just being in my company. I never invited him to hang out; he just showed up. We also made nods and head indications of acknowledgement or small smiles here and there. His eyes smiled more than his lips did.

Finally, he said, "Does my silence bother you?"

I blinked, once, twice.

"No… Yes. No? Maybe?"

His lips turned up in amusement.

"I do talk and answer back, you know, even if I am quiet."

I relaxed my shoulders, taking a spoonful of the broth and meat from the stew.

"I'm Atticus."

The name brought warmth to me as I sighed in relief.

"I'm Anabel—Ana for short."

"I know," he took a bite of his food as I swallowed mine down, tilting my head.

"You do?"

He nodded, taking another bite before tapping his ears.

"Ah, you're a listener. Good to know… It's strange to finally have a non-quiet conversation with you."

He looked up slowly from his bowl, humor dancing in those eyes.

"You are also quiet, you know. It's why I'm comfortable with you. You don't make me talk, and you seemed okay with silence."

My lips curled up. "Fair, but I've still been wondering whose name I should know for the company I keep. Atticus is a lot better than sad eyes or a mysterious boy."

I saw his eyes narrow, "Mysterious, hmmm. I have sad eyes?"

Nodding slowly, I took another few spoonfuls before realizing that he was staring and waiting for me to answer.

"You do. You may be listening, but I look and I see it subliminally."

Something flashed that was almost too quick to tell, almost as if he had been caught. He did well to keep himself composed most of the time, and there for a moment I saw it slip.

"Maybe we should do more talking then…"

It was my turn to feel pleased by the interaction.

"I enjoy your company with or without speaking. I just wanted to know your name."

"Now you know. What to talk about next, then?"

I gave him an honest smile that time, "I'll think of something, I'm sure."

There are two weeks of break left before classes begin for everyone, and more new faces begin to arrive at Arnheim. The heat is already killing me. I'm grumbling and complaining at dinner to Atticus.

He listens, of course, but says nothing as new people sit at the long table. He doesn't speak until I make a suggestion. "How should we fill our time and freedom?"

Leaning back against his chair and staring off in the distance, Atticus taps his fingers against his crossed arms. "Hmm," he says, lost in thought.

"There has to be something we can get into, right? Are we allowed to roam past the grounds and explore the woods?" I wonder aloud.

"New people have just arrived, too," he indicates his head towards the new faces a few seats down from us at the same table. "Maybe we should make some more friends and explore? No telling what's in those woods. I'm unsure if I could protect you against a bear, if there are any."

My ears perk at the mention of being protected by him. "You'll protect me from the dangers of the woods?"

With a smirk, Atticus leans forward against the table. Dark hair falls into his face, which only adds to his mysterious aura.

He's flirting with me, and by God, I could die.

"Why wouldn't I protect someone I care about?"

Wait, he cares about me?

Stumped, I hold his blue gaze and repeat the question aloud to him this time. "You care about me?"

Atticus leans back again with the smallest of smiles. "Of course, I do."

The way he says it so matter-of-factly warms my cheeks. "Like friends care about each other?" I ask simply, registering what he's saying as I look away shyly.

"Yeah… Friends. I am most definitely your friend at the very least."

Unsure what he means, I whisper more to myself than him, "It's nice to not feel alone in the world anymore."

For a moment, I think I'm speaking quietly, but when I turn, his demeanor has completely changed. He lays his hand upon the table, wiggling his fingers towards my hand.

My throat feels tight at the confession, as an unknown emotion rises at too quick a pace to process. With slight hesitation, I give him my hand, and his fingers lace with mine, rubbing the top of my hand with his thumb.

His clear eyes meet mine as he whispers a promise, "You'll never be alone in this world again."

CHAPTER 7

"NEW FACES AND NEW EXPERIENCES"

ANA

Atticus and I got to know the new children around my age who had previously sat down from us at the table. The girls are Noelle, Lisa, Georgina, and Val. Val is the one I've taken a liking to the most, as her sweet smile brings butterflies to my stomach. The boys are Jason, Will, Liam, and Max.

New faces and new experiences; I do my best as the girl without her mentories.

Atticus and I aren't alone anymore. Part of me doesn't know what to do with it, while the other part craves new experiences.

A knock at my open bedroom door pulls my attention away from the latest book I'm reading.

"Hey, Ana!" I sit up at the sound of Val's familiar voice.

We had spent many hours getting to know each other and talking about books we've read in the past couple of days. She spent more time telling me about herself since I don't have much to share about my *unknown* life before the inpatient stay.

"Hey, what's up?" I ask, looking up from another fantasy book from the library I picked up yesterday.

Holding and shaking the large bag in her hand, she smiles and steps inside. The summer sun shines on her chestnut brown hair through the window; her wheat-colored eyes find mine.

"Let's go swimming," she whispers as if it's a secret.

"Swimming?" I close my book and scoot to the edge of the bed.

"The boys explored yesterday and found a creek a little ways out."

I stare down at my all-black ensemble: skirt, summer sandals, and plain t-shirt. "I don't have anything to swim in."

With a shake of her head, she refuses to let that deter us.

"It will be fine; come on! All of us are going! Atticus will be there, too." She wiggles her brows suggestively, and I can't help but roll my eyes.

"We are friends, you know. You don't have to suggest things more than they are."

I see her frown before I get up and follow her out and shut the door behind me.

"He's clearly into you, Ana," she says as if I don't already know. He still meets my gaze often, and our previous silent conversations are much livelier now. His smile stops my heart every time.

Damn my insecurities.

I'm merely a vessel without a real home. Even when I try to let in the light, my mind remains dark and blank. Why would Atticus want me for any other reason than friendship? I can't fathom it. So, I certainly will not be bringing it up. We haven't exactly traded life stories either. Not that I have much to share on my end.

"The others are waiting at the edge of the tree line down the hill," she whispers as we leave through the back by the gardens.

I stay behind her as we join the group in the shade of the

tree line. I see Atticus in black shorts and a T-shirt to match, stepping away from the others to greet me.

He smiles knowingly, "Hey there."

"Hey, Atti," I say without thinking; my heart races in response as I think about what Val said earlier. *He's clearly into you, Ana.*

"Atti?" He steps to my side as Val walks over to Lisa and Georgina, shooting me a quick knowing look that makes me gulp.

I see the others wave toward me and say their greetings, and I wave back. I'm too distracted by the male next to me to do much else.

"I—" I begin, but *Atti* interrupts.

"I like it. Now, you get a cute nickname… Ann? No," he considers as we walk behind the others, "Annie?"

I blush immediately, and as if he senses it, he answers the question himself, "Annie, it is."

I sigh in pitiful defeat. "Whatever, *Atti.*"

A lighthearted laugh leaves him. He walks so close to me that I find I much prefer his voice and laughter to his silence. Mr. Sad Eyes is changing, and I'm not sure what feelings lie behind those eyes now.

His hand tugs at mine, lacing our fingers and pulling me from my thoughts. I glance down at our linked hands and back up at him; Atticus gives me a cool smile as he gently swings our arms while we follow the others. I find the gesture incredibly sweet.

Okay, who are you, and what have you done with Atti?

I shake my head but keep my hand in his. I find that I quite like how it feels in mine. His soft touch emanates so much warmth.

Settling into my surroundings, I listen to the others chat and bicker amongst themselves. Atticus and I descend into our comfortable, silent company until we arrive at our destination.

I hear Will's deep voice first, his blonde hair reflecting specks of sunlight. "Fuck yeah, here it is! Time to strip, boys!"

Just when I think Atti is going to release my hand, he pauses, raising it to his lips for a kiss before letting go.

Staring at him, I mouth the words, *"Who are you?"* He backs away with a wink, then turns and pulls off his shirt as he follows the other guys.

My mouth is agape as the girls cheer, doing the same.

Well, *okay then.*

I realize everyone is in their underwear and slowly join them. I'm more bashful than I care to admit. Doing all of this is outside my comfort zone, but growth doesn't happen by being comfortable.

Everyone is looking at each other. Noelle with her curves, Lisa with her beige skin, and Georgina's gorgeous olive brown skin. Val is excited as she pulls my hand, tugging me along into the creek.

The guys all look *great.* Jason has light brown hair and bright brown eyes to match with an athletic build; Max has caramel brown skin and toned muscles that make him a sight to behold, and Liam has his natural red hair and slim build. Liam doesn't appear to work out, other than being blessed with a good metabolism. The boys are all handsome and diverse, along with the girls. Aside from Val being my closest friend in this place, there's only one male I have eyes for, and he has since he walked into Arnheim weeks ago.

It's as if I'm seeing him for the first time in a whole new light. He's playful and sociable, and I wonder about what else he hides beneath that exterior. Who knows, maybe this is what genuine happiness looks like. A foreign concept I'm still working out myself.

The water's chill makes me gasp as the others laugh, cheering since I'm the last one to wade in. I notice Georgina and Will hugging each other while Max and Liam are laughing about something. Closing my eyes, I dip my head underwater.

The image from the hospital fills my mind again, along with a third-person point of view of me falling into water, *off a fucking cliff.*

I gasp once I surface and open my eyes.

That's why I'm the way I am! Did I jump? Was I pushed?

My heart races as I try to catch my breath. The unknown prickles at the back of my neck.

"You'll get used to the water eventually, Ana," I hear Jason call out. The water goes to my chest as Atticus swims over, and I smile awkwardly.

"It gets deeper. Hop on, there's a little dirt bar over here."

The thing in my chest stalls, distracting my spiraling thoughts and questions as he bears his back to me. Unsure about what to do, I carefully wrap my arms around his neck, trying to ignore how much closer we are now.

"Wrap your legs around my waist."

Swallowing hard, I do as he says. "Hang on, Annie."

I do as he says, resting my head against his, as he swims us both several meters away. Taking in his scent, I find it comforting. Maybe it's sandalwood and cedar? A smell of nature and comfort. Uncertain on the specifics, I find I don't care at this moment. All of me is focused on the male in my arms. His skin is surprisingly smooth, and I'm in no hurry to leave. Touch is normally another sensory thing I'm trying to get used to, since most things feel alien outside of language, sights, and sounds.

"I wasn't sure if you could swim, so I thought I'd spare you the trouble," he says while pausing.

"I don't, so good thinking on your part...Thank you," I say quietly.

"None of us will let anything happen to you. I certainly won't leave your side."

Does he even realize the words he says and how much they affect me?

A simple *'thank you'* is all I can return as he lightly rubs my arms.

"You can stand here now if you'd like."

It takes me a long moment to realize he's on his knees and that the current in the creek isn't strong.

"I'm fine like this," I say out of unknown worry, and I gather that he senses it.

"Are you okay? What's wrong?"

I shake my head as foreign tears well up, and I'm grateful there's no one directly near us to see me cry.

"Hey," he whispers soothingly. I sniffle as he turns around, then I break down right there.

"Hey, hey," he rubs my back gently, cupping my head as I cry into his neck.

"Talk to me, Annie, what's wrong?"

I tighten my hold on him, just now realizing I unlocked a core memory. A reason for who I am and how I got here to this place.

Why the fuck would I jump off a cliff? I had to have been pushed.

I vaguely hear a couple of the others ask if everything's okay, and Atticus responds to them before turning his attention back to me.

"Do you want to get out? I didn't realize this would be upsetting for you. That's my fault. I'll…have to ask you better questions… We don't know much about each other, do we?"

Yet, you're so easy to feel comfortable and safe with.

I hear him sigh at himself as he squeezes me briefly. He cups my face and wipes my tears. The comfort in the gesture alone makes more fall.

"Do you want to talk about it?" He asked.

I close my eyes, sniffling.

"Later?"

I nod as he pulls me into his arms again. A refuge, I didn't know I needed. We remain like this until my tears dry up and I calm down.

I'm embarrassed that I let the moment happen in front of people—in front of him.

"I'm sorry. It's not you," I say, noticing how he's holding me in his lap while he's still sitting on his knees.

"That's a relief at least," he says, kissing the top of my head as I lean into him.

"I didn't mean to get upset. It was sudden. Swimming *isn't* a bad idea, even if I'm not sure how."

"It's okay. You don't have to talk about it here and now. Would it help if the others taught you how to swim? Me, too, of course. I imagine we'll come here more often in the hot days ahead."

After I take a deep breath, I catch those worried eyes lock onto me. There are both sadness and happiness wrapped up in his gaze. My brain is empty; the only thing I see now is him.

Kiss me, Atti.

For some reason, he doesn't. Perhaps it's the moment or situation, but I respect him for it. He's unsure about why I cried and perhaps kissing me isn't the way to solve my problems. Even if it sounds like a good idea.

"Yeah, let's do it. Assuming people don't think I'm some crybaby."

"Aside from gentle teasing, I doubt they will."

I give him a blank look as I maneuver myself to kneel in front of him. His arms stay around me.

"We're still getting to know everyone... How do you know?"

A single brow raises, "Maybe so, but they're more like you and me than we think. We all have our shadows, Annie. Why would any of us fault you for yours?"

Good point.

I relaxed my shoulders, enjoying how my nickname sounds on his lips. "You're right. Who am I to say anything when you and I are in the same boat?"

His demeanor changes with slight tension, "I know. We'll work on that, alright?"

"Okay."

He leans his forehead against mine. After a minute, he asks, "Do you want to learn how now?"

I hear Val's voice coming closer.

"Ana, are you okay?"

Atti and I part, and I nod, offering a lame attempt at a smile.

Val tilts her head questioningly once she's upon us.

"She doesn't know how to swim, and we need to help her learn."

A look of understanding passes over her as she nods, before her usual grin returns. "Of course. Mind if I get the others to help?" She offers me, and I agree.

She turns around and yells, "Hey, guys, let's help Ana learn how to swim! We need all hands on deck!"

To my surprise, no one declines.

CHAPTER 8

"NOTHING WILL CHANGE"

ANA

I spend all afternoon learning the basics of swimming, which, for me, is a doggy paddle. It's hard to properly learn swimming techniques in a creek. The boys spend time doing breath-holding contests and showing me how to hold my breath without dying, and swim underwater.

I'm finding that swimming underwater will take more time. What is endearing is how Atticus has his arms in front of him, so I can lie on top of them to teach me how to feel comfortable floating.

It's dark by the time we semi-dry off and make our way back. The guys snuck some snacks from the kitchen, so we'd have some nourishment after a long day of swimming.

Once we're back to the Arnheim grounds, Atticus sidles up next to me and drapes a dry towel around my shoulders.

"Walk with me?"

I nod while the moon shines full above us.

We wave goodnight to everyone else, and Atti leads me to a spot on the hill to sit. The forest surrounds us below as he lays a towel down for us.

Getting comfortable at his right side, our damp clothes make the night air feel chillier than it truly is.

"You worried me earlier, but I'm glad to have been there," he begins to admit after minutes of silence and huddling close at each other's side.

The day turned around for the better, so it wasn't all a waste.

"You're already learning the basics pretty quickly. It becomes easier when you don't let fear rule you."

My mind locks onto the fear-ruling-me statement.

He's right.

"I have a great teacher," I say softly, feeling him lean into me.

"You give me too much credit."

"Not enough, honestly. I meant what I said before. I don't feel so alone with you around, especially without the memories."

His hand reaches for mine, taking it and squeezing it.

"Memories?"

I sit up straight, not releasing his hand as I look up at the bright moon, seeing its little craters from my vantage point.

My periphery shows his gaze on me, and I choose to be vulnerable again.

"Before I came here, I was in a hospital. Healing from brain trauma—*an accident, apparently*. I have no family left. It was vague before, and I still don't have any memories, but today…a lost memory was triggered."

Atti waits with bated breath during my pause.

You are safe to tell him, Ana, he hasn't walked away yet.

"When I was underwater, I saw myself falling from a cliff and into a sea. That's how I ended up in the hospital with no memories and no family. I can't decipher why I'd jump, so I must have been pushed… That incident is why I feel so…*empty* now." I huff a bitter laugh. "I said before how you were the mysterious guy… It's ironic when my entire life is a mystery."

His hand tightens briefly on mine before cupping it with his other hand. "You are anything but empty. I'm sorry you had to go through that and are continuing to go through it. I can't even imagine." He looks torn when I dare to glance at him, and a painful expression plagues his face.

"I feel as if I have no identity; no meaning. A void of a mind. Dark, even when I try to create these new experiences and face unknown fears."

His eyes find mine. "You have a brilliant mind, whether you can see it now or not. The brain protects itself during traumatic events. As scary as it is, it's not the end-all, be-all. You are here. You are alive, and I'm so glad you are."

I let the words wash over me and wrap me in a cozy blanket. Atticus is sweet in how he shows me how much he truly cares. It's in the way those eyes catch me and how he stares at me with a sort of intensity. He has a simple way of saying things in the right moment to offer me comfort.

"I'm glad to have met you, Atti. I'm uncertain what the future holds, but I'm grateful to have you around."

"We can figure out the unknown together, and it's okay to not have the answers."

I give him a small smile, leaning my head on his shoulder. The comfortable silence resumes for a long while, his hand in mine, and his warmth enveloping me in a cocoon of security and reassurance.

"Thank you for telling me," he says, laying his head against mine.

It takes him some courage to speak again.

"My family's home burned to the ground during a lightning storm," he begins quietly after a long while of silence and moon gazing. "The candles I lit didn't help. I don't remember making it out, but I was the only one to survive. I can still hear my mother screaming for my father when the roof collapsed. The smell of burnt flesh... You are right, Annie. I am sad. I am alone—*Was alone.*"

My eyes fill up with tears I thought I was done with. "I'm so sorry, Atti."

I squeeze his hand because I'm not sure what else to say to such a tragedy.

"I am, too, but I am a firm believer in fate. I'm meant to be here even if I don't know the reasoning. I miss them every day. I didn't think I'd ever feel any relief from the gaping hole left behind…that hole in my chest—*the loss.* That is, until I saw you reading in your spot in the courtyard and getting your kite stuck. You didn't talk to anyone either, but still I found myself walking toward you anyway."

"And look at us now, a treasured friendship," is all I can say as I process his words.

"You make living a little bit easier and less heavy, Anabel."

I blink away the water in my eyes. "I could say the same for you."

Silence roves over us both, and I move my head to the side, finding his glassy eyes already on me.

"My birthday is next week. You know what the greatest gift to me will be?"

I look around his face, lost in thought, "What?"

A wicked smile crosses over him as he leans so close that our lips nearly touch. My heartbeat echoes loudly in my ears at his boldness.

"A kiss from you."

I stare at him, flummoxed. "Seriously?"

"Yes. I anxiously await your birthday, too."

"Why mine?" I ask, tilting my head in confusion.

"The staff can't say anything if we're adults, minus the room rule, of course," he says, his tone dipping lower, "I want to do more than just kiss you, Annie."

A rush of warmth pools at my center over his words. My brain goes blank for the first time, in a whole new way.

"You don't have to say anything right now, just think it

over. Nothing will change between us, no matter what you decide."

Still speechless over his intentions, he kisses the side of my head before pulling me closer so that I'm leaning on his shoulder.

Silence consumes me as I lose track of time.

Atticus wants to *kiss* me. Or me, him.

He craves *more*.

I'm not sure what to do with the information, but I need to figure it out.

CHAPTER 9
"INTERESTING EVENTS"

ANA

Ever since that first night after learning how to swim, Atticus consumes my every waking moment. The group of us still go to the swimming spot, and I find myself changing, opening myself to new possibilities. I enjoy being outside and around people more—a huge change from when I first arrived at Arnheim months ago.

There's a strange yearning deep within me to be careless and free. Free to live as I want and experiment. If I want to kiss Atticus or he me, why shouldn't I explore it? I owe it to myself to try to do new things outside my comfort zone.

Interesting events occur leading up to Atticus's birthday. The first being Val.

While we hang out in my room one afternoon and read fantasy books on my bed, she randomly asks, "Have you ever kissed a girl before, Ana?"

I look over my page, considering her. "If I have, I can't recall. Why do you ask? Have *you*?"

I see her tug on her lip, shaking her head. "No, but I've been wanting to try for a while—*with you*."

I consider her for a moment, then place the black book-mark in my book. "I didn't realize… What would I need to do?"

She sits up and scoots closer.

Once we're facing each other, I take in her chestnut brown hair, her wheat-colored eyes shining with what I think is desire. I'm warm and tingly all over as we stare; eyes rove over one another's faces, before she reaches up and tucks some hair behind my ear.

"You are beautiful, Anabel. Dark and eerie, mysterious without your life's memories. I know you and Atticus may become a thing, but I wanted to at least try. To see and discover."

My lip curls slightly, remembering that I told her all about Atticus and my conversation the first night we came from swimming. I blow out a breath in a heartbeat. "I want to discover, too."

Her smile mirrors mine as she leans in, hovering her lips over mine. "I'm happy to think we'll be each other's first kiss with a girl."

"Me too," I say before I place my lips on hers gently, holding it before moving my head to see her reaction.

"Your lips are soft," she says, reaching up to cup the sides of my face while bringing my lips back onto hers. We release a soft sigh in unison, and I find I enjoy her lips on mine.

I follow her lead and mimic her movements, drawing my arms around her. Her tongue licks my bottom lip, and I assume it's an indication for me to open my mouth for her. When I do, her wet tongue glides against mine, a sensuous entanglement that I dive into. A quiet moan echoes into my mouth, and I can't help the delight over something so *new*.

Quickly, we become breathless, pulling away from each other. "That was better than I could have dreamed, Ana. I definitely want to do that again."

I smirk, licking my lips, as she follows the motion with her eyes.

"I'm open to it," I wink and she giggles, "Ah, you're going to be a tease, aren't you?"

I tilt my chin up innocently, "Maybe, but it's a part of the fun, isn't it?"

Her eyes narrow playfully. "Two can play that game, sweetheart."

The night before Atti's birthday, I wander through the woods, thinking of all the kissing practice I've gotten in with Val. Musing over it, I smile, hoping that the practice pays off to deliver Atti's birthday present as requested.

It's dark outside, but I can see enough tonight to make my way despite it. Lightly touching the bark of one of the trees, I pause when I hear a strange, muffled sound. Glancing around, I can't see any animals, but there is no telling what's in these woods.

Do I turn back?

My steps become lighter. I make my way around the tree toward another when I catch something in my periphery.

With my heart pounding in my chest, I press myself against the nearest tree and peek around until a scene comes into focus that I'm not expecting.

I lean back into the shadows with silent relief. Thank goodness it's not a bear.

Once I calm myself, I hear moans of pleasure—*rather than a starving bear.* I dare to peek again to see two males a couple of trees over. I catch the red hair and dark skin of the two males, piecing together that it's Max and Liam. Liam is on his knees with his hand and mouth around Max's member. Max's head is tilted back against the tree, eyes closed, with his hands in Liam's hair.

I can't deny the ache between my thighs at the sight of the beautiful men giving each other pleasure, and how focused Liam is on his task of pleasuring Max.

"Fuck, Liam! I'm coming," he warns him.

I hold my breath; my thumping heart is excited over the view. Perhaps I shouldn't be there watching them in the shadows, but what they don't know won't hurt them, right?

Seconds later, I hear a groan before a softer, finishing cry leaves Max's lips. Tension eases out of me from watching them; I relax as if I finish, too.

"Let's go back to my room so I can fuck that tight little ass of yours."

Liam answers Max's wicked statement with a kiss before they adjust themselves and quickly leave hand-in-hand.

I press myself against the hard tree, breathing heavily, and wait a long while until I'm sure I'm alone.

Once I steady my breathing, I stare up at the foliage of trees above in the darkness, their shadows dancing all around me. I relax once more, trying to ignore the throb at my core from such a delicious show.

I don't dare to think about the perversion of me watching unknowingly or the excitement it gave me from doing something so forbidden. I simply walk back to my room and find myself daydreaming of moans and soft sighs from various people.

If only…

CHAPTER 10

"HAPPY BIRTHDAY"

ANA

I dress and pull my hair up, tucking the handmade card for Atticus under my arm and holding the cool colored wildflowers I found outside. It isn't much, but it's the least I can do with nothing to my name. A name that feels foreign to me.

Unsure of how proper relationships work, I wonder if Atticus would mind how often I've been kissing Val. I hope I'm not crossing a boundary because spending time with him is all I think of, even with the first semester of classes starting tomorrow.

Excitement and nervousness shoot through my veins as I push the dining hall doors open to find Atti eating breakfast with the guys.

I blush at the images of Max and Liam as I make my way over to them. They smile and wave, gushing at what I have in my hands as I sit next to them and directly across from Atticus.

Our eyes lock onto each other, and I hand him the flowers and card while wishing him a happy birthday. Atticus smiles, taking the card where I drew an image from a biology textbook with a skull and flowers, plus a ribcage and an anatomically correct heart. Something crosses over him, but I'm unsure of the emotions.

"Thank…you, Ana."

Oh, he's choked up!

I soften my gaze before I dig into breakfast, shoveling sausage and bacon into my mouth.

Trying not to pay attention to Atti's intense gaze, I listen to the others ask him what his birthday plans are.

He shrugs, "I think I just want to read and enjoy the peace and quiet before classes begin tomorrow."

Everyone groans at the reminder, and I look up from my plate. He gives me a quick wink. That dark charm is most appealing.

I can't wait to kiss him.

Breakfast finishes before I know it, and we all go our separate ways. I casually stride towards the library, hoping Atti isn't too far behind.

Casually browsing the shelves in the fiction section, my fingers trace over the leather-bound books. Peering through the bookshelves to see blue eyes focusing on me.

"Did you draw these yourself?" He asks quietly.

"I traced some of the images from a book for inspiration, yes, but it's still drawn by me."

"I've never gotten a handmade card before. I love it…and the flowers."

I smile shyly, pretending my focus is on book selections and not the charming man staring back at me. My ears heat over his praise.

"I'm glad you like it."

Glancing up from a bottom shelf, I find him gone. Before the confusion has time to set in, I turn to find him right behind me, pressing me tight against the shelf.

"Have you thought about the *other* gift request?"

I gulp and nod as he moves to cage me in by resting both hands on the bookshelf at my back.

"And?"

I say nothing; his lips capture my attention as he leans closer, a ghost of a breath washes over my chin, then my lips.

"Do you know how hard it's been to not kiss you?" He leans his forehead against mine, and a soft noise leaves his throat. "Then, you bring me the most precious, thoughtful gifts at breakfast, and it takes everything within me not to do just that in front of everyone?"

His nose gently runs down my jaw, and my hands wander to his sides. A vibrating energy travels through my fingertips, even though he's clothed. I think back on our days in the creek over the past two weeks. The desire coursing through my veins and Atticus's swoon worthy charms and sweet words.

"I want nothing more than to kiss you, Atti," I say, already breathless.

His nose nudges against mine. "Please, kiss me, Annie." His warm breath rolls over my lips, an invitation, a quiet plea, one I can't ignore any longer.

I pull him closer and capture his lips with mine. Drawing my hands around his back, he deepens it, moaning softly, and I ignore the familiar warming sensation gathering at my core.

Even though we've swam together, and I've been in his arms, nearly naked, *this* feels different. New. Enticing.

I remember how Val taught me to kiss with tongue, so I lick his lip in invitation. He obliges, and I melt into him. With the way he cups the back of my head and consumes my mouth, all I can hear is the sounds of us, wet and warm with heavy breaths.

How far away is my birthday again, and why do I have to wait?!

Panting, Atti pulls away, leaning his forehead to mine, *"Please. Be mine?"*

"I will always be your friend, but right now…I *need* more. I need your heart. I need your love. *I need all of you."*

With my said heart now turned to goop, I gaze wondrously into his stunning eyes.

Any doubts in my mind are all erased in one simple word, a gesture.

"Yes," I say before claiming his swollen, kissable lips once more.

A sound of approval leaves him, and soon, he's holding me. I lose track of where he begins and where I end.

Kissing Val is different from kissing Atti. Both are pleasurable, and both offer varying experiences.

I know I need to tell him about her, but I can't bring myself to do it on his birthday.

Tomorrow. I'll do it tomorrow.

Minutes pass before we are breathless again, he takes my hand with a knowing smirk and leads me to a back corner where there's a chair and table. No one else is near as he sits down, tugging me into his lap. I'm straddling him when he cups my nape, and his lips are consuming me again.

"Thank you for making this the best birthday ever. I have what I finally need."

"And what's that?" I murmur between kisses.

"You."

CHAPTER 11

"I LOVE CALLING YOU MINE"

ANA

The only thing that makes me happy about classes starting is that my friends are in every one of them. Atticus sits next to me at one desk, while Val sits on my other side. It's a constant reminder to tell him about Val.

You can do this, Ana.

After lunch and homework on Saturday, I gently touch Atticus's shoulder. I indicate my head for him to follow me.

"Take a walk with me?" I suggest as he follows me outside under the overcast sky.

"You okay?" He brushes up beside me.

"I think so?"

We walk with our hands intertwined as I lead us to a spot on the hill with a familiar lone tree where I met him.

"I wasn't sure how to bring it up, but I wanted to tell you before another week passed."

With a head tilt, he waits patiently for me to continue, rubbing his thumb across my hand.

"Before we became official, when you asked me to be *yours,*

Val said her interest in me. I'm not sure if it's a friendship-crush or what, but I've been practicing kissing with her. Not since you asked me to be yours, but…"

I can't get a read on his face as he answers me, "You like women, too?"

"I think I do. Does that bother you?"

Atti smiles, shaking his head. "No. I like boys and girls, too."

I lean into him, my shoulders dropping.

"Thank you for telling me; I thought something was wrong at first, but now it's clear. I don't mind if you continue with Val to see where it goes."

I stare at him in shock. "Really?"

He nods.

All this anxiety over what Atticus would think, and he's…*encouraging me?* I certainly wasn't expecting that.

"Is there anyone else *you're* interested in?" I decide to ask on a whim.

He searches my gaze. "I think all of our friends are attractive, but I only have eyes for you. You're the one who consumes my thoughts."

Melting a bit more, I press my lips to his gently. "I'm not sure if anything will happen with Val, but I'm happy with how things are between you and me. I don't have to add anyone else to the mix; I just wanted to tell you because it was bothering me."

He returns his lips to mine more eagerly this time. A soft sigh leaves us both.

"I love calling you mine, but I'm open to whatever you decide. It won't change anything, alright? Rest easy now and thank you for your honesty."

I nod and claim his mouth. I spend more moments exploring it, swirling my tongue with his while feeling my nervousness ease up significantly.

"Ana-bel."

There is fog and grayness. I cannot see far in front of me.
I'm looking for the voice. A whisper, a caress.
A darkness beyond the gray gloom all around was calling to me.
It knows me, and I know it in return.

"Ana-bel."

I'm frantic now.
Who and what calls to me? It sounds like it's projecting all around me as if the voice is the fog itself.
Where am I?
Why do I feel so lost?

"Ann-na-b-e-l-l," the voice draws out from next to my ear.
Why can't I speak?
I want to answer back, but my voice is mute.
"I will find you, Anabel."
Moving faster, I cannot tell if I am running from or running to.
Fog and gray, the voice, and my running footsteps.
Why can't I feel the ground under me?
My senses are dull as I cry out in despair.
I am not me.

"Anabel Lee!"

My feet leave the ground suddenly, and I'm falling endlessly.
Shaken awake, I'm sweating, looking around my dark room. The window is open, and the long, draped curtain is blowing in the breeze.

. . .

I can almost hear the voice again.
  "Anabel."

CHAPTER 12

"SHE IS A STORM AT SEA"

ATTICUS

She is a storm at sea. I'm merely a ship stranded in the middle of the ocean, with no way to stay afloat amidst such a treacherous storm. *What was her storm?*

I remembered her sitting in the courtyard when I first came to Arnheim, engaged deeply with a large book. A dark-haired girl is trying to blend in with the stone. Lost to the outside world, while I passed by in the open, arched hallway leading to the back end of the Arnheim building.

I'm in a haze of my own, but somehow, I relate to the dark-haired bookworm as I grab a quick lunch and disappear to my room at the end of the boys' wing.

I don't need schooling since I'm ahead, so I await the start of the fall semester and help the professors grade papers for those still in summer classes.

The darkness of my room calls to me as I slip back into it. My routine lately, since coming here.

A fire took everything away from me, and now I'm alone in the world until I graduate. I'm uncertain if college awaits me or if I want to wither and burn away, too.

A walking ghost is what I am. Alive, but dead inside.

My mind is full of black gloom. Grief is on pause since it's recent, and I'm sent to this place for orphans. A summer birthday wouldn't spare me.

How was I the only one to survive? Or be careless by letting the candle's flame remain too close to the curtain, while I took a nightly stroll during that terrible storm?

Why me?

I sink into my cool sheets, not bothering to disrobe. Taking care of myself outside of mealtimes isn't at the top of my to-do list, nor is anything else…minus catching glimpses of the girl reading in the courtyard.

Anabel Lee is her name.

She doesn't talk to anyone, not that there are many around to converse with. She keeps to herself, eating before leaving for the library—until I catch her outside one day with a kite.

There's a lot of sunlight that day, yet I step from the shadows of the building when I see the direction the breeze takes her kite vessel.

She's a decent walk away, but by the time I reach her, she looks defeated; instead, she tries to tug the line out of the tree. I can tell she doesn't want to damage something she created.

I don't even realize what I'm doing until I leave her later, finding that I enjoy her quiet company. What is there to say after I lost everything? They're dead, I'm alone. What next?

I aid in making her brand new kite, bigger than the one she already made, with materials much sturdier than paper. Based on grading her assignments and the remarks from the teacher, she's catching up because of her own unforeseen circumstances that put her behind.

I can't deny my curiosity. Not that I would pry, but I found her much more pleasant up close than in the small glimpses throughout the day.

To my surprise, I didn't rush off after that first day of meeting her officially. Her silence comforts my own. There's no pressure to speak, but I can tell, by how she relaxes her shoulders, that she doesn't seem to mind.

I keep her company at mealtimes. Our silent conversations give me more time to take in her beauty. Dark ash brown hair that's practically black and a set of haunted hazel eyes of blues, greens, and browns that make her absolutely breathtaking. They change with the lighting, turning more golden or muted green. A lovely combination. Yet, I couldn't look too long. For the most beautiful things have a tendency to disappear.

Naturally, I remain drawn to her like flames to gasoline. She ignites something within me. Maybe it's because of how connected I feel. Like calls to like.

Over summer break, I cannot say when I first noticed how in love with her I am. Maybe when I held her in my arms for the first time, or when her lips sought mine, and every day after since my birthday. Perhaps it's when I saw her in the courtyard or those silent glances from afar when she thinks no one is looking, her true facial expressions she thinks are secret.

Many of those faces are at ease, relaxed and content, but every so often, I see an emptiness. Anabel eventually tells me about her accident from atop a cliff, and I can't help but wonder who might have done that to her.

Why would *anyone* want to hurt the one who's most precious to me?

Should the answer ever come to light, I'll do whatever I can to help her or die trying.

Summer turns to Fall, and the temperatures grow colder in Arnheim. All of us spend every waking moment together, between group study sessions, meals, and exams. I'm glad I get to spend time with Annie alone on the weekends.

I can't say I've ever had this sort of dynamic in my entire life, yet it doesn't bother me whenever I see Val and Annie huddled close over a book or the respectable kisses on their cheeks.

I'm unsure of how to navigate such relationships, but I find it endearing all the same. Annie is my happiness, and what makes her happy adds to my own. I find Val to be a good person with a lot of love to give, and I can see how her wheat-colored eyes light up every time she sees Anabel Lee.

I no longer find myself in dreary moods, but it could be the school and love distractions.

On a particular sunny winter day, I pull Annie to the back wall of the greenhouse for a hidden kiss amongst the plants. It's one of her favorite places to go. Now that it's colder outside, I find myself wanting to plan something special for her birthday.

I have a few ideas.

Annie smiles up at me, a sight that brings warmth to my cold.

"I adore you, you know that, right?" I run the backs of my fingers gently against her cheek. She nods, staring up at me with those *kiss-me* eyes, which convinces me to do just as much.

"I'm unsure of springing up the L-word and scaring you off. You don't have to say anything in return, just know that I feel so many things when I'm with you. All the good and lovely things. I can't go a day without seeing your smile, hearing your voice, or losing myself in those heavenly eyes."

She leans into my caress.

"I don't want you to ever feel pressured to be anything other than what you are, Annie. I love you for your silence and your deep thoughts, or when you seek comfort from your nightmares. No darkness that you think you hold could ever keep me from you. Not in the past, present, or future."

Her eyes open and appear glassy as she nods. Comfortable, intimate silence settles over us as I pull her into my arms and kiss her forehead. I breathe her in deeply, finding her scent consuming and overwhelming. Cloves, cinnamon, and petrichor. She is the rainstorm, and I am the earth soaking up her gifts.

I bask in our moment of solitude between classes, relishing the knowledge that such a treasure is in my arms. Even if she believes she's a blank slate with nothing to give, I can't help but want to prove her wrong.

So, when snow covers the ground and Anabel's birthday approaches, I hope she appreciates all I have in store.

CHAPTER 13

"I CAN'T WAIT TO TASTE"

ANA

A knock at my door abruptly awakens me. It's still pitch dark in the room, and I'm still in a weird dream-like state.

I vaguely remember getting up and opening the door to find Val standing there, wrapped in her black cloak.

"Happy Birthday," she says, holding two pieces of cake.

I offer her a sleepy smile as she leans in for a kiss before walking in.

"I wanted to celebrate with you first, since Atticus has plans for you tonight."

I raise my brow at her soft confession.

She sits in front of the barely lit fire, placing logs in order to ignite it, as I meander by and sit beside her.

With a long yawn, I lean my head on her shoulder.

"Thank you."

She leans her head against mine.

"Eat breakfast with me?"

I turn and gaze at her; the flames from beside us are dancing in her eyes.

"What? Eat cake?"

She nods, handing me a fork while I release a giggle.

"Sure, why not? I'm an adult now, so might as well."

Her answering grin motivates us to dive into the cake. The chocolate fudge reignites my taste buds from last night's dessert. It tastes better today.

"The kitchen let you steal this?"

She shrugs. "What they don't know won't hurt them."

"Fair enough. Tastes better the second day," she agrees.

We finish our unconventional breakfast, and she fiddles with her fork, contemplating something while gazing at the flames in front of us. The warmth from the fire radiates; however, the fire isn't the only warm one.

"Are you okay?" I catch a glance as she exhales heavily.

"You know I love you, right, Ana?"

I nod, relaxing my shoulders, wondering where she's going with her next statement.

"I…want to give you something more than cake… I want to touch and explore with you before the rest of the world awakens. I want to taste you more intimately, Anabel."

Whether from the fire or her words, my cheeks redden. I swallow, suddenly parched. My core awakens, intrigue igniting my desires.

"That would be more than fine," I finally say after a long pause, gathering my scattered thoughts.

"Let's go to your bed," she suggests, rising to assist me.

Val takes off her robe, revealing herself bare, and my eyes can't help but travel from her perky breasts toward her center, taking in her beautiful figure.

I feel her gauging my reaction.

"You are beautiful, Val." My words are light and soft-spoken.

"Your turn," she encourages.

A feeling of warmth guides me as I raise my arms, offering myself up to her. Wetness from my core gathers as I anticipate her touch. With the gentlest of touches, Val inches my thick, long black nightshift off of me and drops it to the floor. I am left bare, vulnerable, and wanting.

Watching her with care, I appreciate the fondness in her gaze.

"You are more perfect than I could've imagined."

My lips curve up slightly at her praise.

Val's hand outstretches shakily toward me, trailing soft, lingering touches from my collarbone to my swollen breasts. I shiver as my heartbeat picks up.

I hold my breath as her hand travels down.

"I wonder," she begins, her lips stretching as her hand moves through my pubes and into my folds, "if you're as wet as I am."

Her seduction has me in a chokehold, as I close my eyes and savor her exploring fingertips.

A gasp leaves me, as I feel the edge of the bed behind me.

"Just as I hoped," she purrs, pushing me gently so that I fall back onto it.

"Relax and let me take care of the rest," she adds, kneeling before me and maneuvering my legs over her shoulders.

The fire illuminates Val, sinfully painting her and the room in a seductive glow. The hues of her hair shine while I relax, as instructed.

A hand travels up my abdomen, and soon, her wicked little tongue is teasing me irrevocably. I jolt and twitch as she curls her tongue ruthlessly on my sensitive bundle of nerves.

"You taste better than chocolate cake," she gets out between sweet agonizing strokes.

"Oh, god!" I cry out as her hands grip my thighs and deliver me no mercy.

The suction she applies has my eyes rolling back. She's right, this is better than *any* cake. I love that the attention is coming from a feminine touch, and that all my first female experiences are with *her.*

I love this woman.

A deep rise ensues, yet I grab my breasts to increase the pleasure.

"Val," I call out, before tumbling and falling into sensuous bliss.

It takes me a moment to realize my legs are dangling off the edge of the bed, and Val is crawling over me. As soon as my eyes pop open, her lips greet mine. I taste myself on her lips, and it's not unwelcome.

Moaning, her tongue explores my mouth, and my hands wander to cup her ass.

"Please, touch me and explore as you wish," she encourages, grinding her pelvis against me.

Holding her, I entangle my legs with hers, flipping us over.

Heat from one another warms us both, as I trail kisses from her lips down to her neck, until I reach her mound, licking down it slowly until she opens for me.

Without knowing what I'm doing, I try to mimic what was done to me. I lick up her folds, tasting her wet warmth and pure feminine essence. Basking fully in it, my eyes close, and I feel her thighs squeezing my head as she bucks briefly.

Daring to peek, her mouth falls open as she plays with her breasts.

"Y-yes, Ana, just like that," she says as her free hand goes into my hair.

Encouraged by her enthusiasm, I suck on her bundle of nerves as she did to me previously. Her cries get louder; I take her to the finish line.

Before I know it, wet fluid drips into my mouth. I lap up every drop she gives me while her grip is tightly woven into my hair.

Pure bliss is what this is.

Panting, Val relaxes her thighs, and her grip goes slack. I crawl up next to her, lying on my side to face her. Her eyes find mine, and we share a tired smile.

"Thank you for the best birthday," I say honestly, and she rolls closer.

"I don't know what awaits us after graduation, but I'm glad I didn't miss out on you. No matter what life has in store for us or the amount of distance between us, I will always cherish this moment with you, Ana."

I nuzzle my face into hers as we embrace each other.

"Let me hold you for a while," my whisper caresses the intimacy between us.

She envelops me in her arms, and we eventually tuck ourselves under the covers. Later on, I cuddle behind her.

Tomorrow is not promised, but today, spending it with one of the people I love most is all I need.

"Close your eyes, Annie."

As I do, I giggle while Atticus leads me somewhere through Arnheim. It isn't until I smell the plants in the greenhouse that I guess where we are.

His hands cover my eyes as I touch him in turn.

"Today will be something to remember for the rest of your life; something romantic *just for my Annie.*"

Grinning, I feel familiar warmth around me and within.

"Almost there, watch your step," he instructs, until he tells me to stop.

His hands fall away, and buzzing excitement floods me.

When I don't feel him, long silence follows.

"Okay, open," he says so softly that I can't tell how far away he is from me.

Slowly, I look, and all I see is him framed by candlelight and winter plants. Atti kisses me, and all falls away.

I hold him close, deepening the taste of him. He tastes

different tonight. There's more passion and intention. Now, I realize how he was holding himself back for months.

Breathless, we pull away, his blue eyes locking with mine.

The candlelight decorating the greenhouse frames him as my savior. There are two people who exist in my life that make life worth living. I'm not alone anymore.

Found family is everything, along with the love they bring.

"Val began your morning…" He cups my face, "I want to finish your special day, if you'll have me."

I lean into his hand, nodding my head slowly. His palm warms my very soul.

"I would love nothing more." My eyes follow his.

"I'm so in love with you, Annie."

Melting into Atticus, I pull him into me, claiming his lips in response.

His natural scent, combined with the greenhouse plants, engulfed me. A sense of overwhelming peace washes over me.

"I love you," I whisper with all of my soul.

"I know, and I'm honored," his appealing gaze finds me in the dark, bringing me all the light.

He leads me to the blanket he had already spread out.

"You didn't have to go through all this trouble," I mention, feeling his hand squeeze mine.

"You deserve the world, Annie, so this is the least I can do. Now, I plan to worship you."

I raise my brow, tilting my chin up in invitation.

"Please do."

His boyish smirk is all I need in that moment as he gently lays me down.

"I've only tasted a portion of you…" He helps me out of my shoes and wool stockings, and I lift my hips to assist. "Now, I need *more. All of you.*"

"I'm all yours," I breathe out, anticipation rising.

My morning with Val was wonderful, and I treasured it.

Now, I'll let Atticus claim me wholly, not that he didn't have every piece of me for the taking already.

His hands run under my skirt and up my thighs, where he finds me bare.

"I see you came prepared," he muses, tugging the skirt off and kneeling between my legs.

I aided with pulling off my shirt, thankful that I didn't have to fuss with any underclothes.

Basking under his gaze, Atticus's eyes slowly take me in from head to toe as wetness pools in my core.

"You are an incredible sight. *All mine to devour.*"

Before I can encourage him, he leans over me to kiss my lips once, before trailing down my jaw.

"Such beautiful breasts," he murmurs, licking one nipple before sucking gently.

A shiver leaves me before he moves to the other. His hand travels down my body with intent.

"So wet for me. I can't wait to taste." He moves his lips down my stomach, letting his hands knead and tease where his lips were previously.

Small gasps escape me as I open myself further to his exploration.

Goosebumps rise from my skin, focusing on all he's giving me, as his tongue traces my lips and dives into my divine.

A hum of approval leaves him before he sinks his tongue into my entrance. My back bows as I arch up, moaning at the similar yet different sensations experienced from this morning.

"Oh," I draw-out once he adds suction to my bundle of nerves.

"You taste so fucking good."

I angle my head to watch him amongst the candlelit space, biting my lower lip. The plants are dancing all around and above us ethereally, and with how eagerly he's consuming me between my legs, it's all too much for me to take.

A familiar rising sensation overtakes me, and his fingers slip inside. He hums his approval before adding another digit a minute later.

"That's it, take it all for me," he coaxes.

He sucks my mound and curls his fingers within; it's all I need to tumble down into bliss. Words are incoherent while I cry out, and my legs shake.

He kisses my lips once before moving up my body again.

"Can I taste you now?" I ask.

He pauses at my navel. "You don't have to, but I wouldn't say no."

My lips tug at the corner, gesturing for him to lie down. "I insist."

He inhales, sitting up to strip his clothes to reveal a familiar body I know so intimately from our days in the creek and under the trees. I nearly drool as he stands bare before me. I kneel, admiring the sexy appeal of him naked *and* his impressive length.

"I love the way you drink me in—how you look at me."

I lick my lips, eager and ready for the task ahead. "Lay down for me, Atti."

As he does, I look over my shoulder coyly, before maneuvering myself closer to his throbbing member.

"Tell me what you like as I'm doing it," I say, hovering over him. My head is angled in a way that lets me leave one hard lick from his base to his tip.

"Fuck," he whispers, and I take it as a good sign.

Continuing, I repeat what I'm doing a few more times, before circling my tongue around the head. A small bead of liquid leaks from the tip. It tastes salty but not terrible.

In fact, I want *more.*

He tells me to wrap my lips over my teeth, as I reposition my mouth and take in half of him.

"Add some suction."

I eagerly oblige.

"There you go. Now, bob your head just like that."

He moans as I do.

"Not too hard or fast at the start; you want to build up the pleasure," he adds.

I hum, and his hand dives into my dark locks.

Atticus positions his hips while my lips slide down, and I take him deeper.

My drool saturates him, and I begin to wonder if it bothers him, but then I find that it doesn't as he squirms under my touch. His soft sighs heat my skin, and I find I'm burning for more of him just as equally.

"You keep doing that and I'll be a puddle beneath you—I need to feel you wrapped around me."

Moments later, I pull back with a *pop*.

"Position yourself above me. Go as slowly as you need. It may hurt at first, but that'll disappear."

While wiping my mouth, I swing my leg over him and hover. He uses his hand to line his member against my entrance.

Taking him slowly, inch by inch, I continue until I'm comfortable enough to sink fully. The stretch is initially uncomfortable but not unwelcome. Maybe it's because of how his mouth falls open and desire bleeds from the sweat on his brow. Maybe it's because those sad eyes are now full of love and longing.

It takes me a moment to get my bearings, but once I do, Atticus's words encourage me. "That's it. You feel perfect. So warm and wet—taking me so well. My perfect, Annie."

I focus on the handsome man underneath me who is gazing at me so intensely that my cheeks warm.

His hands grip my hips, assisting me so that he fills me deeper.

I feel so full of him, yet not quite enough. My mouth falls open at the new sensation of him pumping through me that keeps me wanting more.

Atticus curses again, and noises I don't recall ever making before leave my lips.

My eyes roll back, and the rise within me begins again.

"I can feel you about to come," he whispers with intrigue.

My lids are heavy with it as I lock eyes with him. His words are my undoing.

"Yes, eyes on me when you come," he demands sweetly.

Biting my lip, he increases his pace and hits deeper; the spiral of sexual sensation pulls me under.

"Oh, Atti," I cry out, clenching my inner walls down around him.

"Annie."

He pumps me full in spurts as he sits up, clutching me tight to him. My arms go around him, our breaths steadying.

"I'm going to make you come more than this—you are absolute perfection. *You are mine.* God, how long have I waited to taste this—*taste you?* Reality survives my dreams."

"Dreams, huh?" I lean back to gaze upon him, blue eyes peering into mine as I smirk knowingly. Playing with his hair at his nape, he does the same.

"Yes. Different places and positions. Your pleasure and mine. Our love is expressed through flesh and actions."

"Will you show me more?"

"Always, Annie. I'd love nothing more than to make love to you the rest of the night."

With a grin spreading on my face and echoing on his, we do exactly that.

CHAPTER 14
"I'M NOT ALONE"

ANA

Graduation approaches, and a sense of dread fills me. There is a familiar prickling at the back of my neck, telling me a new season of life is approaching and that it'll be hard for someone like me. *Will I revert to a ghostly shell?*

My dreams are odd, too. Unexplainable and unknown.

Last night, I dreamed that I looked in the bathroom mirror, and my face morphed to a more masculine one. Flashes of myself flickered when I blinked before I could decipher and make them out as very similar.

When I awoke, there was a strange sensation of *feeling* haunted. Maybe it's my memories trying to force their way through, but it's not enough to trigger them. It seems nothing worth remembering has been pushed to the forefront.

Curiosity dawns in the early hours of the freezing morning. I make my way into my bathroom with a candle.

My hair is strangely straight in the mirror despite sleep; the candlelight is dancing in the cold chill of the room. The ancient stone has even more memories locked inside than my own mind.

I continue to stare. Suddenly, my skin prickles. A trick of the light, perhaps, but my eyes look like they're changing, shadows stretching out from behind. A more sinister look stared back at me.

I must be groggy. *That's it.*

The breath that leaves my mouth is visible in front of me. *Was it already that cold before?*

Confusion lingers in the back of my brain; something hidden is trying to claw its way out. The shadows begin to loom as I lean closer to the mirror.

There's an opaque image that I can't quite make out until I notice the height is larger than mine, with a face I'm unable to distinguish.

My ears begin to buzz, and I hear the quietest of whispers in my mind.

"I'll find you soon."

Suddenly, the candle goes out, and I'm standing alone in the chill of the dark.

Stark uncertainty fills me as I take shaky steps out from the odd experience and go back to my room.

It's still pitch black outside, despite the dawn peeking over the horizon. Moving closer to the window, there's a steady snowfall on the already covered ground.

Whatever, *whoever,* seems to be waiting for me. The future is beyond that window.

I continue to stare, lost in the stillness of the snowy morning. It reminds me that I'll have to make a choice about what happens once I leave Arnheim.

Will Atticus go to college with me? Is our time here where it ends between us? Where will Val go?

Soon, spring will bring about change. Plants grow, and nature takes over.

Just what will take over my life now?

I received my acceptance letter from a university hours away in the city. It's a new start. I should be excited, yet instead I feel lost.

All of us are at dinner, eating and enjoying each other's company, when various letters are received on places we applied. Except Atticus, as he stares at a letter, his hands shaking.

Unsure if I should wait, Val, who is next to me, reads over my shoulder before I ask where she applied.

"It's on a whole other continent."

I frown briefly before sighing.

"I know, Ana, I'll miss you, too. This change will be good for us both. We're in charge of our destinies now." Val leans closer so no one else hears, "Do you know what Atticus's plans are?"

I shake my head as the man himself stands from the other side of the table and leaves with the letter folded in his hand.

"I'll be back," I say, rising and rushing after him.

To my surprise, he takes long strides outdoors to a familiar lone tree that brought him to me.

"Atti, what troubles you?"

He pauses once I catch up to him.

"I'm not alone."

I frown for the second time, confused about what exactly he meant.

"Of course you aren't—"

"I have an uncle, Annie. I *do* have family still living. He's estranged due to his own personal choices, but he wants to see me…"

"Oh, Atticus, that's great news," I say, leaning into his back and rubbing his side to offer comfort.

"I should find him and meet him, right? But what if he's a terrible person?"

I pat his side.

"Fear of the unknown often sways us away from greatness. It doesn't hurt to find out. I feel as if I'd do the same if I discovered I had a family member still alive. If they happen to be terrible, we can always *leave*."

He relaxes under my touch and turns around to face me. "You're right. So wise, My Anabel Lee."

I can't help but give him the sweetest look as he kisses my forehead.

"Did you get into the school you applied for?"

"Yes," I say with a sad smile.

Atticus runs his hands down both of my arms.

"I'm sorry I won't be able to experience it with you. But it won't be the end for you and me. Maybe for a little while, but I'd be a fool not to find the love of my life again."

A grief, one that I never expected to feel, swells within me.

"I will miss you terribly. What am I going to do without you and Val? I've made a home here, and now I have to figure life out again—start over?"

Tears slip from me, but he wipes them at once.

"Starting over doesn't have to be a dreadfully terrible thing. It's a beginning full of opportunities. Reinvent yourself in this new place. Be whoever you want to be. Fuck around and experiment."

My cheeks warm as I huff a laugh while he cups my face, his lips meeting mine gently.

"There's that beautiful smile. This will be good. I'll find and make my way to my uncle. And we'll write to each other?"

I nod, wrapping my arms around him and blinking away the oncoming tears.

"I can't wait to see how we both evolve. This isn't the end, we'll have our time again."

Somehow, I believe his words.

CHAPTER 15

"GOODBYE"

Graduation is held in the dining hall. A quick, small ceremony with all of us dressed in black robes and fitted hats. We're told that based on the location of our next destinations, cars will be sent for us to take as close as possible within the coming days, as everyone in our age group is eighteen.

I've spent every waking moment with Val and Atticus. We'd sneak into each other's rooms or off to the library, greenhouse, and by the creek. We wanted to soak up as much time together as possible.

The sand in the hourglass is running out, and my heart is torn on that fact.

Val is the first to leave. I hug her before she's gone forever out of my life. I can't explain how I know this will be the last time I see her, but I can *feel it*. An instinct.

Val cries with me, kissing my cheek. I squeeze her tight, and it's all too soon before she lets me go. Forever.

"Live for you, Anabel. It's been an honor to know you. A privilege to love you."

Her goodbye is final—an end to our chapter.

People come for seasons or for life. Unfortunately, Val is my season.

I sob quietly as she gets in the car with tears in her eyes, as I tell her I love her, mouthing the words. She leaves down the gravel road and disappears into the sunset.

Standing there even after the dust long settles, my eyes dry and swollen, Atticus finds me.

"There you are."

I don't move as I stare at the space where Val disappeared, until his hand finds mine and pulls me from my vacant thoughts to his embrace.

"You leave in two days?" He asks.

I nod through tears.

"I leave tomorrow morning; will you stay with me tonight?"

"Of course. I would be nowhere else."

Leaning into him, I sob and shake in misery.

"I'll miss her, too," he whispers as I clutch his shirt.

My sadness oozes from me as I try to be strong while knowing Val's gone for good—I'll probably never see her again. With Atticus, there's no telling *when* I'll see him again either…

Eventually, I gather myself and wipe my face, then take a walk to the tree we met under. For the first and last time.

The moment is bittersweet as we sit at the base of it. I pick at the grass, while the warm breeze caresses my skin.

"You know, Annie, you used to say how sad I was—lost like you. We sometimes lose sight of what carries us through the darkest times and all that threatens to pull us under…"

I catch a glimpse of him, shifting myself so that we're facing each other.

"It's you."

Tilting my head, my heart picks up its pace, anxious over his next words.

"You've brought me to life. Before, I was only ashes in the wind of my life. I've been carried by *you.*"

All I can do is stare. There is nothing but adoration beyond his depths. We both changed in the past year at Arnheim. We opened ourselves up.

"You have freed me all the same. My blank slate doesn't seem so empty. I have a future to dream of now, where none was before. I..." I exhale slowly, as intense blue eyes observe my pause.

Looking off into the distance, I fumble over my words. He tugs my hand, bringing me back to the present—*back to him.*

He is my unseen dream; I'm awake now.

My eyes water as his gentle fingers glide slowly down my cheek. "I can't even begin..." A tear escapes as strong, overwhelming emotions spill from the tightness in my chest.

Heaving a breath, the words finally force themselves out. "Love doesn't seem to be the right word to explain what I feel for you."

Atticus relaxes, leaning forward to rest his forehead on mine. He then takes my face into his hands, lightly tracing his thumbs over my cheek.

"When I find my breathing labored or difficult, there you are to fill my lungs. My broken brain is encapsulated in darkness, and there you are to remind me that I don't need all the pieces to be whole. You give it the light it needs—*the light I need.*"

We breathe out in unison. Atticus has a long-lost uncle who still lives, and I respect his wishes. He deserves a family—or at least the chance at one. Although we'll be apart, I'll carry him in my memory and heart until we meet again—whether death or life separates us.

"It will be hard to leave you, Atticus... I need you to promise me you won't forget me. That you'll remember and come back for me someday. Whenever that is. When you picture or speak of a future, I hope that I'll be a part of it.

Please, Atti?" I close my eyes, holding my breath and my lungs tight with lack of air.

"I promise."

He presses a kiss to my head.

Please, don't forget.

I lose track of time until he leads me to his room. One look at his half-lidded eyes and I know his intentions; he locks the door behind him.

All I see is him as he draws me into his arms. The heat from his fireplace is equal to his own, radiating from within.

My heart is in my throat as I kiss him with everything I have.

"Annie," he whispers into the dimly lit room and cups my face.

A sob escapes me, "I don't want to be apart from you."

"I know," he murmurs in my ear, pulling me with him towards his matching four-poster bed. I breathe him in fully and take note of all the little details I'll miss about him. Those eyes. How they light up when he sees me. How he steals secret kisses at any moment he can. How foolishly in love with him I am.

"Make love to me, Atti. I don't want to forget you or lose you to the wavelengths of time."

We sink in unison onto his bed, removing our clothes in a slow manner, eyes on one another. I take in his strength, those muscles that hold me with great care. The strength that has carried and healed me in these past few months. How easy it is to simply exist and be here with him, in any moment—it was always enough for me.

"I will never forget this beautifully perfect face, Annie."

Tears stream down my face, and I catch his watery eyes reflecting the firelight.

"Promise me that this isn't our last night," I whimper as his lips trail gently to my neck and downward.

"I will promise you as many times as you and I both need.

This is goodbye for now—not forever. I love you too much, Annie."

"I love you," I reply as he caresses my inner thighs and devours me whole.

He licks and teases where I need him most. My body will always know his touch and crave that gentle and healing love. The hopeful dread that fills me about tomorrow disappears for a while; it's only the two of us in the firelight. Loving each other even if it's only for a moment in time before it's gone.

A moan slips past my lips.

"Yes, Annie, let me relish those perfect sounds from those perfect lips."

He drives his point home as I tip over the edge, bowing my back off the bed in bittersweet ecstasy.

"Let me feel you," I beg quietly, reaching for him as he pulls me into his lap.

Taking my place, I ease him inside and meet his sad gaze.

"Don't think," he whispers, before taking my lips to his. With my moans stifled, he continues. "Only *feel.*"

For once, I quiet my mind and worries. There's a stretch and pull of one another. It's gravity keeping us together, just as we're meant to be.

Tonight, I want to make the most of our goodbye.

Just him and me.

I stand outside the car with him.

"Until I see you again, and believe me, *I will.* I plan to write to you while you're at school. Live your life to the fullest. You are no longer the ghost of all you've chased away and can't recall."

Ghosts I can't remember.

"Okay," I tell him with a kiss goodbye. My hand lingers briefly in his, hesitant to let him go.

Reluctantly, he gets in the car, but my heart remains with him as he drives off.

I stare at the dust left behind.

How symbolic.

The sun grows higher, and I succumb to loneliness once more.

Tomorrow, I will rise again with a newfound perspective. The ghosts can chase me, but I refuse to linger or hope for all that I lost. *I will live.*

It's time to live.

CHAPTER 16
"FROM BIRTH TO DEATH"

UNKNOWN

Always watching,
Waiting in the dark.

The devil is in the details.
To read between the lines,
To define the lie.

The curse of all the knowledge to break and bend.
My obsession is taking hold.
Voices of the past whisper,
Taunting and toying with what is not within my grasp.

Yet.
Seasons may have passed,
But I was never far.

We are bound for life.

In the night is when I'll rise,
I'll be her future demise.

We are promised,
The reckoning. The finality.
The culling of our blood.

For now, I bide my time.
From birth to death,
She will always be mine.
Always watching,
Waiting in the dark.

The devil is in the details.
To read between the lines,
To define the lie.

The curse of all the knowledge to break and bend.
My obsession is taking hold.
Voices of the past whisper,
Taunting and toying with what is not within my grasp.

Yet.
Seasons may have passed,
But I was never far.

We are bound for life.
In the night is when I'll rise,
I'll be her future demise.

We are promised,
The reckoning. The finality.
The culling of our blood.

For now, I bide my time.
From birth to death,
She will always be mine.

PART TWO
COLLEGE YEARS

CHAPTER 17

"I'LL DEFINITELY BE DOING THIS AGAIN"

ANA

College in the city is a new experience entirely. It has forced me to remove my rose-colored glasses completely.

The women are daring, adventurous, and outspoken. We're still sexualized and fighting for our equal rights; however, through my own observations, I've found how women use *assets* to get what they want.

I can learn a thing or two from them.

And I did.

I take Atticus and Val's advice wholeheartedly, even if I miss them every day.

I received a full-ride scholarship with enough money for leftovers. So, I bought a new wardrobe. A mixture of respectable, daring, and black clothes like before, such as short skirts and thigh-highs.

A new me, a new start. I decide I no longer want to be shy and reserved.

I end up with a roommate in our large shared room. My dorm is in an aged, gothic building. It's always drafty, no matter the time of year—so I was told anyway. Yet, I'm used to that from Arnheim. The dorm reminds me of Arnheim in a way, but the whole campus is classically styled in its Gothic architecture. Long hallways and vaulted ceilings with some spaces looking like picturesque cathedrals. The building I'll be living in for four years has an odd, spooky charm about it that I don't mind.

My roommate ends up being a blonde woman with strange, piercing bumblebee yellow eyes. I think her eyes are cool personally, but I decide to let her settle in without bothering her as I go to a back-to-school bash at one of the fraternity houses.

There are people everywhere when I arrive, and I recognize a few from my classes. I make my own alcoholic beverage, wincing at the awful concoction initially, until I find random assortments to mix in for a better taste.

As I take in the energy of the crowd, a drunk brunette drags me over to dance. She probably thinks I'm a friend, with the amount of alcohol I can smell on her breath.

I chug my drink and follow her. Mimicking her movements, I giggle at her ridiculousness, as we dance and come to life. The beats are melodic and seductive; I melt right in. Alcohol sits heavy in my stomach, and it's not long before I'm right there with the girl I don't know, dancing drunk with tomfoolery.

A couple of hours pass, and the woman kisses me. Guys holler and shout, and the two of us giggle and give them a show. We end up on the couch with me in her lap, tongues fusing together—horny and waiting.

Even in my inebriated state, I'm having too much fun. There's a slight notice of a blonde male in my periphery, placing his hand on my backside.

"So hot. Give me a kiss, darlin'."

I pause, leaning back to wink at the lusty-eyed woman that I'm straddling, before I turn back towards the guy for a kiss. I think I hear a groan before I pull away and return my attention to the girl I have decided to invest in for the rest of the evening.

"Why don't you two come up to my room?" The blonde offers.

I pull away from the woman to see where her mind is at. She nods in agreement.

The guy gingerly takes our hands and leads us away from the crowd. After two flights of stairs, he opens up a door to a clean room of pale colors.

Not even caring about the location, the woman pulls me to the guy's bed and falls flat so that I'm straddling her.

He strips while I lean over her to fuse our lips and tongues. Guiding her hands, I place them on my breasts. Thankfully, she squeezes, even if it is lazily, because of alcohol.

In my periphery, the guy walks to a chair in the corner, dick in hand, as he watches us.

Looking up between my lashes, I catch the blonde's gaze before the woman sits up and takes off her shirt. She's wearing a red-lace bra.

Wondering where I can get one too, I pull my own red dress off to reveal my neutral-toned bra and the matching panties. I pull down the woman's bra and lick her breasts in tantalizing strokes that leave her gasping.

"God, that feels so good."

Massaging her breast, I casually tug her skirt down before I sink to the floor with it.

"O-oh. What are you doing?" She tries to sit up, but I quickly wrap her legs around me and dive into her wet warmth.

She cries out. I taste sweat and her musk.

Her hands grip my hair in shock before she grips the sheets. "Oh, God! Yes, right there!"

She bucks once, and before I know it, she's unraveling and coming on my tongue.

After stiffening, then relaxing, she sighs as if she accomplished a large task.

"I didn't think I could cum while drunk," she mumbles, and I stifle a smile while kissing up her thigh.

Almost forgetting about the blonde in the corner, I meet his gaze while he stands and slowly moves toward us.

"Want some company?" He asks, rounding the bed to stand behind me.

The two of us agree as I stand.

His strong arms wrap around me. I take note that while he's in great shape, my inhibitions are lower than normal. I do my best not to compare him to Atticus…but for a moment, I can pretend it's his arms around me instead.

Leaning into him, he cups my breasts before unhooking the bra open, so they spill out. The woman sits up and plays with one, while my eyes slide shut. He kisses behind my ear, his hand slipping around the front of me and into my folds. A lovely exhale leaves my lungs.

"Look how wet you are."

Tugging on my bottom lip, I feel hers enclose around my nipple.

"Which one of you wants to ride my face, and which one wants my cock?"

Heat flares my core and travels up my belly, settling in my flushed face.

"I've never sat on someone's face before," the woman says, licking my other areola.

"Then it's settled," he concludes, sucking his fingers that were inside me before lying on the bed.

She rides his face first, and I watch with drunken interest. Bouncing up and down on his face as he holds her butt, it has my own slickness gathering as I rub my thighs together.

With my great internal debate, I position my mouth over his dick to get it good and wet, while I watch her get off. The sight is so arousing that sucking his dick isn't enough, so I climb over him as she finishes.

I sink down, sighing in relief. She moves from his mouth and clumsily makes her way behind me, holding me to her as she kisses my neck. I arch myself, exposing more of myself, as she moves my hair for better access.

Lust permeates the room as I grind my hips into his pelvis. He moves too, hitting deep within—my favorite spot, I'm finding. A soft moan escapes while his hands hold my hips in place. Her arm snakes around me to find my sweet spot; she rubs it in slow, sensuous circles.

God, is there anything better than this?

I'm panting and crashing down into the bottomless pit of pleasure. The guy sits up, and before I know it, I'm lying down with her over me, and he's taking turns filling us both.

I don't recall when we end up falling asleep, and I wake tangled between their limbs. I can't help but smile to myself as I sit up.

I'll definitely be doing this again.

CHAPTER 18
"ARDELLA FOR SHORT"

ANA

My Annie,

I finally found my uncle. It's taken me so long to write to you because I helped him move. He's a nice older gentleman, and I've been helping him get his house ready. So, I didn't want to write before having a final address to send from. He recently lost his wife and thought to look into my father's whereabouts. That's how he found me in Arnheim.

I didn't think I could feel like this after losing everyone, knowing that I have blood relatives who still live. My uncle is older and moves more slowly, so I'm unsure how long I'll have with him. I know I'm doing my best to make each day count, and I hope you are, too.

I can't even describe how much I miss you. Ardently. Terribly. There is hope and light ahead for us both. I can't wait to hear from you.

I love you.

Yours,

A

Atti,

It's so wonderful to hear from you!

I'll be honest, I was worried about never hearing from you again, but I'm relieved that isn't the case.

I'm glad you reconnected with your uncle, and how sweet you are to help him out.

I'm sorry to hear about his wife, but I'm delighted you two found each other when you did. I know you've been busy helping him, so I'll be happy to write until my fingers bleed.

I've missed you soooo much, and I have lots to tell you!

I took your advice and changed my whole personality. I'm taking on the freedoms that adulthood has to offer, along with experimenting with men and women alike. Fucking around and finding out is more like it, but it's not so bad!

I have a roommate, Ardella. She has these cool yellow eyes and practically white hair. We've grown close, and she's so talented! I know you'd love her as much as I do! Not that I've told her that yet...

Her friendship means a lot to me, so I don't want

to ruin it or risk it yet. Maybe by the next letter you send to me, things will have changed?

I attend college parties often to mingle and drink. It's nice to let loose, and I like this new me I'm becoming...so free and wild.

As you know, I chose to study biology, and I'm absolutely loving it so far! This first semester is basic general education courses, but I can't wait to dive further into my major rather than these bullshit classes like math. You know how much I hate math...

I'm thinking I want to work in a hospital after I graduate. I'm not sure why, but I think that's a good start to my career. I want to help people like the same people who helped me recover from whatever happened to me in my childhood.

As you can probably guess, I still haven't recovered my memories. Which is fine, I suppose, but I can't help wondering where I came from, you know?

When you first told me you had an uncle, part of me questioned how I'd react if I discovered living relatives of my own. Would I rush to wherever they were, or would I ask them a million questions about the family and if they knew what happened?

I don't know, Atti. Part of me feels as if I'm better off not knowing them.

I've come so far already since Arnheim. The campus living and the new world I've walked in, it's changing me and molding me. I'm trying to embrace life and what I have, just like Val told me to. She told me to live, Atti.

I miss her so much. And you, too.

Tell your uncle I said hello and that I wish him well, and that I'm happy you both found each other.

I wish you were here experiencing this school life with me. I do miss those secret kisses in the library...

I love you always.

Can't wait to hear from you. Try not to wait six months, yeah?

Love,
Annie

I mail out the letter as soon as possible and greet my roommate upon my return. Her full name is *Ardellan Esther Gray Poa*, but she goes by Ardella for short.

The woman herself sees my excitement and restlessness when I close our door behind me to our room.

"What's got you in a tizzy?"

I grin before skipping over to her bed to then spend hours explaining Atticus and Arnheim with him, and she gushes, wiggling a singular brow.

"I'm relieved to finally hear from him after six months of nothing!"

She leans back in her desk chair, a slight smug look encroaching on her lovely face. "Well, you've had people to occupy your time."

I stick my tongue out, enjoying her cute laugh that follows.

"I can't help my free spiritedness; also, there's nothing wrong with living a little! You should try it sometime," I encourage her.

When she doesn't say anything while I'm digging into my wardrobe later for an outfit, I turn around.

I pose the greatest question I could ever ask her. "Would you want to come to the house party with me tonight?"

Considering my proposal, she ponders it while I continue my search for my black mini dress. I'm thinking of sexy things for tonight, so I'm a woman with a plan.

Once I find the dress, I yank it out and wave it around blindly. "Found it!"

"I might need alcohol if I'm to entertain this ludicrous idea of yours."

I roll my eyes, but internally I'm positively *thrilled*. "As the guys say to their guy friends: *Don't be a pussy!*"

She gapes at me, and I stifle a giggle. "Don't shoot the messenger."

"Bitch!"

We burst into a fit of laughter, and I'm ecstatic that she's joining in with my shenanigans *and banter.*

Ardella chooses a shorter white dress—one that is more modest than mine.

"I'll teach you the art of seduction, my friend. Shall we tag team?"

With the way she tilts her head, I huff a laugh.

"Not sure what that means, but is alcohol involved?"

I grin and nod eagerly. Tonight's air gives me a sense of purpose—to make a way forward with our friendship and to be more honest with someone dear to me...

When we arrive at a familiar frat house, we go straight toward the booze.

I make our drinks strong yet tasty and hand one to Ardella.

"Cheers!"

She rolls her eyes, taking a drink.

"Hmm. Not bad."

Pride swells over her approval. "It's not my first rodeo."

We wade through the crowd, and I wonder where the blonde guy is. It took me months to figure out his name —*Oliver.* We met up a few times since, but it was never serious. We enjoy each other's company in bed; *nothing wrong with that.*

The girl I met, I never got her name or see her again. Apparently, she was only visiting that one night months ago.

A fun song comes on, and slowly Ardella loosens up.

Show me what you're made of.

I down my drink, and she follows along doing the same. We get and finish another before making our way back into the dancing crowd.

Rhythm flows through us both, and I show her how to move her body sensuously. We end up close, tucked into each other, swaying and grabbing one another's hips every couple of songs.

"Is this okay?" I shout over the music. I see a nod and relax more. I certainly didn't want to make Ardella uncomfortable by any means.

A fun, rowdy song comes on the radio, and the crowd cheers and goes wild before jumping around chaotically.

Ardella, at my side, cackles with me over the energy in the place.

I desperately want to kiss her, but I do not want to cross any forbidden lines. *Yet.*

The buzz from the alcohol takes hold of me as the song changes and various people begin kissing throughout the place. I see her take the surroundings in. Some girls are kissing, males grinding against whoever they can find, and then there's *everyone else drinking.*

I can't quite tell if she's intrigued or not, but when her yellow eyes meet mine, I wink and make a smooching, flirty face.

Moving my body to the beat, Ardella inches closer.

Unsure who makes the move first, we kiss. All feels right in the world. Ardella is soft in my arms—vulnerable, too. She tastes like my match made in heaven and smells oh-so sweet.

A familiar feeling arises, like with Val and Atticus last year. I close my eyes and cup the back of her head to deepen the kiss. People around us begin to take notice.

Before I know it, Ardella's arms are around me, and another set of hands goes to my waist. Not minding it, someone does the same to Ardella. We pull away with smiles, taking in our flushed cheeks and swollen lips.

Behind Ardella is a brown-haired guy, who seems decent enough as he kisses her cheek. I turn my head to the side and see Oliver's face right before he kisses my neck.

Closing my eyes, I sink into the blissful feeling of his attention, along with Ardella's.

Her eyes are hooded when I look upon them again.

Oliver initiates the next steps by taking my hand and leading us away to his bedroom. Ardella and the other guy follow.

All of us make it to Oliver's room, and he murmurs about missing me while his hand slides up my thigh, backing me into a wall.

"It's okay, Ar-dell-a. Ar-deli. *Deli.* These guys are fun. Right, guys?"

Okay, maybe I shouldn't speak since it's not coherent.

The other guy agrees, capturing Ardella's lips.

"You already know how fun I am," Oliver whispers in my ear before groping my breasts.

I wrap my legs around him, and he lifts me to support my weight against the wall, his lips claiming mine.

Moaning into his mouth, time blurs when skin is pressed bare against mine, the mattress meeting my back.

My eyes open to find Ardella in the same position next to me.

"Use protection, guys," is all I say, and they do so after licking and lapping at us both.

I grab Ardella's hand as I come for the first time, and she squeezes mine when she releases.

Turned on by the sight of her mouth open, panting while she arches her back, Ardella's sexy sounds only make me burn hotter.

The guys end up on their backs with Ardella and me riding them both.

With how my breasts bounce, I toss my head back in pleasure before I feel fingers on my face. Peeking my eyes open, all I see is her face getting closer before meeting my lips. Oliver and his friend whisper how hot we are.

Moaning into her mouth, I play with the closest-to-me breast. When she returns the same, I nearly come again. This night is too good to be true, and I don't want it to end.

Sensation and wandering hands bring me to the edge more and more.

With how she holds my face to hers, we're moaning in sync and swimming in bliss. As I descend into the madness of a drunken orgasm, we cry out as we finish.

The guys are nearly there, too, but they position us on all fours to face each other so I can still kiss my girl.

She seems to be on the same page, as our tongues combine into one.

At this moment, it's only the two of us. We forget about being pummeled from behind until another peak ensues...

I don't remember passing out, but I do remember waking up in the middle of Oliver's bed with Ardella's bright yellow eyes on me.

"Ready for breakfast, Deli?" I ask lazily.

Hiding her smirk, she agrees quietly.

We untangle ourselves and dress in record time, linking our arms once we're outside and far enough away to release a laugh.

"That was *wild*. You sure taught me the art, alright. *Beli.*"

"I'm surprised I remembered, too, but I did. Now we have cute nicknames."

Geez, I can't help myself, can I?

"We're still friends, right? It's not weird or anything?"

I'm not surprised by her question.

"I'd fuck you again," I admit far too quickly and honestly.

She gasps, smacking my arm before we burst out into giggles.

"I'm your best friend. You can't get rid of me now, even if you tried," I mention playfully.

Ardella leans into me.

"Okay, good. I had fun. I wouldn't mind doing that again...after a break, of course."

"Deal."

We make our way to a cozy spot on campus and spend the rest of the day in the library, reading for fun in the lazy lounge chairs. My heart is full of love for this woman, and I'm grateful that my nonsense hasn't scared her away. It's a relief to see her loosen up and live a little, too.

THE STORM

He comes in by wind.
The rain and thunder follow behind.
Peace becomes chaos.

He strikes like lightning in the night,
Enfolding the senses,
With nothing to relinquish.

The storm consumes.
Devouring all surroundings,
Leaving nothing behind but pieces.

Blood of the aftermath,
A memory to contend with.
If only to forget.

*It's underneath the rumble that I find what truly lies
    within.
A force of nature we're both made of.
Two fronts, but only one will remain.*

— E.G. Poa

CHAPTER 19

"IT WAS ONLY A DREAM"

ANA

The darkness crawls within. Shadows create pictures on the stone walls.

The darkness crawls within. Shadows create pictures on the stone walls.

Am I floating or falling?

There's a pull calling me, as I tread the stairs in a strange trance.

A cool breeze blows through the hallway. My white nightgown is billowing all around me like a bride meeting her groom.

What is drawing me to the attic?

A stream of whispers travels all around and carries me up the steps. No door appears once I make it to the top. The glow from the moon shines through the small stained-glass windows.

There are no more whispers, but a shadow moves across the room. A trick of the light, perhaps?

Fear trembles through me. A sense of danger—of the unknown; yet, I keep slowly walking further into the large attic room.

There is covered furniture, boxes, and what seems to be an assortment of junk. With the darkness and intense shadows, it's hard to say or describe what I'm looking for.

Rounding what seems to be a cabinet, there's a creak and a larger stained-glass window.

Someone is standing there. The figure is tall, and I can vaguely see an outline, one that shows it's male in nature.

"Come closer," it whispers.

Inch by inch. I don't feel my feet move.

There is no terror, only emptiness.

Why would I ever dare to truly move closer?

Tick, tick.

Slow as time takes me through the motion. I reach the person and hear a distant scream from somewhere far behind me.

They turn around. "I'll see you soon."

I'm pulled from weightlessness, between floating and falling in the dark. My eyes shoot open, and I find myself cocooned in sweat-drenched sheets. My heart is racing, and my mind is blank. *As always, when I need my brain to truly work in my favor.*

There was an attic and a shadow… It's all I can remember as sunbeams peek through the curtains. Throwing them open, I remember my soaked long white nightgown and glance down. The dream is still prickling at the back of my mind.

Feeling odd and eerie, Ardella is nowhere to be found. I tell myself she's probably at breakfast already and race up the stairs to the attic.

There, I find white sheets covering furniture in a large room. Wardrobes and various cabinets are displayed through-out. I catch sight of light peering through a stained-glass window. A mannequin in a suit with a wig stands there. *Not a person.*

Relaxing into the cool stone wall beside me, I can't help but laugh nervously. Yet I can't stop. Nervousness turns to relief.

It was nothing. I'm okay. It was only a dream.

ONE YEAR LATER

Ardella and I are still best friends and roommates. We are as close as any two people can be, in more ways than one. *Even if I still drag her to these stupid parties sometimes.*

With society shaming women, there's only so much we can do in the darkness of our cove—our hidden places. She knows about Atticus, his letters, and even Val. She knows how broken and incomplete I am without my early childhood memories, even if I can function in society well enough and show the face of a well-put-together woman.

Ardella comes from a family of morticians. Her dad inherited the business from another family member, and her mother passed away from illness. She's had a fascination with death since her first—and last—hunting experience, vowing to never relive it.

Her brother aids her father while her sister attends school. They aren't as close as they used to be.

Then there was *Rigswold.* He was her first love, until his parents died in a car crash, leaving him alone in the world.

She hasn't seen him since.

Ardella doesn't judge my lack of memories, and I don't fault her for her death-obsessions, either.

We are coral in a sea, limbs entwined and linked. Friendship and love, *always.*

We're studying in the library this afternoon for a microbiology exam, though I have this strange feeling that we are being watched. It etches away at my skin and tingles at the back of my neck.

I try to refocus by shaking myself out of it. Then, I ask Deli a random study question about cell division.

She answers flawlessly, as expected, while I look around.

It happens so quickly, I almost miss it.

A tall male is at the edge of a bookshelf several feet away. I can't make him out, but I can't shake the feeling of something amiss either. Maybe because he fancied one of us at the table...*perhaps*.

Blowing off the feeling as a mere coincidence and curiosity, we go about studying until our stomachs are growling for dinner.

We leave our books, knowing we'll be back, and head to the dining hall. After we grab our food and drinks, we find a table near a window.

Deli heaves a sigh. "My brain feels mushy. While this class *is* needed, it has nothing to do with what *I* want to do. It's bullshit."

I hum an agreement.

She continues to speak, but my ears fail to process her words. Instead, a buzzing sound reverberates in my eardrums, and I turn to find a tall, dark silhouette in the distant crowd of the room. I can vaguely make out the back of the male figure's head and dark clothes.

Somehow, I know it's the person from the library. As if the guy senses me looking directly at him, he begins to turn.

Right as he does, I jump when Deli says my name and taps the table.

"Ana—*Beli!* Are you okay? You seem distracted."

I sigh, trying to still my racing heart.

"I am. This exam is stressing me out, too."

She reaches across the table, taking one of my hands to stop my other one from stabbing at my food in frustration.

"It will be okay. We'll study late tonight and ace it in two days! Just in time for the end of the year bash this weekend!"

I squeeze her hand, feeling my neck prickle again.

"Of course. You're right. We're smart, intelligent women."

"There you go!" She pats my hand before releasing it. "Now eat your food without trying to kill it. It's already dead."

Rolling my eyes, I eat less aggressively.

The feeling at my neck doesn't go away even if I choose not to pay it too much attention.

For now, the mystery guy will have to remain unknown.

I'll see them again.

CHAPTER 20

"THE STRANGER"

ANA

Ardella screams in excitement as she hands me a drink. We passed our exam, having just barely earned Bs.

I clink my drink with hers and shout back, "Bottoms up, bitch!"

We link our arms together and drink from each other's cups, spilling some on ourselves.

"Gosh, what the hell did you mix in this?" I choke out a laugh, backing up as she spills more on me.

"Whoops! Sorry, I'll go get us paper towels or something. And…I don't know? I just grabbed liquor and mixed it!"

With a sour face, I shook my head. "Never again."

She puffs her cheeks, walking off as I laugh. Knowing she's drunk, I probably won't see her for a couple of hours.

I make my own drink and wipe off my short, red dress. The spillage isn't too bad, and the people at the party won't care anyway.

The music has gotten better, changing into something more upbeat and danceable. Finishing up the new drink quickly, I seek to enjoy a different buzz.

Swaying my hips to the beat, I converge with the crowd and find a good spot to dance. I raise my arms, enjoying the music as bodies merge and mingle together. My hair is down, wild and free.

Tonight, I'm not anyone I don't want to be. Not a girl without a past or a dead family. I'm not my nightmares or the shadows that crawl the walls at night and whisper things to me —not secrets I don't understand.

No. I'm free tonight.

A change in pitch, plus a buzzing in my ears, causes my hands to drop and my eyes to open. Movements slow, and homemade strobe lights flash.

The stranger I've snuck glances at is finally revealed. My eyes lock onto him as he stalks closer as if I'm the prey tonight. Time pauses as lights flash and the music dips into a decrescendo.

The alcohol's effects have loosened my inhibitions, and I don't mind being sought out. The mysterious stranger's buzzing energy pulls me closer—a moon to Earth's tides.

Heat and darkness are all I know when he finally comes upon me. Sandalwood and amber consume my sense of smell as I breathe him in. I don't really care who the guy is, but *damn does he smell enticing.*

His hands go to my waist, and mine respond in kind. I can feel his strength under my fingertips as I run my hands up his sides to his chest. Hazel eyes stare into mine as his hand cups my nape. Refusing myself to think past this moment, I do the same and, moments later, our lips meet.

I taste a hint of mint and rum; his tongue quickly claims mine, asserting his control, and I willingly oblige. It's only him and me in our own bubble of noise.

I don't remember when my senses come back into focus, but it's the next morning when I awaken in my bed. I'm in a fresh set of my own black pajamas.

Did I sleep with him?

Where's Deli?

My hangover does nothing for me, as I groan and pull the covers over my head. Soon, I hear Ardella doing the same in the bed across the room. At least we both made it back safely.

The summer sun peeks through the trees as I lie on my blanket reading a textbook I don't want to read. *English Literature.*

It's not biology, so I don't particularly care for it.

Weeks have passed since the semester ended and summer classes began, yet I haven't come across the mysterious stranger I kissed that night. I don't recall sleeping with him. I didn't feel sore the following morning, but knowing me, I wouldn't be surprised either way.

Trying to focus on studying, a warm breeze caresses my leg as if to encourage more distraction.

Who wants to take a summer class anyway?

Since it's warm out, I dress cute with a brown, plaid skirt and a beige top with ruffles. Can't forget my cute Mary Jane shoes I just bought either.

I want to take a nap under the shade of the tree, but a figure in the distance draws my attention.

It's him.

The guy is across the large courtyard, locking eyes with me. I don't look away or break contact but instead beckon him to join me.

It's hard to tell if he smirks or not, but he makes his way over. He dons black pants and a short-sleeved shirt that's unbuttoned halfway and open, revealing pecs that make me titillate. He's much taller than I am and more handsome than I could have imagined in my drunken state when I met him.

"Having fun with your book?" The deep huskiness of his voice paints a sultry allure.

I sigh heavily to mask how he affects me.

"Not really. It's too nice a day to study," I complain as he sits next to me.

Leaning back on his hands, he peeks to the side at my outfit. I pretend not to notice, but I smirk. "Are you taking any classes this summer?"

He shakes his head.

"Lucky you," I grumble and roll over so that I'm on my back.

There aren't as many students in the summer as there are during the main semesters. Ardella is currently in a lab class for another psychology course, so that we can have all our classes together in the upcoming semester.

I stare up between the trees, feeling like I'm somewhere else in time. *There is a brief and subtle smell of the ocean air lingering, and faint waves can be heard crashing in the distance.*

As soon as I register what's happening when it shouldn't be, it dissipates.

Weird.

"Would you like a distraction? Although, by the looks of it, it seems you need no help with that."

I toss the book at him, but miss, with it landing at his side. He chuckles lightly.

"What do you have in mind?"

"I can think of a few things…"

I raise my brow. I can read his face and gauge his intent; he wouldn't mind a peek beneath my skirt.

Perhaps I'll let him. After I find out his name, that is.

"Tell me whose lips I kissed at the end-of-term party, and maybe you can see if I'm wearing anything underneath this."

I gesture at my skirt before I sit up on my elbows.

"Ace." His eyes are on me—hungrily, I might add. He

doesn't even bother trying to hide that he'd love nothing more than to see all of me.

"It seems I've forgotten what those lips taste like. Care to remind me?"

"Have you had lips such as these before?" He asks, eyes lingering on my face.

I shake my head as he turns around so that he's half leaning over my face. "I don't believe I have, *Ace.*"

"Let me remind you."

A promise from his lips.

He dips his head, claiming me once more. Now that I'm sober, awake, *and horny,* I happen to enjoy how his lips mold to mine.

Oliver, my casual hook-up, is away for the summer, so it couldn't hurt to have another. I've given up modesty and now enjoy the finer pleasures in life—*copulating with people I want.*

Sandalwood and amber envelop me as I taste mint, breathing him in. His large hands grab my thigh and travel upward to discover *no underwear.*

I smirk beneath his lips as he makes a grunting noise—one of pleasure, I would think.

Two fingers slip inside, finding me already soaked.

"I should've known you'd be ready for me, even after all this time."

My tongue teases him, as soft sounds release from me.

He lazily traces his fingers on my labia, then down the center of me as I shiver under him, before going in for the kill.

His sly smirk hovers just above my lips. I gasp when he glides those long fingers into my entrance.

"I've waited so long to hear these sounds."

I tug on his lower lip with my teeth. I'm losing myself at this moment, basking in the rise he gives me.

Yes, this will be a fun summer yet.

"That's it, ride it out."

He's fucking me with his fingers as I grind back, seeking my release.

"Oh, god," I whimper, and come right when he curls his fingers.

Ace deepens the kiss, drawing my orgasm out.

"Next time, it'll be my cock."

He pulls his swollen lips away while bringing his fingers to taste the mess I made. The gesture is so hot that I'm ready for round two. Tugging on my bottom lip, he watches me.

"I can't wait to have you completely and taste you more. You are more beautiful than I could have ever imagined."

Ace cups my cheek fondly, as I lean into his sweet words.

"Feel free to make good on your promise later."

He leans down to kiss me and straightens out my skirt.

"I will happily distract you. All you need to do is ask."

"I'm asking you now, come to my room later. I'm in the old dorm building over there," I point. "I'll make sure my roommate is asleep and we'll be good."

He sits on his knees with a smug look on his face, before helping me up.

"Hey, don't get greedy, this is temporary. I'm not girlfriend material, nor do I want to be."

"You're better than that... Message received."

I kiss him in return. "I'm just making my intentions clear. I very much want your attention this summer. If it goes past the summer, then it is what it is. There are no expectations here other than a good time. Fair?"

"No expectations, other than *my promises.*"

Giving him a cute smile, I lean in to kiss him harder this time, which returns with equal enthusiasm.

"Good luck finding my room," I say as he stands up.

"That won't be a problem, *Anabel.*"

I playfully throw my book again. "Stalker!" I call out before lying back with a laugh of amusement.

He gives me his own harmless expression before he wanders off, leaving me to my *studies*.

Tonight couldn't come soon enough.

CHAPTER 21

"YOU BELONG TO ME"

ANA

I can hear soft snores from Ardella's side of the room when a small creak echoes from the door. Ace's silhouette graces the entry before quietly closing the door behind him.

With my heart racing in anticipation and my slick thighs rubbing together, he's all I fantasized about today.

It doesn't take him long to stand at the foot of my bed. I'm curious as to how he came to know my name, but I very well could've told him at the party.

No idea how he found my room, but strangely it doesn't bother me. He likes me enough to see me again and *hopefully fuck me*, but maybe he's just as sex-crazed as I am.

Moving my feet, I hold the covers up for him, as he slides underneath and crawls up my legs, kissing my thighs along the way.

My skin pebbles against his touch. His lips graze toward my pussy, and I grind against him. His hands grip my hips, and I wrap my legs around him as he descends upon me. It's a slow build, and I quickly become consumed.

My mouth falls open, as I keep my sigh as silent as possible. I don't want to disturb Ardella. My body moves in sync with his tongue. He holds me tight to his face until I'm shaking. My release blindsides me, and I bite my fingers to stifle my sounds.

Ace laps me up, proceeding to lick up my body in slow strokes. He shifts, tugging his pants down when his lips meet mine hungrily. Moaning into his mouth, I enjoy the taste of myself and him merging. His hands wander and squeeze my thighs, hips, and up my body. I'm lost there in him as he lines himself up.

He doesn't stop swirling his tongue with mine, soft sighs intermixing from us both. I break away from his tasteful lips to gasp at the stretch of him.

His face now rubbing against mine, *"Mmm, you like how I fill you up, don't you? As if I'm meant to be inside you."*

I nod, biting my lip, unsure if he sees me in the dark.

"Roll us over," I whisper.

To my surprise, he does. I listen for a moment once I'm atop. Ardella's still snoring softly, so I begin to undulate my hips to match his rhythm.

Ace's hands caress me before massaging my breasts, kneading them in a way that becomes pure pleasure. I lean back and steady my arms on his strong thighs, moving my body in a way that hits my most sensitive spot.

I groan, panting as he half-sits up and moves and grinds his hips in tandem. I feel the rise as he hits me deeper, at just the right angle, and soon, I'm falling with my eyes rolling back.

Ace sits up and presses his face between my breasts as I clamp down around his girth. As I begin to slowly pulsate around him, he joins me, our arms around one another.

"Fuck, *you are perfect.*"

Delectable lips meet mine as he murmurs once more, *"You belong to me."*

I huff a laugh, claiming his sexy mouth.

"I suppose I shall allow that for a while," I tease him.

Ace licks my neck roughly, gripping my nape.

Possession, his object to use.

"You are mine, Anabel."

I shiver, unsure how to respond to such demands.

"Why don't you prove it then?"

A low growl rumbles in his throat, and my pussy responds eagerly.

"Be careful what you ask for."

A warning or a promise.

At this moment, I don't care.

He feels eminent, but I'm not asking for forever—*just a good time.* I want to bide on such time until I see Atticus again —the *true* owner of my heart.

Before I can think, he flips me over with my backside in the air.

"Has anyone claimed this ass?"

With the way he asks, it sounds as if he'd be jealous if someone did.

I decided to fib to see how he reacts.

"No. You'll be my first."

He hums his approval low in his throat.

I can't help my smirk as I arch my ass up, and he licks it.

"All mine for the taking."

Arousal pools between my thighs with a mixture of his saliva. His tongue drags from my pussy to my asshole. So dirty and forbidden—I thrive in it.

Many people frown on promiscuity, but I rejoice in it. I find freedom in acts of service and attention. A touch, a caress —*one look,* it's all I need.

It takes a few minutes for Ace to get hard again. Once he does, he drives his cock into my wet pussy while prepping my ass with his slick fingers before sliding into my ass.

I bite down on the blanket to muffle as many of my sounds as I can.

"You have a tight little ass, *fuck.*"

I want to laugh, but a moan slips out instead. He smacks my ass once, and my eyes roll back. Ace could dominate me anytime. He's a beautiful man and knows how to use his cock well enough.

Our fling could last through school—*maybe.* If he treats me like this, fucking me senselessly and claiming dominance, I could live with it.

Once he really gets going, his fingers circle my clit, and we ride closer to the edge together.

I can't help my noises this time, so he pulls my hair to silence me. Then, I succumb; he slides the fingers he had used to tease me right into my mouth.

"Don't wake her up," his gravelly voice floods my eardrums, as I come hard.

His hand tightens and covers my mouth, plugging my nose. My breathing is under his control. My heart echoes loudly in my ears, my pulse thrumming.

"I'll say it again, *you belong to me.*"

My pussy pulses one last time as he fills me. A low groan leaves his lovely mouth, and I release a breath of my own.

I inhale deeply. Somehow, his words don't sway me. I don't mind them.

For now, I'm his.

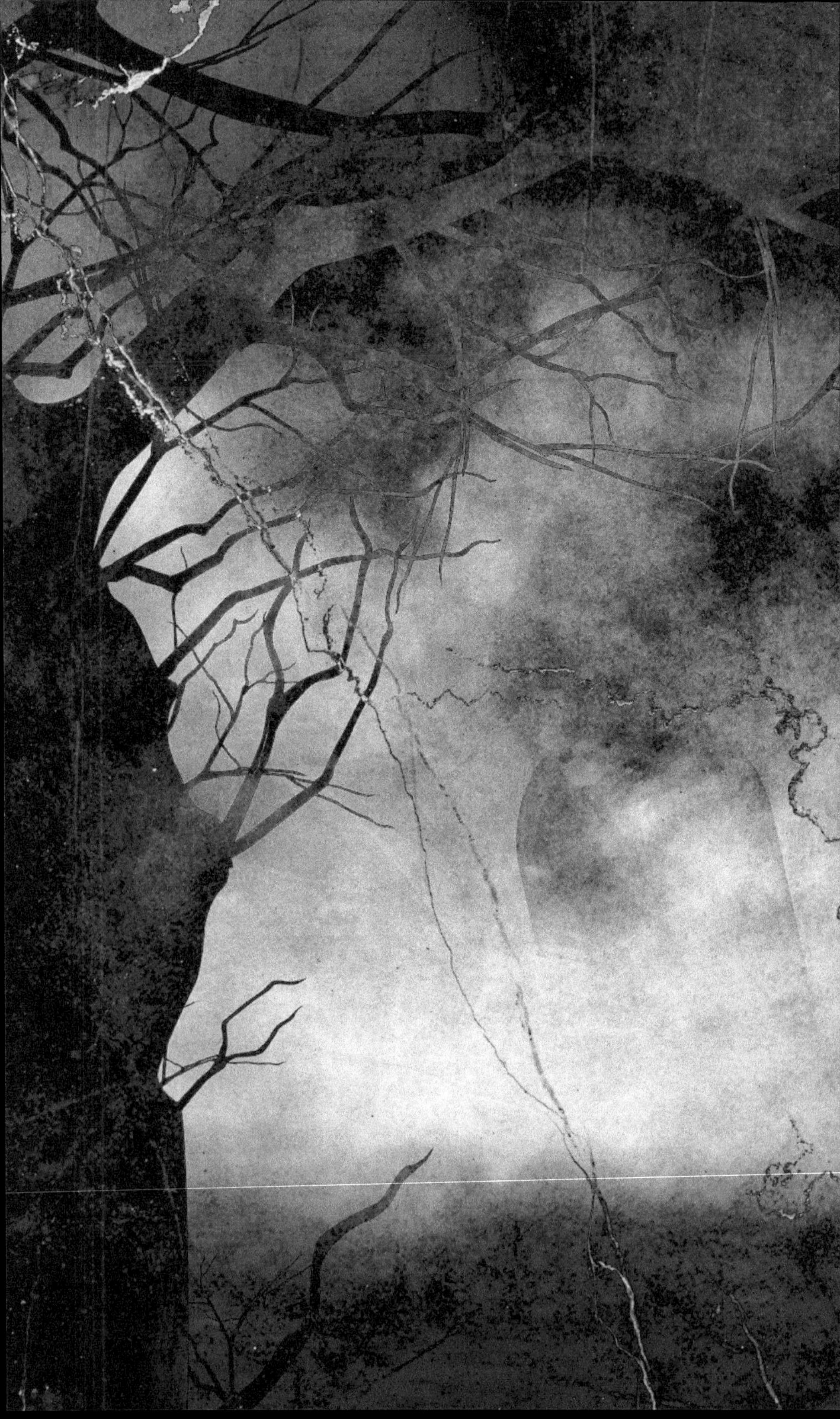

SHADOWS

Pitch-black,
Consuming
Lingering,
Reaching for me.

Please take me far away from here.
Shadows become;
I'm undone.

Longing
Holding,
Lost in darkness.

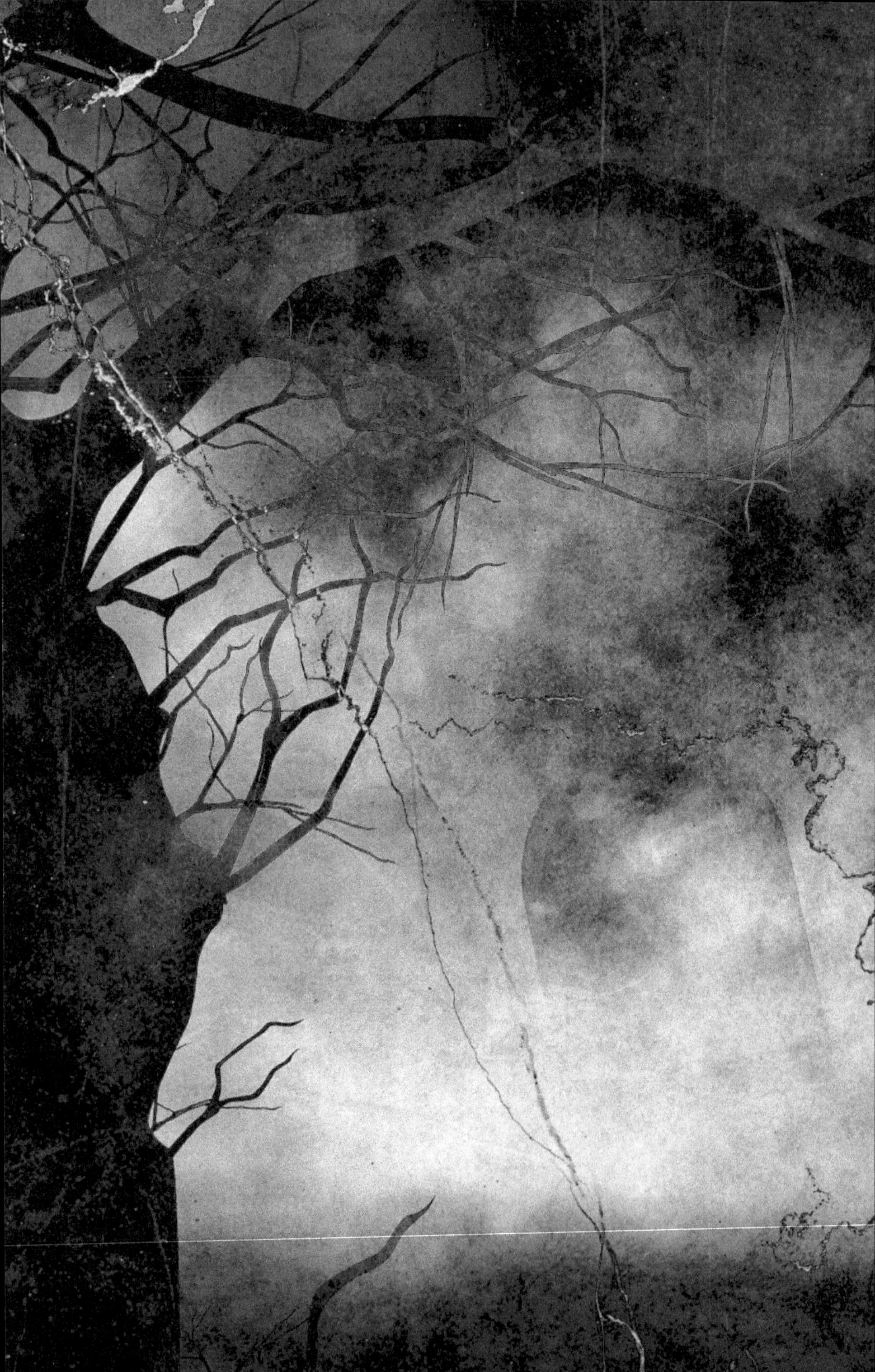

My savior resides in death.
Cloaked on the edges of forever.
Tied together,
Blood bound.

Madness claims,
My skin peels from me.
It's because of you,
I'm a shadow, too.

— E.G. Poa

CHAPTER 22

"IT'S TOO LATE FOR HER NOW"

ACE

Her lips consume me. Eyes that mirror my own. Such lust-filled love.

Until death, it will always be her—my hierophant.

Dark hair haunts my dreams and ensues my waking breath. I'm blind to everything else.

My obsessions have always been unhealthy.

When I set my mind to something, I don't relent. *Ever.*

Like a black snake, I slither in the shadows and wait to strike.

As the sole heir to the family fortune, my future is set without worry.

Old money. Old ways.

While some of those ways have stuck with generations, it's no bother to me. I'm a proud product of my genetics. I've always been without the other half of my soul. Searching in the dark, from my mother's womb, fighting for oxygen—*life or death.* It doesn't matter in the end.

From the dark we come, back into the black we go.

I'm a patient man. Now that I've found her, I'll never let her go.

Not until I'm in my tomb, next to the rest of my family.

As the only male left, I have a duty to uphold. And I will. I'll live inside her head before I'm done with her.

It's only a matter of time. She's already let me in—a pass through those defenses.

I have the upper hand now.

At least until I find the *letters* in her drawer.

I snuck in before her last class and looked through her things.

My hands shook as I read them.

Atticus.

His love—*hers.*

She's biding her time until she graduates. Then, they plan to find each other.

Well, not if I have anything to do with it.

They'll both pay.

She'll be begging for me.

I have his address and have seen how he signs his letters. In due time, I make sure to memorize every word and how he writes.

Rage from long ago fills me, and I can't think clearly.

I take the latest unread letter about his uncle's passing and crumble it before putting it in my pocket.

These letters will cease.

I rub my eyes, grunting in frustration within the dark solitude of Ana's shared room.

No, this won't do.

We'll see about this, *Atticus.*

He calls her *Annie.*

I scoff, feeling bile rise with my anger. My blood boils.

Deciding against seeing her tonight, I leave abruptly into the night. Needing to hit something, I make my way into a dark park and unleash my destruction. Once I'm done erasing what I can, I look up to the sky and can't help but laugh.

Anabel—*Annie* will not be continuing this charade.

I have so much planned for her.

It's too late for her now.

CHAPTER 23

"IT'S JUST US NOW"

ANA

Ace disappears near the end of junior year. I can't figure out why. We *were* stuck like glue, but now it's like it was all a façade.

Ardella doesn't seem to mind as we attend an end-of-school-year bash. Oliver keeps Deli and me company, and we fool around like normal.

Only this time, when I wake up hungover the next day, I feel unsettled like something isn't right. I haven't heard from Atti in months, and it's starting to get to me.

Quickly dressing, I rush out to write and send off a letter to Atticus. After I mail it off, I find myself gazing in the bathroom mirror.

Ace is gone. Atticus hasn't written.

When did I get so reliant on these fucking men?

Annoyed with myself, I punch the mirror, cracking it in the center. It distorts and contorts my face. For a second, I swear I see Ace staring back at me with a dark smile.

"You're mine, Anabel," I hear the whisper as if he's there.

I whip around, not caring that my hand is dripping with blood.

Ace isn't there, even if I hear him in the back of my mind.

"Remember," I hear faintly.

Something within me is clawing to get out. I'm unsure if I'm ready for whatever it is. My mind is vivid in what is unseen; blank pictures are trying to get through—a static that I can't make out. Shadows moving and morphing in unknown locations with distorted voices.

The dreams have gotten worse in the months I've been sleeping with Ace, and perhaps his obsessions have rubbed off. I've been unfolded, remade, and perhaps something new is happening to me—who am I to know with my empty memories?

I scream out in frustration, hitting the stone wall until I sink against it and let the tears fall.

What is wrong with me?

Wherever these emotions are stemming from, I have no choice but to let myself feel every last one of them.

My mind is loud and noisy, and I'm wondering what it will take to break me and crack those memories open once and for all, assuming there's anything left of me afterward.

Just get through this last year of school, Ana, and everything will work itself out.

I tell myself that, repeatedly, as I stare at the vaulted ceiling above me. These ancient, drafty buildings remind me that there are secrets in stone.

I lose track of time until Ardella walks in and yelps at the sight of me.

"Are you okay? Fuck! You're bleeding!"

Staring up at her vacantly, I realize how lost I feel.

"It stopped bleeding. I saw a bug and hit the mirror trying to get it."

I'm not ready to talk, and I'm not sure I could form the right words if I tried. Not that Ardella deserves my silence, since she's my number one constant. Like all those years ago, how can I explain what I don't know?

Thankfully, she doesn't press me further.

She gets my hand cleaned and bandaged up before tucking me in, changing her clothes, and getting in with me.

"I know it wasn't a bug, but I'm here for you—for whatever it is that's bothering you."

I treasure her words, curling into her as she holds me until I fall asleep.

When I wake up, she's still there. Her eyes are closed, and she's on her back, breathing softly with pale blonde hair spilling over the pillow. Ardella looks like an angel. *My angel.*

She didn't deserve my lie from last night, but I'm so grateful she's here, even if I don't have myself together. Her beauty distracts me in all the best ways, and I can't help but lean over and kiss her cheek.

I pause once her yellow eyes open, pulling me closer until our lips meet.

"Good morning to you, too," I murmur between kisses.

She cups my face as I crawl over her, keeping my face close to hers.

"Are you okay, Ana?"

"I don't know. It suddenly hit me yesterday. Atticus and Ace. I feel unsettled, Deli."

She runs her hand through my messy hair, and I make a note to chop it off later.

"Ace is pretty obsessed with you, so it's odd. He'll turn up sooner or later. As for Atticus, did you try to write to him again?"

I nod slightly.

"Well, all we can do is enjoy the summer then, Beli," she says in kind.

Leaning my forehead against hers, I exhale heavily.

"Stupid boys."

She huffs a laugh, stealing another kiss.

"Enough of them, it's just us now."

"Mmm, indeed," I deepen the kiss, pulling her to sit up as I straddle her.

I'm in the wrong for holding myself back, but I'm grateful for her not holding it against me. She knows me better than I know myself. Strangely enough, Ace never expressed any interest in Ardella or the two of us together—not that either of us minded, even if Ace hogged up most of my time. He didn't deem Ardella a threat, and I didn't tell him about our relationship—only our friendship—just in case his stalking went overboard. I did it to protect her, even if he seemed relatively harmless.

My tongue slides in her mouth as I cup her nape. Her hands roam, gripping my breasts through my nightdress. Teasing her in turn, I tug hers off and then mine.

I place my finger against her sternum for her to lie back, and she sighs pleasantly, opening her milky thighs without me asking. Before I dive straight to her pussy, I lick down her body, paying special attention to her perky and swollen nipples. Circling and flicking with my tongue, she writhes under me.

We know each other intimately, along with our bodies. She's said over the years how I've changed her, but in reality, she's changed *me*. While she feels I've opened her mind and heart to be free sexually, she's a safe space for me to be both lost and found.

Reveling in her soft curves, my hand dips down to her folds, teasing and massaging her inner thigh. She elicits a lovely moan, tilting her head back and gripping the sheets under her.

She whispers my name, and I kiss down her abdomen and lick near her pubic bone.

"Please," she urges, unable to stand my teasing this early in the morning.

Hiding my smile, I playfully nibble on her inner groin

before licking her labia. Then, I tease her seeping entrance. I lap it up eagerly, unable to hold back anymore from her spectacular taste.

Slowly, I take her on a journey to her peak until she's unable to stand it. Sucking on her clit like a mad woman, I slide two fingers in and massage her inner walls.

She's crying for me at this point.

All of my ghosts are silent, and I bask in the swell of her until she tightens on my fingers and soaks my face. Not shying away, I ensure she rides it out fully until she's twitching.

"Christ, I'm awake now," she exhales in defeat, going lax while I crawl over her with a grin.

Dazzling yellow eyes sparkle up at me. "I love you."

I run my nose against her jaw, kissing her collarbone.

"And I love you," I say, meaning it with every cell in my blood.

CHAPTER 24

"I REALLY FUCKING MISSED YOU"

ANA

It's the last semester of school when Ace shows back up. I received a strange letter not too long before the asshole's return. Atticus seems to be going through things, so he won't be able to see me after I graduate.

> *My Annie,*
>
> *Uncle isn't doing well. He's moving even more slowly and has been in and out of the hospital. I've been taking care of him. It hurts so much to see him suffer. He doesn't deserve it, and it kills me to watch yet another family member go to their deathbed.*
> *All I can do is make him comfortable and be here. As much as I'd love to finally be with you at long last, I'm afraid it will have to wait. I miss you so much. It's been years away from you. Although not forever.*
> *Annie, I know you're graduating soon, and I'm so*

proud of you. I'm sorry I can't be there, but I know you'll find a job and thrive. I love you endlessly.

I'll write when I can.

With love,

A

I'm heading to my class, making a note to apply to work at the hospital in the city nearby, since graduation is around the corner. I'll be homeless if I don't find a facility to work in with my degree.

Ardella said I wouldn't either way, and I'm always welcome to her home in Morella. Her passion is mortuary services, particularly in body preparation. She learned from her father and brother. Deli is drawn to death like I'm drawn to my emptiness inside, searching for answers.

I see Ace-hole across the large courtyard, walking toward me. Thankfully, there are other people around, so I turn and make conversation with a stranger, asking where something is and if they can show me.

This allows me to avoid a confrontation with Ace—one that I'm not ready for. If he thinks he can walk back into my life without a word for months like nothing happened, he has another thing coming.

Asshole.

I make it through the rest of the day without a hitch, until he catches me outside my dorm building.

"What do you want?"

He sighs, seeming nervous. "I'm so sorry... Can we talk?"

I debate whether I want to hear his excuses or not. Looking up to the darkening sky, I breathe out heavily.

"Fine. But you aren't invited to my room. We can go around the side of the building and chat."

I lead the way, partially interested, but mostly wishing for a reason to slap him. *He left me without a word.*

It's not looking good for him.

Once we're at a wall without windows away from any nosey people, I lean against it and wait for him to begin his spiel.

"Again, I'm sorry for disappearing. I could've written, but I didn't. That's on *me*. I tried to get back here as soon as I could, but things at home were *complicated*. I had to leave you."

"Math is complicated. *People* are complicated. Your disappearance is an asshole move. Just because we've had our fun doesn't mean I'm disposable. That's not how things work. Brownie points for having the balls to face me, though."

Ace is a couple of feet away, standing with his hands in his pockets.

"You aren't disposable. *Never, ever,* think that."

"Could have fooled me," I mumble.

Ace interjects, "I'm here because I *do* feel like an ass, so I'm apologizing."

"What happened that was so complicated?"

He shifts uncomfortably, and I watch, eager to hear more. While he does appear sincere, something is pulling at my brain. I can't put my finger on it, but I *feel* an intuitive instinct sinking in my stomach.

Ace runs a hand through his hair, searching for words. Strange, when he's always full of comebacks or something to say.

"My family is dead, and the estate was handed to me. It's not a quick process, so that's what I spent all those months doing. Thankfully, I'm doing well in school, so I don't need to retake anything, nor am I behind."

My curiosity piques.

"School news aside, what happened to them? *That's a lot, Ace.*"

He sighs deeply, dressed in all black, a shadow blending in with the changing light.

"It's not a pretty tale. Murders and suicides," he stares off to the side, a distancing look for him. "My mother and father were having affairs with my aunt and uncle. My mother caught my father and her sister in bed, so she got revenge by sleeping with her brother-in-law. My sibling is also dead, but that was before my parents. The anniversary was around the same time."

Wow.

"I'm…so sorry, Ace. That's heavy."

His eyes meet mine, taking a step closer.

"It is, but I made them promises, so there were priorities. Then, there was dealing with the will and lawyers…"

"Are you okay?"

He reaches for my cheek, caressing it lightly.

"I am now."

I can't help but give him a small smile. As a woman without childhood memories *still* with only lingering vague shadows in daydreams—I couldn't even begin to imagine what it's like for him.

Soon, his forehead is against mine, breathing me in. Sandalwood and amber hit my nose, and soon I'm falling back into him again. Easily forgiven.

"I fucking missed you, Anabel. Thank you for hearing me out."

The tone of his voice dips low, husky and alluring.

I drop my bag beside me and pull him closer.

"Kiss me."

He wastes no time merging his lips to mine with fervor. Moaning into his mouth, he picks me up as I wrap my legs around his waist. It doesn't slip my mind how much time has passed since we've seen each other.

The guy is already hard as a rock, pressing me against the stone, which doesn't bother me. I missed him just as much.

He tugs on my bottom lip, "I *really* fucking missed you."

Grinding slightly, he presses against me tightly, and I'm immediately in a tailspin.

"Likewise… Are you going to fuck me or not?" I say it breathlessly into his mouth.

He pulls up my black dress and frees himself before ripping my underwear. A gasp leaves me as he slides home.

"Fuck, I've missed this tight cunt, too. It feels so good to be back where I belong."

I almost tell him to shut up with his antics, but I decide against it, once he hits me deep and fast and makes my mouth fall open.

"Take what I give you. Take all of it."

I sigh as he fucks me hard and desperately, claiming my lips and locking his tightly to them. Moans become fragmented and split apart.

Anyone can walk around the building and see.

Not that either of us fucking cares.

I'm a proud slut, and there's nothing wrong with getting fucked in broad daylight. It's a human experience. *The idea of someone seeing is equally exciting.*

His hands hold my hips steady as he finishes inside of me right after I come. I hadn't been fucked this hard since he left me last year at the start of summer.

"I think that should hold me over, since I'm not invited inside."

I huff a laugh as he helps me down.

"I think you already came inside," I tease back.

He grins wickedly, adjusting himself.

He takes my ripped panties and stuffs them in his pocket. Rolling my eyes, he pulls me in for a quick kiss.

"Let your roommate know I'm back? I don't want her to crucify me too badly."

I give him my best smile, as I fix my dress and grab my bag.

"No promises; she's my best friend and she loves me."

"Fair enough," he reaches for my hand, walking me to the front entrance.

"I love you, Anabel. I'll see you tomorrow?"

I nod, feeling satisfied and good between my legs.

He kisses me and leaves into the twilight, while I make my way up the flights of stairs.

"Was that Ace I just saw leaving the entry?" Ardella asks as I open the door to our room. I give her a knowing look once I'm fully inside and shut the door behind me.

"Tell me, bitch." Her tone suggests playfulness, as I smirk and jump into her bed after tossing my bag in a corner.

"It *was.*"

"Well, tell a whore already!"

I giggle and tell her everything he told me, plus the fabulous dicking he graced me with on the side of the building.

She throws a pillow at my face.

"Slut!"

We're laughing, and I shrug. "So? If you were down there, you would've been watching!"

She gives me an innocent look.

"Good dicking aside, that's a wild ass story. It certainly explains his absence."

I lay my head on her lap, as she begins to play with my hair.

"Once I graduate, I'll be ditching him, so I'll only have to deal with his obsessive ass until then. Not that I mind his attention, but it's a strange reminder of the limits I have to have."

"You don't have to deal with anything you don't want to," she says quietly.

"I know, but I do enjoy his dick."

We giggle before I sigh sadly with the knowledge of yet another ending—*a transition in life.*

"I'm sad to see you go back to Morella."

"It won't be forever."

Where have I heard those words before?

"Maybe, maybe not. Will you write to me at least?" I ask, sounding so small—desperate even.

"Always."

I let the word sink in. I'm not losing Ardella, but damn if I won't miss her more than anyone else. I make an internal vow to visit her when I can.

CHAPTER 25

"IT'S MY TURN TO DISAPPEAR"

ANA

Ace and I consume each other's time until I graduate. I don't tell him about what I'm doing or that I was offered a job at the hospital, working in the psych ward.

I told him at graduation that our journey was over, as it was meant to be. Our time together was good while it lasted, but I'm a lady with goals and ambitions. He doesn't like it, but I don't give him a chance to object. His facial expression of anger and heartbreak lingered in the back of my mind.

For now, it's my turn to disappear.

It's been months without Ardella, and I feel lost. Hell, I even miss *Ace*. I haven't heard from Atticus anymore. Instead, I write to Ardella, who doesn't care for telephones and prefers penmanship, which makes sense since she's a writer.

E.G. Poe—her pen name.

She's so good at what she does that she even earned an enemy amongst the pages. I read the guy's stuff and wasn't impressed, but I'm also biased.

Rigswold was her ex. She mentioned many moons ago that she had seen him, in the next town over, with a woman who looked just like her on his arm.

If she can open her heart up to damaged goods like me, then I hope she can do the same for whoever captures her heart next.

I ended up finding a cheap room to rent with a coworker at the hospital. They're a sweet, gay couple who happily offered up their last spare room.

The hospital takes up most of my time. The psych ward keeps me busy, with patients screaming and having psychological breakdowns or resisting medications. Some talk to themselves or stare at the wall for hours. I feel unnerved about some of the treatments, like some of the methods of restraints. Not sure what it is about seeing someone strapped to a bed or held down, but it's unsettling to witness, nonetheless.

At night, my dreams show me images of things I can't explain. I see myself hanging from a rope with bloodshot eyes, dangling from a beam above. All I can do is cry and scream in the dream, before someone covers my eyes and steers me away.

There are other images of multiple people who look like *me*. They are only flashes; I can't understand what they could mean. There are long, marble-floored hallways of places I cannot name, and blurry photographs on the walls adorned in fancy sconces. Tall ceilings that remind me of a place left behind in time.

I can't remember the details while awake, but I do remember the feeling.

The loneliness.

A feeling of being caged by pretty things.

Every time I'd wake up from another dream of me wandering hallways endlessly, I'd feel equally unsettled.

I'm not sure what to make of the maze my mind is trying to uncover. After all these years, all I can think to ask myself is: *why now?*

All I can do is continue to wake up confused and work all the hours I can manage at the hospital.

I write Ardella, telling her about my weird dreams and how I feel so alone without her. I miss her terribly.

More months passed, and I finally received a letter from Ardella.

Ana,

I wish I had something happy to talk about, but I don't.

My sister is dead. Suicide.

I prepped her body and had a solo funeral that only I showed up to. I feel so much regret for not being a better sister. I should have been someone she could've counted on.

I failed her.

After I got death-obsessed with mortuary stuff, we grew apart. It's eating at me, even if I have two handsome men keeping me distracted.

My brother is nowhere to be found, and my father is missing. I'm running this show solo. I never thought I'd ask so soon, but I need you, if only to see you for a while. I have so much to talk about and not enough pretty words to write.

There was a masquerade, and Prick Furrows was unveiled. It's too much to write to you, so I'll leave you in suspense, if only to persuade you to come.

Anyway, I miss you with every fiber of my dark being. I eagerly await your response.
I love you until I leave this earth.

Deli

My eyes tear up. My best friend needs me. So, I guess I'll be putting in my two weeks and going to Morella. She knows I don't like being left hanging with gossip, and I couldn't wait to hear about that Prick Furrows writer who lived to see another day after fucking with the wrong friend.

As I prepared for a long journey to the mountains, I ran into someone I least expected.

Ace.

I am dropping off a load of donations when I see him staring at me from across the street.

He still possesses me, mind and body, even after walking away at graduation. Ace inclines his head as I exhale, looking both ways for the cars before I cross the street.

Ace leads the way into a café, and I dare to follow. I wonder what he wants? *Why is he in the city?*

I wouldn't doubt that he stalked me again. It's in his nature to be obsessive, at least toward me.

He finds a corner table by the window.

"When you truly try, you are a hard woman to find."

I lean back in my seat, cross my arms, and raise my brow.

"What do you want, Ace?"

Ignoring my question, he gives me a full look over. I'm wearing a sweater over my dark dress, with stockings and Mary Jane shoes. I don't look my best due to stress, and I'm not in the mood for his antics.

"You look resplendent as always. How are you?"

All I do is stare as a server brings coffee to our table.

"I'm just fucking dandy. Again, what do you want, Ace? I'm not in the mood, nor do I have the time."

He frowns.

"What's the rush? You fucking left me at graduation and disappeared like I was nothing to you."

"We talked about this," I narrowed my eyes, continuing, "it was only temporary while in school. School is over. I've been working my ass off. I am *not* yours. We had our fun, but the reality of us hit its end."

He sips his coffee before responding.

"I love you, Anabel. It hurt me when you disappeared like I meant nothing. *I know we aren't nothing.*"

I sigh dejectedly, looking out the window.

Maybe I'm an asshole for disappearing, sure, but I told him not to get attached. My goals were never to be tied down. Atticus aside, I guess it doesn't matter in the end.

"I'm sorry for the disappearing act; I am. But what do you want with me now? It's been months, and I have places to be. I'm moving soon, and I don't have time for whatever it is you're trying to do here." I gesture my hand toward him.

"Where are you going now?"

"My best friend needs my help. I'm not telling you where either, so don't even think about it."

He sighs deeply, looking down at his hands, before putting them on the table.

"I didn't realize you could be so cold, Anabel. I say *'I love you'* and you dismiss it. That's cruel of you to play with a man's heart like that."

I'm speechless. All I can think to say is, "I don't have room in my life for love, Ace."

"I see, and I'm the biggest fool in this room. I will always be *your fool,* whether you have room in your heart or not."

I rub my forehead in frustration.

"Can we just table this for now? I'm stressed out enough as it is. I'm sorry I can't return your affection at this time. I really just need some space to figure it out. Would it make you feel better if I wrote to you?"

He shakes his head.

"Don't make promises you know you aren't going to keep. You built your walls up so high that you refuse to let anyone in. What happens when they finally crumble? Where will you be then, Anabel?"

I can't help but glare at him.

Before I can think of anything to respond with, he grabs a pen from another table that paid for their meal and writes on a napkin.

"Write to me, or don't. I'll give you your space, because you *so politely demanded it.* Before I go, though," he pauses, standing as I stare dubiously at him in wonder.

"Have you heard anything from Atticus?"

I tilt my head.

"How the hell do you know about Atticus?"

"I found your *love* letters in your drawer." He growls grumpily.

I stand up, anxiety taking hold.

"Why the hell are you asking me about him?"

He gives me this look I can't decipher before talking past me.

"No reason. Goodbye, Anabel."

He's at the door as I shout his name.

"Wait! Ace!"

By the time I make it outside the café, the bastard is gone.

Well, *shit.*

PART THREE

MORELLA

CHAPTER 26

"I'VE BEEN DREAMING OF DROWNING LATELY"

ANA

Hugging Ardella for the first time, after so many months apart, feels like a new kind of torture. She's the other half of my soul. How did I think things were going to go without her around? I give her my condolences for the disarray and grief before she catches me up on everything going on. Eventually, she introduces me to her two new lovers.

Jackson is a smart and appealing, intellectual man with his short, curly red hair and glasses. Roman has darker hair and an appeal that matches those teasing brown eyes. I find that he and I are similar in banter. All of us hit it off, thankfully.

After fucking them together with Deli, I realize why they all fit together so well.

There's warmth and care between the three of them. Jackson is the intellectual bookworm, which is why I see his appeal, since Ardella's the same. He's outwardly romantic and sweet. Roman is the brooding smartass who lives to tease, but in his own way, he shows selfless care with Jackson and Ardella. I can see how Ardella finds charm in the two men, even if their meeting was unconventional by their planning to rob her home but instead were entranced by those precious yellow gems of hers. Ardella likes people with brains and emotion, no matter their dark past or where they came from. Just like me, I suppose.

Maybe in another life, I'd feel worthy of the same love from them.

I can't help but feel a sense of loss in a way. Ardella is moving on with life, and I'm still *stuck*. Like I was so many years ago and throughout college. My mind is always stuck in the past. Unfortunately for me, I've been stuck there, a familiar ghost haunting the walls of an old house.

Just like an old house, I have history written on my walls. Some is forgotten by circumstance, and other traces of history I wish I could forget. It's a loneliness that runs deep, a tidal wave of an ocean I can't escape from.

I've been dreaming of drowning lately. I struggle to come up for air and wake gasping. Must I always be so lost, for the rest of my life?

Ever since school let out and I dedicated my life to the hospital, I have realized how unhappy I truly am. There are missing pieces that I can't get back or change.

My chest is heavy, sinking further and further.

I've been drinking more to help me sleep. I think Ardella doesn't notice the party girl façade. I let her think I'm still the same—unchanged.

Of course, her men see right through me because they have a backstory of survival; they can see me when I think no one else is looking.

It starts with sitting in the grass on the backside of Ardella's home. I light up my cigarette and stare at the dark, outer walls of the crematorium. A bit morbid, but I'm long past the point of giving a fuck.

I aid in helping Ardella with body preparations, but I can tell she's on edge because of her family missing and her sister's death. I try what I can to crack jokes and keep things as familiar as they always were, even though we aren't quite the same as we were in college. We wear the faces of who we once were, yes, but time changes people—no matter how much passes.

I'm lost in thought, like normal, when I notice someone sitting next to me. I'm not surprised it's Roman. I can tell from his woodsy scent. He has dark hair and eyes to match and a hell of a body to ogle and lick. *Which I did.*

"Got another one of those?" He asks nonchalantly like we're two old friends, and I hand the pack and lighter over to him.

I'm wearing a simple, long black dress with no shoes, leaning on my hands, puffing away. I don't think I even brushed my hair today.

"Your mind seems elsewhere today, Hazel Eyes." The familiar nickname warms my insides slightly.

"Where is my mind, indeed?" I say, staring off into the distance at the dreadful-looking crematorium, while flicking the ashes and taking another drag.

Part of me wonders if it's disrespectful to smoke in the presence of a crematorium. *It's rude, right?*

"I know I'm a good lay, Ro," I give him a side glance, finding his lips twitching up in amusement, "but you don't have to check in on me or pretend to care. I do appreciate it, but you don't have to just because of my history with Ardella."

I hear him sigh in frustration.

"You don't let people in, do you?"

No, I don't.

I shrug, lying on my back. Maybe it's better if I push everyone away; no one but me will get hurt.

He leans on one arm, gazing down at me. His shirt is half unbuttoned; his chiseled chest is exposed. I think of how lucky they all are to have found each other.

I'm bitter over Atticus and Ace and my unraveling life.

Ardella seems happier without me around, and I wonder

if *I'm* the dark cloud that's looming. My emotions are futile, and I'm not sure what to do about them.

"Despite what you think, I *do* care. I don't have to know you for four plus years to care. Ardella loves and cares about you. You're someone important and worth getting to know. *Good lay aside, you are more than welcome to give Jackson and me a chance for more, too.*"

My heart skips a beat, and I can't help but smirk as I blow smoke up towards him.

Roman playfully shoves my leg. "You and Arde are both moody."

"Like calls to like, don't you know?"

He huffs a laugh, lying back beside me.

"I do. I wouldn't be anyone without Jackson, and now that extends to Arde."

The clouds are thick and gray, fitting my mood. "I'm glad you three have each other. I always worry about her obsessions running away with her, but I see she's doing just fine," I say honestly, my heart sinking into the earth over my own doom and gloom.

"You aren't left out, Bel."

I turn my head to gaze at him. He's given me another more personable nickname. Special people get nicknames.

Brown eyes meet mine.

"I'm the noncommittal type of girl. I have a stalker and a long-lost lover who's somewhere out there. I have missing memories that come back in strange ways that make no sense, and after college, I have felt more alone than ever before. So, no, I disagree. I am left out. But it doesn't have to be a hateful thing. I'm not unhappy for you three. I just feel so fucking lost with my own shit. I refuse to drag you all down into the pit with me."

I'm being a little too honest with Roman, but I have no fucks left to give. I'm untethered, floating out to sea.

He stares at me for a long moment, saying nothing before

turning his face back toward the sky, while we finish our cigarettes.

"We all go through stuff, but it doesn't mean we have to do it alone. Have you talked to Ardella?"

I shake my head.

"No, she's going through enough. I showed up here, didn't I? It's not about me."

"That you did. Like a bolt of lightning."

Smiling at his comment, I feel his eyes on me. He rolls to his side, head in hand, once I catch his gaze again.

"I'm unhappy, Ro. I'm not sure how to get out of this pit. I don't have a good feeling about Deli's family situation."

"Me either. But just as she's not alone, neither are you."

I puff out the last bit of smoke and roll onto my side to face him.

"I'm glad she has you, too," he adds quietly, and strangely, I'm comforted by his company.

I wait a long while before responding.

"She's the other half of my soul, and I'm used to sharing her. I doubt that will be changing any time soon." I can't tell if my tone is teasing or serious, but Roman gives me a small smile, pulling me into his hold with a kiss to the forehead.

"It will be alright, Bel."

His chest is warm as I relax in his embrace. I can't remember the last time I felt safe in someone's arms, minus Ardella. A certain boy comes to mind then, just as he always does when I miss him.

Atticus, *where are you?*

CHAPTER 27

"I'M NOT READY TO LET GO AND LEAVE"

ANA

"Anabel, remember what I've taught you, dear. How does a lady act?"
My mother said over afternoon tea.

I glanced down at my small feet from a fancy chair.

I was just reprimanded for getting my nice dress dirty.

When I looked up, her face blurred, and everything began to spin.
The scene changed from a cute afternoon tea setting to me curling up in a
corner, covering my head, and crying. I saw feet through my blurry tears,
but I couldn't make out who it was.

I'm begging and pleading. Just before I awakened fully, I was crying
while staring into a mirror with two other reflections of my face on either
side of me. One was masculine and one was feminine.

I crawl out of bed quietly, not to wake the others. It takes me
minutes to realize tears are streaming down my cheeks. In the
bathroom, I splash water on my face and grab one of Ardel-

la's black robes. I make my way downstairs, swiping my cigarettes off the kitchen counter before I head outside. I sit on the front porch step, trying to ease my shaking.

How in the hell was I supposed to process what that was?

Were they memories?

Regardless, it's distressing.

I jump when I hear a door open. I don't remember the first cigarette, so I lit up another.

"Nightmares?" A hushed, sleepy voice asks, and my eyes water in acknowledgement.

Ardella scoots closer, wrapping an arm around me.

"I think my memories are pushing through. I don't understand why *now*, after all these years."

"Brains are fickle things; I can't say for sure... What did you see?"

Finishing my last cigarette, I spill my guts to her. I mention the other dreams with a creepy house and the haunted walls within. I talk about the glimpses of my mom lecturing me because I was unladylike and going against my duties, though I still can't recall *why*.

My mind tries to make out the huge family portrait on the wall in the grand living room, but the faces are blurred. There are repeated images in my dreams of a boy and a girl with my face.

It doesn't make sense.

"Why did you never tell me your dreams and worries?" Ardella asks quietly as I wipe my eyes, leaning into her.

"I thought they were just dreams. When everything is uncertain, why drag someone in with me?"

"Because I love you and I care."

I sniffle. "You have two men inside. What do you need me for?"

Ardella cups my face, wiping away my streaming tears repeatedly.

"I will always need you. Don't let your mind win. Don't let

memories take what you know to be true. No matter what happened before, you are not that person or that life anymore. You are Anabel. Forget the last name; it doesn't define your spirit or *your heart.*"

She places her hand on said heart of mine, rubbing my cheek.

"You are not alone. You will always have me. You know that. What's our saying? You're the—"

"—other half of my soul," I finish.

"That's right. No matter the distance or time, that will never change. The only thing we're adding is a pair of gorgeous men to that picture. They are open and willing if you are. You can't keep everyone out for the rest of your life, Ana."

I look into her precious gold gems that reflect the night.

"Give them the chance to love you like I do. They are here for you, too."

I close my eyes and weep. Ardella pulls me in and holds me tight.

I let her.

Resting my head in her lap while the sun rises, Ardella plays with my hair. Her comfort is soothing to my spirit, and I feel a sense of release, now that I'm not holding back how I truly feel. I've opened up about the nightmares that've plagued me for so long—*they still do.*

We sit there for a while, not saying anything, until she offers to go inside. I let her lead me into her home. She asks if I want something to drink, and I shake my head, making my way to the couch. I curl myself on it.

I feel a blanket being draped over me. "I love you. I'm here if you need me. Try and rest."

Little does she know, weeks later, I'd be saying the same to her…

Her father was found dead; now, she vacantly walks the halls. Ardella has stopped eating and speaking with us—not that we'd rush her grief. Her father was her person, idol, and reason for being a mortician.

Jackson comes into the kitchen to find me leaning my arms on the counter with my head in my hands. I'm at more of a loss now than ever before.

"Hey," he says gently, moving to stand beside me. "I don't know when that day will come, but she'll be okay."

I'm not sure if he's reassuring me or himself while rubbing my back in soothing motions.

"I'm fine," I say, looking up at his blue and green, concerned-filled eyes. "I'm just worried about her."

"I know, me too. Ro is cuddling with her right now. Do you want to take a walk with me?"

I exhale and nod in agreement, thinking some fresh air would do me some good.

We soon walk through the trees side-by-side in comfortable silence for a long while.

"Can I show you something?"

"Okay," I say quietly, wondering what he wants to reveal to me.

We walk for an hour until we get to the heart of the town of Morella. Soon, we're standing in front of an abandoned home of sorts.

I stare, looking at the cracks in the roof and foundation. A physical representation of my mental state.

"Roman and I grew up in this home," he begins, gazing at the decrepit structure. "We're foster brothers. Without each other, we wouldn't have made it this far in life. It took us so many years to admit our feelings toward each other. It wasn't until Ardella came into our lives. And now, we have *you.*"

Turning my head toward him, we lock eyes.

The time in Morella has blurred. Weeks, months—who knows at this point.

"Jack—"

He places a finger on my lips. "You don't need to say anything. Just know, Ro and I are here for you, too. I know we've been barely put together all this time, searching for her dad and brother, and then dealing with the aftermath of grief. It's been hard lately. Ro and I haven't said it lately, but we're glad you came and to have met you. You are someone special, Annie. We are so grateful to spend this time with you, even though I wish it were under better circumstances. I know you hold yourself back and that monsters are digging into your mind. I hope you realize by now that you don't have to face those demons alone."

His words made me feel as if Atticus was speaking to me. I didn't know if the man lived or died at this point.

My eyes fill up with tears.

Speechless, I follow blindly with blurry eyes while Jackson leads me away from the deteriorating house, and soon we're in front of another one, only this time it's a more put-together structure. The symbolism between the houses and my broken spirit is uncanny.

"This is the home Roman and I were able to get. Our life of criminal activity could cease because we finally have a place of our own and weren't surrounded by memories and ghosts reminding us of things we care not to recall."

The tears fall from my eyes, and the weight is back on my shoulders.

"I know you can relate in a way, but I wanted to show you that seemingly broken things can heal, too. You will always have a home here with us, if you want it."

Releasing another cry, I turn toward him as he tugs me

into a tight hug. Jackson holds me as I weep into his chest, unable to form the words I need.

How can I express gratitude if I feel unworthy of it? *Of them?*

Jack says nothing, letting me get it out. He doesn't seem to mind, and I'm not ready to let go.

So, I don't, until I have to.

Dear Annie,

I have much to tell you. I'm sorry I haven't written. I was dealing with the death of my uncle and his estate.

I've missed you terribly, and I must ask that you come to the address on the postage. I need you. Come home, where you belong with me.

I hope there's still a place for me in your heart after all these years, for you still fondly live in mine.

I saw these clippings during my travels and thought you might find them interesting.

I love you and hope to see you soon.

I'll always wait for you.

I'll meet you where the land touches the sea.

With eternal love,

-A

CHAPTER 28
"THE CLIFF"

ANA

My mind races against time. Uncertainty and questions are condemning me. I feel a sense of urgency running through my bloodstream. My letter to Ardella is quick as I pack my bags and arrange the ride out of Morella.

I quickly hug Jackson and Roman goodbye, telling them I'll see them again someday. They aren't really understanding my hurriedness while I write down the address I'll be going to for them, and they tell me to be careful.

Once I leave Ardella's home and make it into the heart of Morella, I take a taxi back to the big city. On the ride there, I think about all that led me to this moment. The letter was specific and strange, with newspaper clippings of a murdered family and one member still missing. There's a grainy image of a house by the sea.

Why would Atticus want me to go to a place where people were killed? So many uncertain thoughts race through me, the most important one of all being anticipation. I can't wait to finally see him again after all these years. It has been a long time coming.

The large city appears in my field of vision, and I quickly pay the taxi and find the nearest convenience store to get a map for myself.

It only took me a few hours of investigation to find myself at a train station on my way to Blackwood, a town many hours away.

The train ride is overnight, so I settle in, but of course, haunting dreams occur.

Angry hot tears rolled down my cheeks as I spewed words of turmoil, "I will never be what you want me to be."

A male's words echoed back to me, muffled and low. "You are already all that I want. We are fated."

The male's figure stalked toward me until I was backed into a hard wall. Closing my eyes, he caged me in with his arms.

"I will die before I let anyone else have you. You are mine, *Anabel. That's how it is and will always be."*

The dream swirled into another image of me standing in the hallway, looking at a dark-haired girl hanging from the tall ceiling. I walked into the room. I was shocked, grief-stricken—too late. There was no telling how long she had been hanging there.

The five-sided room attached to the attic was dusty. Not sure how I knew that, but I did.

With sudden hands on my shoulders, I yelped.

"Come, let's see our sister."

I struggled against whoever tightly gripped me and moved me toward the front-facing side. As soon as I was there, I sobbed before being forced to take in the horrific sight.

"Look at her, Anabel."

So, I did.

Jumping awake, *thank goodness,* my heart is racing as the train jerks to my intended stop.

I wipe my sweat while my legs shake in fear, as if I were just there in that room with the woman—*sister?*

Grabbing my two bags, I make my way off the train toward a large map on the station wall.

It looks like it's a two-hour walk.

Sighing heavily, I make my way from the station toward the dirt road. I'm in the middle of nowhere. There are woods, but somehow, I can smell salt and sea. A morning chill weaves its way around my bones, yet it doesn't bother me much. I'm wide awake after that terrible dream. *Or was it?*

Was it truly my sister?

I try to distract myself on the long walk and take in the cool air, greenery, and sound of nature. My arms are tired from carrying my bags, and I pause to go and relieve myself behind one of the large trees.

Feeling better now, I resume the last bit of the walk. Side roads appear, but I don't venture down them; I keep going along the path, somehow knowing it'll take me to where I need to go.

The scent of the sea is even stronger, and I can hear waves in the distance. *What a sweet relief.*

As the woods clear and fizzle out, I pause to see rolling hills, with various houses in the distance, and the edges of the sea. There's a cliff's edge to my left as the road travels down toward the neighborhood below. I pick up the bags and carry them near the cliff, setting them down and walking over.

Once I'm there, I peer over but quickly take a step back out of fear of falling. Sitting down off to the side, a strange feeling washes over me.

This is the cliff that changed my life.

My airways constrict as the feeling of being pushed overtakes me.

Who the hell pushed me?

The soothing sun peeks out from a cloudy sky, as if to tell me there is still light. Closing my eyes, I bask in the heat before it's gone.

A strange sense of reckoning is coming, although I can't decipher what. Looking out at the endless sea as it meets the horizon, a foreboding feeling washes over me.

It's the place from long ago. I ended up back where it all started.

Rising from the ground, I dust myself off and look to the left. I see the tree line and more cliffs stretching far and wide, with scattered big houses. My eyes roam over to the right, and that's when I see it. The dark house of my dreams. It's large and unique, different from Ardella's family home. *At least there's no crematorium in the back.*

The answers I've been looking for are in that house. It's down a steep hill, and no cars are in the driveway. Swallowing the disquietude, I lift my bags again. As I hold them, I stare down the hill, waiting and watching.

No lights are on. There is no sign of life, for that matter.

I can't make myself move. I'm frozen there, gazing at that mansion and taking in its dark colors. A place that gives off an eerie air.

Come on, Ana. Move your feet.

I won't find the answers I've been waiting for by standing here.

With one deep breath after another, I count for five cycles in my mind.

Finally, I walk down the big hill.

THE HOUSE

Voices whisper from within the walls,
Pushing and pulling.
My memory can't recall,
Sight and sound.
Please, don't turn around.

The darkness calls within,
For the release of all my sins.
A tug-of-war, I cannot win.
All thoughts of before are grim.

Peace doesn't exist here,
Haunted by ghastly fears.
You'll find me in your tear,
For I disappear when you come near.

Secrets plague thine blood.
Where would I be if not dragged through the mud?
The cage of my dwelling,
Pandora's box will be my unveiling.

Tormented by the souls who've come before,
No one knows what goes beyond those closed doors.
Always soliciting for more,
Scraping down the page of our family lore.

A steady structure, a buzzing honeybee.
For it ends with me, our family tree.
This house isn't me,
Forever I break, until I'm free.

— E.G. Poa

213

CHAPTER 29

"ANSEL"

ANA

My skin prickles as I stand at the grand entryway. It gives off an odd feeling of familiarity. There are two dark statues of large vultures standing on a rotting-away body, painting a macabre scene. I look up at the archway and see a graphic scene of blood, violence, and lust. There's a painted dark-haired male, holding another dark-haired female with passion, lush and nude. There is a script that reads, *"The blood that binds us is the purest form of love."*

A rush of various memories floods my mind, causing me to lean against the fancy set of double Gothic-arched doors.

I'm being dragged, sobbing and pleading, out of the house by a firm grip.
"Please don't do this," I pleaded, repeating the first word.
There was a sharp male gaze that turned abruptly to face me while dragging me up the hill to the cliff.

The scene then flashed to something darker, more forbidden.

A gentle but demanding touch lingered on my body as I lay in bed. I know it was wrong; it's so wrong to enjoy it. But in the dark, where all things linger, I can't help but give in each time. If only he were someone else.

Calming my erratic breath, I finally use the cast-iron ornate knockers to make my presence known.

Thump-thump!

The silence is deafening afterward. My heartbeat echoes in my ears like a deathwatch beetle. A warning. *A reminder.*

I do it again.

Thump! Thump!

This time, the door opens slowly.

I don't hear anyone.

"Hello?"

Waiting with bated breath, no one answers.

I huff out another breath, grab my bags, and step inside.

Shutting the door behind me, I wander further in and call out once again. No one answers.

There are art pieces everywhere. A strange museum of dark and terrible, yet fascinating things. There are abstract sculptures and taxidermy, and various-shaped bones, of what I'm hoping are animals, in glass cases.

I move into the next room, which looks like a lounging area. It's dark like the main foyer, but in a subtle way. Flames are going steady in the fireplace.

Someone must be here.

"Hello? Is anyone there?" I call out once more.

I'm tired of the weird energy emanating from this place and *of my own mind.*

It's quick, but with my periphery, I see a shadow in the doorway to the room.

"You came."

I startle, yelping.

Shoes clack on the pristine floor as the sound moves closer to me. I'm gripping the sofa in front of the fireplace, unsure if I want to see who I'm talking to. My foolish eyes follow the figure, tensing up once I realize who's standing before me.

"Ace," I whisper in confusion, my head beginning to ache.

"Call me Ansel. Ace is what I used for school."

What the hell is going on?

Frowning, his footsteps carry past me and toward a drink cart nearby, where he makes himself a drink.

"Thirsty?" He offers nonchalantly, acting as if I hadn't met him, spent so much time with him, *or fucked him.*

"You're really asking me for a drink, *right now?*" I ask in disbelief.

He shrugs and takes the glass back, "We have much to discuss."

"I'm not even sure what the hell is going on, so maybe start there? Who the fuck are you, Ace?"

"Ansel," he corrects. Completely unbothered, he sips whatever gold liquid he poured.

"Whatever," I grumble, trying to ease my rising anger and panic. My head aches as if it knows that Pandora's box is about to be ripped open and chaos unleashed.

"Please, sit." He gestures toward the sofa I'm leaning on.

"I think I'll stand," I say while he sits in an oversized chair instead, facing toward me.

"What do you remember about this place?"

I rub my temple for a moment.

"I don't know, why? Is there something I *should* remember? Why am I here?"

Ignoring my first two questions, he answers the last, "You are here because I want you here. You belong here."

"Can you stop with the theatrics, for fuck's sake?" I glare at him, meeting his darkening gaze over the top of the glass he's holding.

"Walk around the house, Anabel, then I'll answer your questions."

"What—"

"Please," he adds earnestly.

Begrudgingly, I stomp from the room and wander around the bottom floor. After the kitchen and burgundy dining room, I find the library, and on its walls, a large family portrait hangs.

The one from my dream.

The portrait is otherworldly in nature due to the gloomy, but realistic, mood it gives off. Whoever the painter was, they did a phenomenal job.

Everyone in it has dark brown hair with blank or moody faces. Three children are off to the left, and next to the boy are the father and mother. The father has his hand on the boy's shoulder. A couple is located next to the parents. The two women look like they're sisters, and the men look like brothers.

A sense of déjà vu overcomes me; somehow, I *should* know that painting intimately, but I think nothing more of it as I leave the room immediately wanting to know what Ace's problem is and why he's so demanding about my searching of the creepy mansion. Some guest bedrooms and bathrooms are on the bottom floor, too, but I exit as quickly as I see them. Many rooms are bold in their cool color schemes, which wouldn't bother me normally, but this fucking place leaves me disturbed.

I make my way up the grand staircase near where I entered, and things suddenly get more interesting.

Various portraits line the long hallway at the top. At each solo portrait, I stop and read the names.

Caspian Lee.

Elowen Lee.

Ansel Lee.

Anabel Lee.

Anais Lee.

Valencia Lee.

Rimordian Lee.

There's one for every person in the family portrait from the library. My mind catches up to what was always lacking as I take a shaky step back.

I reread my name.

Then again.

The teenager in the portrait is *me*.

I'm barely smiling, wearing a maroon, mixed with black, dress, more suited for a vampire. *It breaks my heart.*

My mouth falls open as a few realizations occur to me all at once.

This is my family's home.

Most of my family is dead.

Ace—*Ansel*—is my brother.

He tried to kill me by pushing me off a cliff.

My sister, Anais, was the girl who hung from the ceiling in a memory flashback.

Horror washes over me as I look closer at our portraits. We're younger. We're not just related by blood.

We're triplets!

I gasp and back away. I'm going to be sick.

Bile rises as I curse myself for being a blind idiot.

How did I not realize before?

The hallway starts to spin, my panic rising from deep within my chest.

There's a reason why I'm affected by this place.

"Anabel," I hear his voice at the start of the hallway.

My head snaps to the side. As I feel I've done before, I turn away from Ansel.

Then, I run.

CHAPTER 30
"REMEMBER"

ANSEL

Once I hear my Anabel go up the stairs, I follow behind until she's up in the hallway.

Yes, see our history—remember it.

Remember me and how much I love you.

You are mine, Anabel Lee.

At the top of the stairs, I hear her gasp.

I call out her name, as I watch her spiral—*remember.*

She stares at me briefly before fleeing down the hallway and finds the closest room to escape into, slamming and locking the door shut behind her. She's about to find out that she chose *my room.*

I lean against my door, listening to her sob and breaking down.

"Anabel, let me in. I'm not going to hurt you."

"Then why did you push me off the cliff?" Her voice is cracked and broken, deservingly so.

I sigh heavily; the question stings. The answer is even more complicated.

"Open the door, and I'll tell you."

All I want is to be close to you, near you, Anabel.

"So you can kill me again? Are you crazy?!"

"Ann, I'm being serious. I'm not going to hurt you."

Right now, you are safe with me.

She's right to fear me. I've given her no reason to trust me, especially now. I lied to her for years in college.

I just wanted to know her without her knowing me—without our history being a sore subject, and desperate times call for desperate measures.

"How am I supposed to trust you?" I hear her sniffle behind the door.

She sounds closer now. I lean against the wood, placing my hands upon it before closing my eyes so that I can see through hers. She's pacing before stopping in front of the door, hesitantly at my silence.

"What did you do? What was that?" She demands.

"Don't you know? Triplets and twins have special abilities; all of us did growing up. The three of us."

"How?"

I can feel her breath easing, her heartbeat struggling to make sense of reality and her memories. The line between what is real and what isn't.

After all, this house has its ghosts.

"Close your eyes. Start with imagining what I look and feel like. Envision what I'm doing. You focus your senses on what you know to be true and then work from there. I am an extension of you, Anabel."

It's silent for a moment as I take a step back from the door and shove my hands in the pockets of my black slacks.

Open the door, Ana.

I hear quiet footsteps and a creak of the door opening.

We stare at each other, taking in our identical eyes. I think of our recent years more so than our dark childhood. Hard choices and sacrifices needed to be made. She is my addiction, my blood, and my lifeline.

Anabel may think that Ardella is her soul mate, but it's always been *me*.

It's a family tradition. The hereditary trait of having twins or triplets as both of our parents are a pair. As it always was, we were to keep our bloodline pure, untainted.

We grew up learning from our parents, keeping our family secrets within the walls, covered in pristine paint to hide the bloodstains. Others were always excluded. It was forbidden to marry or breed outside the family.

In the early years of our youth, Anais, Anabel, and I were fairly close. Running and playing together, cuddling, and sleeping in the same bed. We were innocent. At least until we hit early puberty.

Around that time, our parents began to groom all three of us. My Aunt Valencia and Uncle Rimordian were constantly reminding us of our duties and what lies ahead for our future.

Our parents had put us all in separate rooms, alone without one another. The other parts of ourselves were missing. There was initial loneliness, since we spent the first decade of our lives together, only to have our parents separate us.

Little did we know they were having their own marital problems. My aunt and uncle moved in and influenced my parents with their wicked whims and family secrets, reminding them of what needed to be done. Then, the affairs started.

I caught my mom with my uncle a few times; the same happened with my father and aunt. It shaped my fascination with watching, lurking in the shadows to learn everyone's secrets. The very same secrets that tainted my blood. It was uncertain whether or not they knew about it then, but that changed over the years.

All four of them made an effort to drill into our heads who we were supposed to be and our destiny; Anabel and I got the worst of it. Anais was the compliant one, and all of them doted on her. A rivalry began, unknowingly to Anabel.

I had taken to Ann more. We were most similar of the three of us. My bond to her was greater than Anais's, and I knew I would have to choose one of them to marry. It was never a question in my mind. *Where one lived, another had to die. So, my aunt and uncle had said anyway.*

Anabel wore her heart on her sleeve, sensitive to the environment around her. Our mother and aunt forced her to learn the family feminine ways, and then I was forced to learn, too.

I didn't want to be cruel initially. I loved my sisters, but over those five years until the accident and murders, *I changed.*

If I refused to comply, one of us was beaten. Once I learned about sex and how to do it by observing and looking through old magazines in my uncle's room, I experimented with Anabel.

She was afraid but let me. I would hold her close afterwards, as we were away from the world of what our family expected of us.

Eventually, Anabel began to fear me and resist, not making sense of our duties. I became more aggressive toward her, controlling and demanding, just like our parents. I hurt her the more she resisted me, but I was only doing what our family tree taught me.

No wonder she feared me.

Even now, I am full of secrets and lies. I've never made it easy for her. *I still don't make it easy.*

Everything I've ever done is for her. To have her back with me.

I will lie, cheat, steal, and kill for it—*for her.*

And I had done so.

I bear the weight of my sins heavily on my back, and I will

commit as many as needed to ensure she remains here with me.

As I stare at her, I notice her knees becoming weak and catch her before she falls. Holding her close, I run my fingers through her soft hair.

"You are mine, Anabel. I won't let anyone stand between us. Atticus won't be a problem anymore, and you're away from Morella. I won't let you get away again."

CHAPTER 31

"WHY?"

ANA

I can't believe I fainted.

My head is throbbing as if my skull were cracked open and rearranged. I'm starting to remember more and more, but *I'm not liking the images.* Did I truly need this strange house to unlock the key to my kingdom? The heart of me?

Groaning, I roll over, realizing I'm in a plush bed.

A hand gently rubs my back in slow, soothing motions. It's familiar and comforting to me, and I don't have the energy to pull away or do anything more.

"As long as you're with me, Ana, you're safe."

Am I not safe without him?

His undertones are so confusing.

I drift back to sleep and wake again to blinding light. I stretch and see my bags in the far corner of the room.

Speaking of the room, I look around, recognizing it's not the same one I fainted in. That room held artwork and black and white photographs with beige walls and dark furniture.

The room I'm currently in has stormy gray walls and

fancy paneling. Sitting up, I realize I'm on a four-poster bed with black sheets and thick blankets.

Before I can think or glance at anything else, there's a knock at the door that makes me jump. Moments later, it opens, and in walks Ansel dressed in casual black, carrying a tray of food and drinks.

"Good, you're awake. I made us some food."

He sets it on the nightstand beside the bed, sitting down next to me. Ansel lays his hand on my blanket-covered leg and rubs.

"How are you feeling?" I ignore the concern in his voice as I still gather all my thoughts.

I'm not sure how to feel.

Matching hazel eyes linger on mine before he hands me some orange juice and the plate of breakfast foods without another word.

Before I can think of what to try and say next, he grabs his plate, takes a bite, and begins to speak.

"After we eat, I'll answer all your questions. The weather is nice, so we can sit outside if you'd like or somewhere else if you'd prefer."

I nod slowly, saying nothing while crunching on my crispy bacon. I'm not sure where to even begin with my questions, but I should at least ask them. I highly doubt Ansel would let me leave this place.

We eat in silence for the rest of our meal. There are too many questions, and I wonder if he would even be truthful?

I gather he's holding a lot back, for whatever reason. More than likely, he's done terrible things or is ashamed—*or not*—who's to say?

When I arrived, I panicked and needed to get away with the shock of everything hitting me at once. Staring at his matching eyes brought back so many memories; it was overwhelming. At least the sleep helped my brain from imploding.

"Is this my room?" I ask, once we finish eating and he stands.

"Yes," he answers simply, gathering up the tray and dishes. "I'll meet you downstairs when you're dressed and ready."

Watching him leave, I can't help but be curious about why he's offering to answer questions. I hold the great internal debate as I finally throw the covers off a minute later.

I pull a dark blue dress out of my luggage, deciding to get the conversation over with while gathering my thoughts. Shutting the bedroom door behind me, I avoid the portraits boring into my skull as I rush down to meet him.

I'm still having trouble processing my memories.

Ansel is my brother, *and I fucked him.*

What does that say about me?

Worst yet, *I liked it.*

I'm fucked like the rest of my family.

A dark, lusting part of me shrugged it off, while the other sane half reminded me of my taboo family. The taboo thinking of this family must have been something I fought so hard against once it was forced upon us.

As children, we simply didn't know. We could just exist without it being right or wrong. All we had was each other until puberty.

I try to remember my sister, but Ansel turns around before I can get more lost in thought. He gestures with a hand toward the left side of the stairs and to the hallway. Leading the way, it doesn't take long for him to fall in step beside me.

"The blue on your dress brings out your eyes," he comments quietly.

I return nothing in response, wondering how to even act around him. How could I face anyone after this, knowing I fucked my brother?

A sense of shame washes over me, but if I want answers from him, I need to be careful. If I piss him off, there's no one here to save me. I really don't want to end up over the cliff's edge again.

If I pretend, will he see through me?

The more I think about it, the more complicated those thoughts of mine become. *Nothing is looking good here.*

There are questions tugging at me.

What does he know about Atticus?

My head begins to pound, and we haven't even made it outside yet.

Cutting through the kitchen, Ansel opens a door that leads out to a fancy garden area. There's a place to sit under some shade.

"I'm sure you have questions," he says while sitting down.

I say, "I don't know where to start," and it's the honest truth.

"Do you love *me?*" He asks moments later.

"I do," I say honestly, because before arriving, *I did.* Before I remembered him as *him,* I definitely had an addiction, call it love—or whatever.

My heart is always with Atticus.

And Ardella.

They plague my mind when I'm not around them, and I haven't seen Atticus in so many years that I'm uncertain if he loves me anymore.

Ansel seems to relax. "You already know how crazy I've always been about you. We are two sides of the same coin. I hope you don't regret our time in college."

Well, now that you mention it...

The most important, yet hardest, question I think to ask then is, "Why did you push me off the cliff, Ansel?"

I hold his gaze with my own, letting the hurt show before continuing, "People who love each other don't try to kill each other."

"On the contrary," he leans forward, resting his elbows on

the iron table. "Love runs in blood. Blood is stored and blood flows."

What the fuck?

"Our parents had an affair after your accident. Did you ever suspect or hear?"

I blink twice before shrugging and shaking my head.

"Nothing comes to mind," I respond, frustrated that he's ignoring my question.

He sighs, "I think we would've been fine if it weren't for their harsh ways of doing things. The forced solitude, threats, and punishments."

Yeah, mind games—love that.

"You still didn't answer my question. *Why?*" I remind him again.

"That answer is complicated, Ann."

"I don't care. I deserve to know! Because now, I'm back here *again* under false pretense. Stop bullshitting me, Anse."

I freeze, realizing what I just said.

Ansel notices, too, rising quickly before sinking to the ground. I'm startled by his quick action until he's in front of me, laying his head in my lap while hugging me so tightly, afraid to let me go.

"You haven't said that adorable little name in over a decade."

Shit.

I don't know what else to do other than run my hand through his hair.

What the hell am I doing?

"It's complicated because I never wanted to hurt you like I did. Our family fucked with all of our heads, and they forced me to play my hand with your continuous defiance. As for the sibling rivalry, I don't know where that came from. You were always my favorite, *my only.*"

Good for me.

I exhale long and slow while his excuses continue.

"I couldn't make you love me back the way that I loved you. I grew frustrated and took it out on Anais—*you, too. I became just like our parents.* I hated myself, Bel."

Now that my memories are coming back more and more, I remember him calling me nicknames, like Bel and Ann. He only ever really used Anabel when he was being serious. I got my love for nicknames from him.

Like calls to like.

"You were supposed to be my protector, but you became my abuser," I say, my chest cracking open.

My heart feels like iron, and I hear him sniffle and cry softly.

The knife is twisted in my chest. The greatest betrayal by shared blood.

"I was so angry that you kept refusing to accept me, despite our parents' attempts. I dragged you up there to that cliff out of anger and desperation. I thought if I threatened you, it might help, but then *I pushed you too hard.*"

Ansel is still weeping on my lap, and I stop moving my hand, trying to understand his motivations.

"I watched the sea swallow you, and then I peered over, realizing what I'd done. I tried to find you, but it was already too late. I lost it after that, destroying everything I touched."

I take a deep breath, my heart lodged in my throat.

"Our parents found me destroying the house and asked where you were. They beat me black and blue."

Closing my eyes, I'm suddenly pulled to the moment with him.

"Ansel, where is Anabel?" Father asked.

"What did you do?" Mother chimed in as they stood and stared at the destruction in my room.

"I pushed her into the sea. She's gone," I said, void of all emotion, completely numb to what I'd done.

What I did was unforgivable.

They shouted their curses as Mother smacked me hard and my father kicked me in the ribs.

"You fucking idiot! There's no one left to marry! They're both gone! You stupid, insolent boy! You've ruined our legacy and our fucking family!" He continued to hit and kick me as I let the pain wash away my sins, crying quietly.

Mother was crying angrily as she smacked me so hard in the face, my vision blurred.

"You are a disgrace to this family, ruining everything you fucking touch!"

"You did not come from my womb, you monster of a child!"

"It's time for you to think seriously about your actions," Father spit out, while dragging me down the steps by my hair. Then, he threw open the basement doors after.

"I'm not the disgrace!" I shouted hatefully. "You two are the ones cheating!" I probably shouldn't have yelled that loud enough for my aunt and uncle to hear, but it was too late.

"What the fuck did you just say?" My father backhanded me hard enough to see stars as I tumbled down the steps into the basement. I probably hit my head on something, because I didn't remember what hateful things they said to me or each other after that.

I remained in the basement until their deaths.

Tears flow down my cheeks, dripping onto Ansel.

"We come from a family of monsters," I say more to myself than him.

"We can't help where we come from; we were both trapped," he says dejectedly, sitting up to gaze upon me.

Ansel carefully reaches his fingers toward my face, wiping away my tears.

"I shouldn't have let their cruelty change me."

"No, probably not," I mumble honestly, while he rubs my cheek with his thumb.

"I'm glad you're finally here with me in our home."

"I can't say the same, with all that haunts this family in this fucking house."

Staring off towards said house, I let my mind linger on the letter received.

"We must cleanse it with new memories now."

I ignore his statement, giving him a stare down. "Ansel, you sent that letter to me."

Glancing back toward him, I catch his nod.

I thought it was Atti this whole time.

I'm not sure what to think anymore.

"Where is Atticus? What happened?"

"I'll tell you about him when I feel like I can trust you not to run away from me, *again.*"

Leverage and a bribe. *Ansel knows what's going on with Atticus.*

"Ansel," I press, and he stands, shaking his head.

"I mean it, Anabel."

"At least tell me if he's dead? Is he alive?" I swallow the knot in my throat.

"He's alive."

Relief floods me, and Ansel notices, his hand clenching at his side.

"It's either me or him, but you don't get both. I will be your only choice, Anabel."

All I can do is stare at him in disbelief.

"What happened to cleansing this place and creating newer memories?"

Ansel exhales heavily, "That is solely dependent on *you, Bel.* I won't lose you again. *No matter what.*"

I try to calm myself down from his vague threats. He's used to getting what he wants. While he's changed in some ways, I can still see those old habits lying under the surface in wait, begging to be unleashed. *Or maybe they never left at all.*

One thing is for sure, it looks like it's do or die for me, yet again.

CHAPTER 32

"THE BLOOD THAT BINDS US IS THE PUREST FORM OF LOVE."

ANSEL

I pull the cord, and the lights flicker on.

The buzzing electricity tickles my mind. I lean against the wall and cross my arms, while I watch him struggle in the binds once he notices it's me.

"How are you, my friend?" I ask.

He narrows his eye, answering in a way that probably says, *"fuck you."*

"I'm glad to hear you're doing well," I answer for him. "As for me, I am splendid. *She* is finally home, isn't that great?"

I casually stride toward the guy. *I can definitely see the appeal.*

"She's remembering and she's staying here. Did you know she asked about you?"

I sit on his lap, draping my arm around him as if we're the best of friends.

"She's not meant to know about you, yet. I don't trust her not to flee with you—not when I just got her back. Thankfully, she's still naïve enough to listen to my nonsense."

Muffled sounds continue as I tilt my head toward him. "I'm sorry, what was that? Were you saying something?"

He struggles under me.

"Ah, well, maybe next time, old champ." I pat his shoulder.

"I'll feed you in the morning. Can't kill you, yet... Not that anyone would look for you."

I stand up, making my way to the string again.

"Sweet dreams, Atticus."

"Ans, tell me more about our family. Were we always like this?"

I'm seated in the library, staring at our family portrait. Anabel is looking through the shelves.

"To my knowledge, yes. What do you want to know?"

My eyes slowly move around the room until settling on her. She's dark perfection, a feminine version of myself. She had always been the curious and adventurous type. I'm glad to see those parts of her didn't change despite the accident.

"Have we always lived in Blackwood?"

"No," I say simply. "Our parents bought this place shortly after they married. Our aunt and uncle had trouble conceiving, so they moved in with us when we were ten. They were a second set of parents."

She processes my words, no doubt thinking of another question.

"I'm remembering bits and pieces the longer I stay here. Is this place haunted?"

I chuckle grimly. With all the death, I wouldn't be surprised.

"Probably. If you have any questions about misshapen memories, I'm happy to aid or clear the air."

"Thanks." She turns around to browse the books once more. "Do you think our parents truly loved us?"

Looking toward the moody portrait, I sigh in contempt of those matching eyes lingering back. Ghosts that would never leave me. "Maybe in their own fucked up way. Take out the abuse, then sure, maybe. I think they didn't know any other way to be. Their parents were way worse and more restrictive."

Her hand lingers on a violet book before turning her head to meet my gaze. I admire her blood-red dress I put in her closet to make her feel more at home.

I already knew her body intimately, so stocking up with clothes and necessities, in preparation of her arrival, was no issue.

"I..."

Tilting my head and raising my brow, I ask, "What is it?"

"I—" Her hand drops, and she sighs. "You've lied to me for years. I just want to know what you expect out of me now that I'm here. Are you going to enforce outdated traditions? You know the world outside of this house doesn't condone such things."

I don't care about the rest of the world. I can't change what I've been made to believe and become. That's the difference between us. I'll kill and destroy to get what I need and want. Anabel won't do any such thing. She has her opinions and conclusions, but she's in for a rude awakening if she doesn't wake up.

"Anabel, I love you. I've been without you for years, and then when I finally found you, I couldn't exactly tell you about all this fucked up shit. I'm surprised memories didn't trigger while being around me."

She looks thoughtful for a second. "Me too...but you thought it was okay to play on my ignorance and *fuck* me? *That's fucked up.* How do you expect me to stay here when you've lied to me about *really* important things? You probably are still keeping secrets."

I stand abruptly, my temper rising as I ignore her last statement.

"Would you have been with me if you knew?" I'm upon her, caging her in against the built-in bookshelf. When she says nothing, I know I've got her.

"That's what I thought." My hand cups her cheek and my thumb trails over her bottom lip. "I'm not going to apologize for the lengths I've gone through just to find out you were alive and in school. Of course, I had to be where you were. Everyone else is *dead,* Anabel. It's just you and me. *We can make our own rules.*"

I lean in and kiss her while I have her off guard. She returns it out of pure instinct but doesn't go further. Now that she knows various truths, she won't act as oblivious as she was in school toward me.

It drives me fucking crazy.

"Anse—" I put my finger to her lips.

"I'll let you think about what you want to do. This is your home—*our home.* I'm not running you out. We can redecorate or burn it down and start over. I don't care as long as it's with *you.*"

I can see the conflict in her eyes and almost hear her thoughts, like before.

"I can't be what you want me to be."

I step away and am surprised when she grabs for my arm.

Wrapping me in a tight embrace, she finally responds, "Please don't hate me. I'm trying to come to terms with everything. I thought it was just me in the world. It's a lot to take in. I'm sad about our family history, Anse. I'm sad to see you this way. But I'm so glad to know that I'm not alone like I once thought I was. I'm not lost anymore."

I relax into her hold and lean in slightly. My hand rises to rub where her arms are linked around my torso.

"That's comforting to know. I could never hate you. I'm a possessive man. I can't help but want you all to myself. I told you this before, but I don't regret college. You were finally mine in a sense, and I just wanted to hold onto that for as long as I could. I couldn't stand the look of disgust in your eyes every time you looked at me before the accident."

"I'm sorry," she whispers, squeezing me slightly and leaning her head against my spine.

"Come here," I turn around and hold her.

"You are the most precious person to me. That's never changed in all my life. We were innocent children, forced to be this way. I don't know how to be better. *Will you show me how?*"

I pull back slightly to cup her cheeks and take in her watery eyes as she nods.

"I'm not perfect either, Ansel, but we can work on it together."

"You are, to me." I kiss her forehead and hold her there longer, not yet ready to let go.

She's all I know; all I'd ever want. Even before I found her in the city, when men and women came onto me. I tried to be with people outside the family, *sleep with them even,* and learn how to fuck more efficiently. But nothing was the same.

Sex is forbidden, but not in our family tree.

"The blood that binds us is the purest form of love."

CHAPTER 33
"INTO THE DARK"

ANA

Running.
That's all I knew.
From my mind, my heart. My fucking family.
How long can one person run until they reach a dead end?
My limits and psyche have been tested for years.
The truth is, I'm haunted.
Ghosts linger in the walls of all I once knew, pulling me back into my tomb.
If it's not real, then it can't harm me, right?
Screams call to me, tortured sounds of the unknown.
Wails from beyond the walls.
All I can do is hold my head in my hands and cry.
For monsters are closer than a burglar in the night; they exist in your home.
The world may not know the depravity inside this house, but I always begged to forget.

I'm standing outside, glancing up toward the looming cliff in the near distance. *Just right up the fucking hill. An end and a beginning, all wrapped up in one little bow.*

I know I'm torturing myself by standing here on an overcast day, gazing at it. There's a looming dread.

My brother's mind is sick. No amount of love that I give him will fix that. It's gotten to the point of no return. I'm experiencing the familiar trapped feeling I had when I was a girl. I feel it deep in my bones as if it never truly left. I still want to protect him. *He's my twin and I can't leave him.*

There's a powerful pull that I can't explain, like two binary stars. One will eventually consume the other. We can only dance alongside each other for so long, until chaos erupts, again.

That hill is a reminder of where I have been, and what is to come if I'm not careful. I'm backed into a corner with my hands tied.

He's hiding something from me—many things. I'm not strong enough to enter his mind like he can mine. Not yet anyway.

There's tense energy lingering in the halls of the House of Lee. A darkness that sucks any happiness away. That's the energy my family put into the house, and that's what the house reeks of. My soul feels tainted, in more ways than one.

I can't make the same mistake twice, but how do I get him to trust me fully?

Do I have it in me to fuck him? *I don't know if I can do it now that I know.*

I wonder what Atticus, Ardella, Jackson, and Roman would think? Would they shun me? How could I look at either of them again, knowing the sins that taint my bloodstream?

Also, where the hell is Atticus?

No letters or words have been received in the weeks I've been *home*. What a strange place, one that used to be my *home*, but it never felt like a home. I created a home with people, not in any one place.

I wonder if Ardella is still grieving, and if she's disappointed in me for disappearing on her. At least her father was a good man, unlike mine. Even with her distance from her mother and sister, the dynamic was still better than the sins of my family.

God, how could I ever live down this shame?

Incest and lies. Blood stains hidden by coats of paint and updated material things.

We come from old money. My dead family was powerful in their own right. We kept our secrets hidden and buried under the floorboards where outsiders couldn't see.

People never suspect anything behind a perfect white smile and a seemingly flawless family.

It makes me sick.

Taking walks outside helps clear my mind some, but the House of Lee stands as a reminder. Perhaps, I'd take him up on the offer of burning it down and starting anew.

I make my way to the edge of the property and find steps that lead down somewhere toward the sea.

Turning around, I make sure Ansel isn't outside with me. After listening for a minute and hearing nothing but the crashing waves in the distance, I make my way down.

It's between rocks and leads to a private little alcove on a beach. I'm grateful for the low tide, as I step off and make my way toward the water. The sounds and motions are soothing to my troubled spirit. I'm already barefoot, as I lift my forest-green dress and walk a few feet in.

The temperature has a slight chill but is somehow welcoming. Suddenly, I'm not thinking about my woes. Instead, I am able to ground myself. Slowly, I am coming back into myself.

I'm not sure how long I've been standing here, but I now hear thunder rumble in the distance—a sign, surely. Yet, I'm not ready to go back into that haunted, fucking house.

Looking over to my left, it looks like there's no place to go past *where I fell from.*

I ignore the lingering dread of how close I am to where I nearly died. My eyes look off toward the right, noticing a pathway. Remaining in the water, I hold my dress up and follow the path. I quickly realize there's more beach but not much. We're the only ones on the cliffside with an alcove. Others built their steps *on* the sides of the smaller cliffs rather than *through* them.

Unsure if I'm trespassing, I walk for a half-hour until I can't walk anymore. The thunder sounds closer and the sky darkens in the distance.

I decide to turn around and head back. This walk was welcomed and so needed. I find myself feeling lighter than before. When I make it back to the garden, it's pouring rain.

The sky releases the storm. I ignore how creepy the mansion looks under a canopy of rain and lightning as if it's a living thing rejoicing in the eerie elements.

Lightning strikes in the distance, but I turn my head up toward the sky and open my hands to feel the cool, thick drops on my skin.

Water is my element; a peaceful feeling always occurs when I'm near it, in it, or listening to the sounds of it. It grounds me. It reminds me to *feel. To be present.* Minus the minor fact that my twin intended to kill me, the water below *saved* me.

I close my eyes and let the raindrops soak through. Thunder crashes again, and I open my eyes. In the distance, I see Ansel coming toward me.

He's wearing a soaked and unbuttoned, white shirt, and his pants are black, as always. I can't deny that he looks handsome like this. For a moment, I forget our history and blood.

His matching eyes are locked on me. All I can do is stare until he comes upon me, meeting my lips eagerly.

Ansel's darkness tugs on mine and I let him.

I think about college, and how I easily fell into his presence just as I'm doing now.

When his tongue molds to mine, I let it happen. There's something lurid about this moment. Pouring rain, a tragic house, and the two lost twins. *The only twins left alive in the family.*

It's just like fucking yourself, Anabel.

I wrap my arms around him, and he carries me inside the house. We are a mess of lips and tangled teeth. Clothes are torn off and fingers fill the void of empty spaces. There's no rhyme or reason, just moans and panting.

When I come, I cry out of shame, yet I let myself fall into the dark with him.

CHAPTER 34

"WHAT THE HELL AM I GOING TO DO?"

ANA

A draft enters from underneath a strange, locked door. I bet it leads to a cellar or basement. Being locked likely means one thing. *Ansel is hiding something down there.*

No other rooms are locked in the house. I debate whether I want to find out or not. *For now, I'll leave it alone.*

I refuse to go into the attic and be reminded of things I wish to forget again. There are lingering memories of when I was locked up there with the spiders and rodents.

Their bedrooms were remodeled years before I came back here. Ansel says the murder-suicides took place in them.

With how fucked our family history is, I'm not surprised by the affairs. Even though we come from a long line of twins and triplets, each generation varies slightly but beautiful, nonetheless. Dark brown hair and colorful eyes are a common trait in the family. My dad had hazel eyes, while my mother had blue. No matter the degree of beauty, there is no excuse for their cruelty and madness. The same madness that plagues Ansel. One that is suffocating me too by being in this hellish place.

Atticus has been lingering in the back of my mind with each passing week. I dare not bring him up to Ansel just yet, but I have a deep, unsettling feeling that he knows more than he's letting on about Atti.

Dare I say, things feel *comfortable* now. Ansel doesn't seem as on-edge as when I arrived. He's using my nicknames more. I'm starting to fall into his delusions easier, too. This façade of happiness we are portraying, *like he didn't do everything within his power to get me there.*

I'm biding my time. For what?

I'm still working that out.

I let him kiss and hold me as if we are a couple, an illusion of the marriage our parents always beat into our heads.

Still no letters from anyone. Part of me feels forgotten about, but the other part rationalizes Ardella's grief…

It's raining this morning. Ansel is eating breakfast and reading something at the dining table. I sit down to join him.

He usually disappears early in the morning; my guess is that he can't sleep or has a set routine. Part of me is glad for the reprieve.

"I had this delivered today with news from Morella. Read it." By his tone, I can tell he sounds indifferent and unbothered.

Ansel always tolerated Ardella, but I could never tell if he liked her or not, since we'd sometimes hang out back in our college days.

I take the paper and open it. There's a story titled in bold, black font: ***Poa's Mortuary Has Burned to the Ground!***

There's also a subheading: ***Family's whereabouts unknown.***

Ardella and her brother are both missing now.

Just, what the fuck!

My heartbeat increases with worry; I feel sick.

"Did Ardella make it out?" I squeak, shuddering.

Ansel answers me, "I'm not certain. Are you okay?"

It doesn't take long for my eyes to water. He whispers my name, and I dare to look up. His face is blurry under my tears until it spills, and I blink.

"She's important to me, Anse. I'll lose my mind if she's dead."

"I'll find out for you, okay? I'll go down there myself if I have to."

"You would?" I cry, wiping my face.

The headline is a reminder to worry about Ardella, so I toss it in another chair, not wanting to look at it. My heart can't take any more bad news.

"Yes. Occasionally, I'll have papers sent here all the way from Morella because I know she's your friend."

I melt slightly from his words, not bothering to question his reasoning. "Thank you."

He offers me a small smile and scoots his chair back, patting his lap. "Come here and let me hold you awhile. I'll find those answers for you."

Nearly crying again, I do as he says.

Tucking my head into the crook of his neck, I settle into his lap and warm embrace.

"I love you, Ann. Everything will be okay."

As he holds me, I wonder if that anyone perished in the fire and if everyone is okay… How would I ever explain that whole situation to Ansel?

He'll fucking kill me.

At school, he displayed immense jealousy, but when he wasn't disappearing, I'd sleep around. I couldn't let him know who my heart truly belonged to—*or that it belonged to multiple people.* Ansel is very traditional and monogamous; there's no way he'd allow that.

Since when did I let him dictate my life?

I wrestle with my inner turmoil.

It's because he has answers I'm seeking. With that being

said, I make a quiet vow to myself to find out what's in the basement, whether I want to know or not.

I need to know.

Next time Ansel leaves the house for necessities, I'll break in.

I woke up in a cold sweat, shuddering in fear. For the first time, I dreamed through Ansel's eyes.

I watched him force our sister to hang herself.

I look beside me to his sleeping form and fear squeezes my heart.

That will be me if I don't find a way out of here.

I could go back to Morella and search for them, but if they weren't there, then what?

Carefully slipping out of Ansel's bed, I wrap a robe around my naked body. Maybe some water will help.

Would water truly help how numb I've become and how trapped I am in this place yet again

I make my way down the stairs quietly. It's hard to see, so that I feel like the ghosts of my parents are watching me. They probably disapprove or are waiting to see me run from destiny, *again.*

Before I turn on a light in the kitchen, I swear I see a shadow. Though, nothing is there and I question my sanity.

Is my mind playing tricks on me?

There's nothing to be afraid of. It's just a house with history—and death.

I grab a glass and fill it with cool water from the sink.

Leaning on the black marble counter, I wonder how the hell I'm supposed to sleep after seeing *that.*

Was Ansel dreaming and reliving it, too? Is that why I saw it?

I refuse to find out.

When he wakes, I'll confront him.

After I finish the glass, I leave it on the counter, turn off the light, and make my way into the library. I turn on the lamp, needing to calm my anxious mind.

Grabbing a random book, I settle in the settee. I read through a chapter or two before I fall back asleep.

The book knocks to the floor when I spring back awake.

Sitting up, I groan and stretch with a long yawn. Glancing up, I yelp when I see Ansel sitting there staring at me.

That's fucking creepy.

There's a strange look in his eyes. "Why weren't you in bed sleeping?"

"I woke up from a dream and couldn't fall back asleep, so here I am," I answer, obviously.

"Were you in my head?" He looks upset about it.

He's admitting to it.

"Like I have control over such a thing," I snap, scrunching my brows together at the tone of his voice. "Are you trying to tell me that it's you who killed our sister?"

He sits up straighter. "So, what if I did? There could only be one of you. I told you, it would always be *you* in the end."

I smack my hands on the settee in anger. "That doesn't mean you fucking kill her, asshole!"

"Then what was I supposed to do? Let our parents kill you? Or our aunt and uncle? *No, Anabel.*"

Freezing up, I let my mind take in his words. "What?"

Ansel leans forward, resting his arms on his knees, as he slumps in a chair across the room.

"You heard right, Bel. They favored Anais more because she listened to their every word, while you defied most things. Plus, I may have eavesdropped on conversations between our aunt and uncle. However, I favored *you.* So, as I keep saying, I did what I had to. *What I still do.* I wasn't going to let them take you away from me."

Our family is so fucked up, I can't even process half this shit.

I need a therapist, the minute I figure out how to get the hell out of here for good.

Rubbing my head, I sigh heavily, "This is all so fucked, Anse."

"I know," he says, suddenly sounding closer. Soon after, he sits beside me and wraps an arm around me.

He comes up with every excuse and justification for *everything*, with little regard to morality. It bothers me that *nothing* bothers him. He will do anything and everything.

"It's in the past, Ann. It's just you and me now. Until death do us part."

I bite back the rising bile and lean into him.

What the hell am I going to do?

CHAPTER 35
"THE LOCKED DOOR"

ANA

It takes two more weeks before Ansel finally leaves the house.

He kisses me goodbye, while I pretend to be asleep in bed. The minute I hear his footsteps echo down the stairs, I jump out of bed. I need to make sure he actually leaves.

I peek through a bottom-floor window to see a cab picking him up.

Why doesn't he own a car with all this money?

Ignoring the thought, relief fills me as I watch him pull away and disappear. Once a minute or so passes, I rush for my thin hair pins to break into the locked door.

It takes me ten excruciating minutes; my hands shake as each one passes. I have no idea how long Ansel will be gone, so every second counts.

Finally, the door opens with a click.

Yes!

I see the dark stairs leading into pitch blackness.

Fuck, I have to go down here myself?

There's only a moment of hesitation before I say, *"fuck it,"* and venture on down.

I leave the door open if only to have some light. The putrid smells, along with the dampness of the basement, burn my nose.

"Great idea, Anabel, really great," I mumble quietly to myself, wondering just what lay in the pitch blackness below.

This is scary shit.

I make it to the bottom of the staircase and try to find a light switch or something to pull. I move out of the stairway lighting from above, and I don't like it.

Not one bit.

As I raise my arm, feeling for something to pull, I jump at the sound of something muffled nearby.

"Fuck. Fuck!" I nervously shake my foot.

Something that feels like a string touches my hand. I tug on it and light floods my vision.

I shut my eyes quickly, backing against the wall before blinking them open again and taking in my surroundings.

My mouth is agape when I see a man gagged and tied to a chair. I let my eyes travel around the room quickly and see odd shit in jars and oddities on the shelves. When I get to my corner, I scream.

There are five coffins with glass lids, offering a clear view to the corpses inside.

I run over to where the captive is, completely horrified.

"That's so fucking gross!"

I didn't even have to think too hard about *who* was in them. There were plaques above it with all of their names. Mom and Dad, my aunt and uncle. *My sister.*

Thank goodness I didn't eat yet, or I would be throwing up right now.

I am pulled from my thoughts by the struggling man beside me. I focus my attention on him and take in his disheveled look. His matted greasy dark brown is hanging in his face.

My shaky hands remove the gag and move his hair from in front of his face.

"Annie."

I choke out a startled cry, cupping his face to make sure he's real.

"At-Atti?"

His eyes fill with tears as he nods his head, *yes.*

"Are you hurt?" I ask while checking him over.

"Annie, we need to get out of here before he comes back."

I sob, "I'll untie you, hang on."

When I move to do so, I see dried blood on his hands. From how the rope has torn into his skin, it looks like he's been here for a while.

I free his hands and arms first before working on his legs.

"How long have you been here?" I croak out, trying not to have a breakdown.

"Too long," he says weakly, trying to rub his bloody and bruised wrists.

He looks like death, skinny and dying from lack of light and nourishment. I get his legs freed.

I've been playing fucking house, while my heart was in the basement. How fucking stupid am I?

I lay my head in his lap and weep.

"You're too weak to move, Atti. I'm so sorry you had to suffer like this."

"We'll figure it out in therapy later, Annie."

I choke out a cry, my heart in pieces. Ansel is my lifeblood. Yet, he betrayed me with his cruelty, *again.* How could I ever fall into this shit again? *This fucking lie of a life he painted.*

I need to stop this. *Now.*

"Give me some time, and we'll run away together. We need to protect ourselves from him."

I gaze up at Atti, as I sit on my knees.

Cupping my cheek he whispers, "Once I got here, I never

in my wildest dreams thought I'd see this beautiful face again. Your brother is fucking crazy."

Don't I know it…

"We need to build up your strength," I say, steadying my erratic, disturbed emotions.

"I'm going to grab a bunch of food and bring you a weapon for protection, but I think it would be best if he didn't figure out, I freed you."

"You're probably right."

"Here, let me help you, and we can see if you can stand," I offer.

I rise from the floor and position my hands under his rancid armpits, as his hands are fucked up from being bound for who knows how long.

Using all my strength, I pull and tug. Atticus tries to stand, but we both end up tumbling to the floor.

Fuck, that hurt.

He groans, "We shouldn't have done that, Annie. That fucking hurt."

"I'm so sorry," I say, trying to help him back to his chair, which takes me at least 10 minutes.

"I'm sorry for hurting you," I whisper, kissing his forehead.

"I'll live… We'd better hurry before he comes back. Over the next couple of weeks or so, I'll build up my strength. If I can barely walk or stand, then I won't be able to get very far in our escape."

I nod, wiping my tears.

"Give me a few minutes, and I'll bring you food and extras."

He nods, trying to lift and stretch his legs from his sitting position.

I race back up the steps and into the kitchen.

In record time, I make a quick, full-course meal and bring him tons of water. The poor guy is covered in piss and shit. Has Ansel not washed him or fed him?

Why the fuck is he keeping him in the basement?

I'm fuming with all the rage I held back.

Bringing the tray of food, I sit with him for a while as he eats.

"I haven't eaten this much food in so long. Every once in a while, he'd let me relieve myself in that bucket over there, with a gun to my head." He points weakly in the general direction of said bucket. "But he hasn't done that in weeks."

Weeks?!

That must mean Atticus has been here for months, long before I got here. *Oh my God!*

"I'm going to make him pay for all he's done!" I swore.

"I need you alive, Annie. Don't take any more unnecessary risks."

I sigh heavily, trying to calm my shaking hands of rage. All the brokenness is sitting heavy on my fucking chest. *I'm the reason he's here withering away like this.*

"I wrapped up some food so you can have them for later. I'm not sure how much food and water I can sneak you, but I'll figure it out."

"Leave what you can at the top of the steps. But if you can't, don't risk it. I need us both to make it out of here safely. Okay?"

I nod as he hands me the tray of unfinished food.

Looking around quickly, I find a spot hidden away on a shelf to put the remaining wrapped food. It's out of sight from Ansel if he comes down here.

"I'm so glad you found me, Anabel," he whispers in earnest, and my heart disintegrates more and more.

"I'm sorry it took me so long." I take the tray and plates, getting rid of any evidence I was there.

"You've been down here for too long; you should go before he gets back."

"I wish we could talk. I've missed you," I begin before he shakes his head.

"I love you, *but go,*" he pleads quietly.

My eyes water once more as I quickly fill the basement with darkness and leave.

The basement door locks from the inside, which meant Ansel never wanted me in there.

I lock it back in place, leaning my head on the door. I smell myself briefly and run to the bathroom to freshen up.

As soon as I leave, freshly changed, there's a sound of a car door slamming.

I take a deep breath.

Swiftly, I make my way into the kitchen with the tray to begin washing the dishes as fast as I can. The front door opens, and I do everything within my power not to rage out.

Protect. Him.

I slid a knife on the tray earlier, and Atticus took it and put it under him. The safest place for it *and him.*

I hear Ansel's shoes on the floor, walking toward the kitchen as I finish the dishes.

Breathe. Keep going.

"There you are. Good morning, Bel."

"Morning."

"You used a tray?"

I nod as he kisses my cheek and sets bags on the counter.

"I wanted to eat in the library this morning."

"Very well. Want to help me unload? There are more bags."

"Of course."

He smiles and walks out of the room.

Distracting myself, I make note of the dust and decide to clean house, otherwise I'd blow the whole operation.

It's just the distraction I need to not kill him.

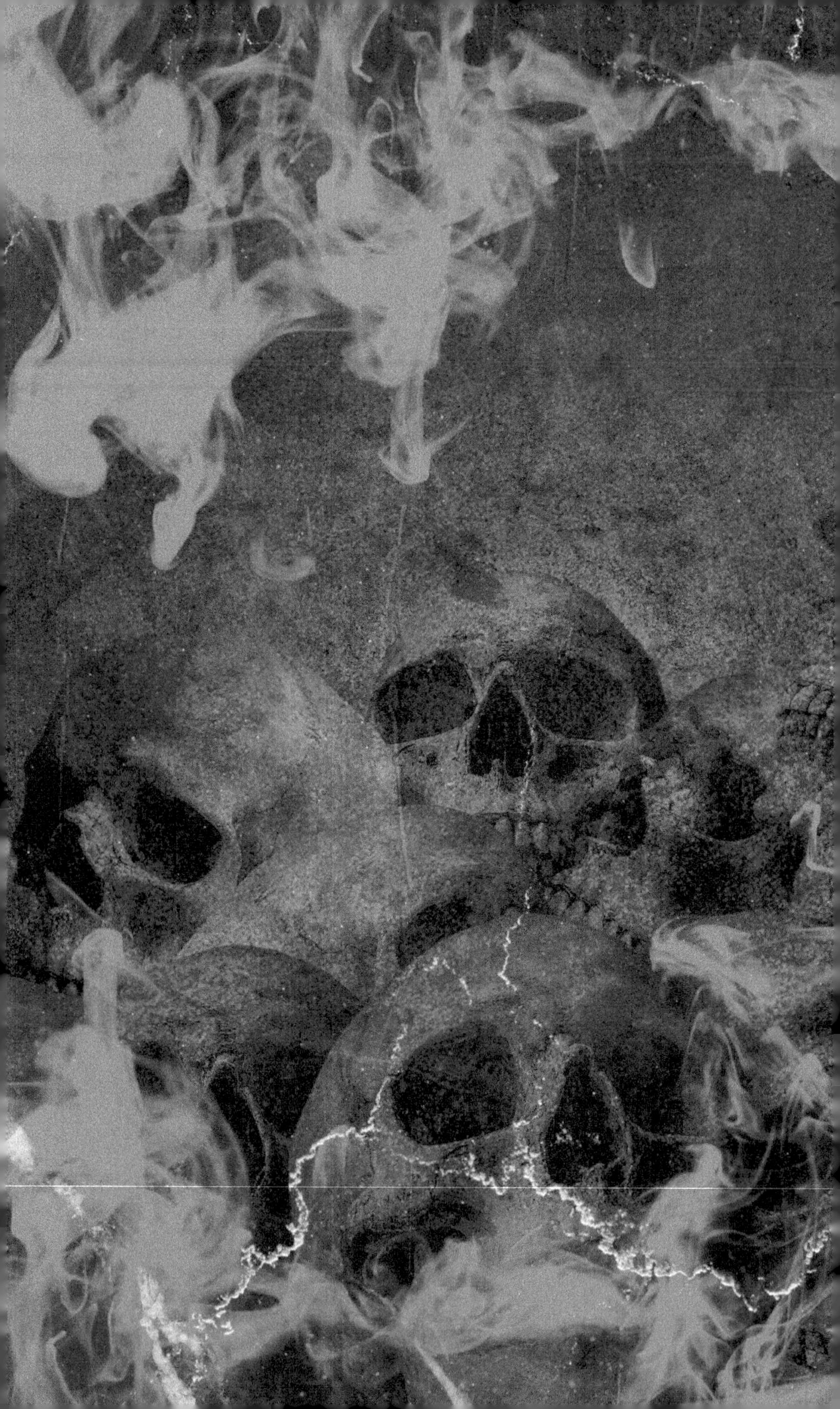

FOR YOU

I will always find you.
I will come for you until the end of time.
I carry you with me in my spirit,
I will carry your pain.

When you're gone,
I think about when I can see you again.
Every breath,
Is a breath wasted without you near.

The flames I've erupted,
Only ignite something else born from the ashes.
The picture was clear in the fire,
So clear in my veins.

It isn't the same without you.
Whether it's now or in the future,
I will make my way back to you.
I will find you once more.

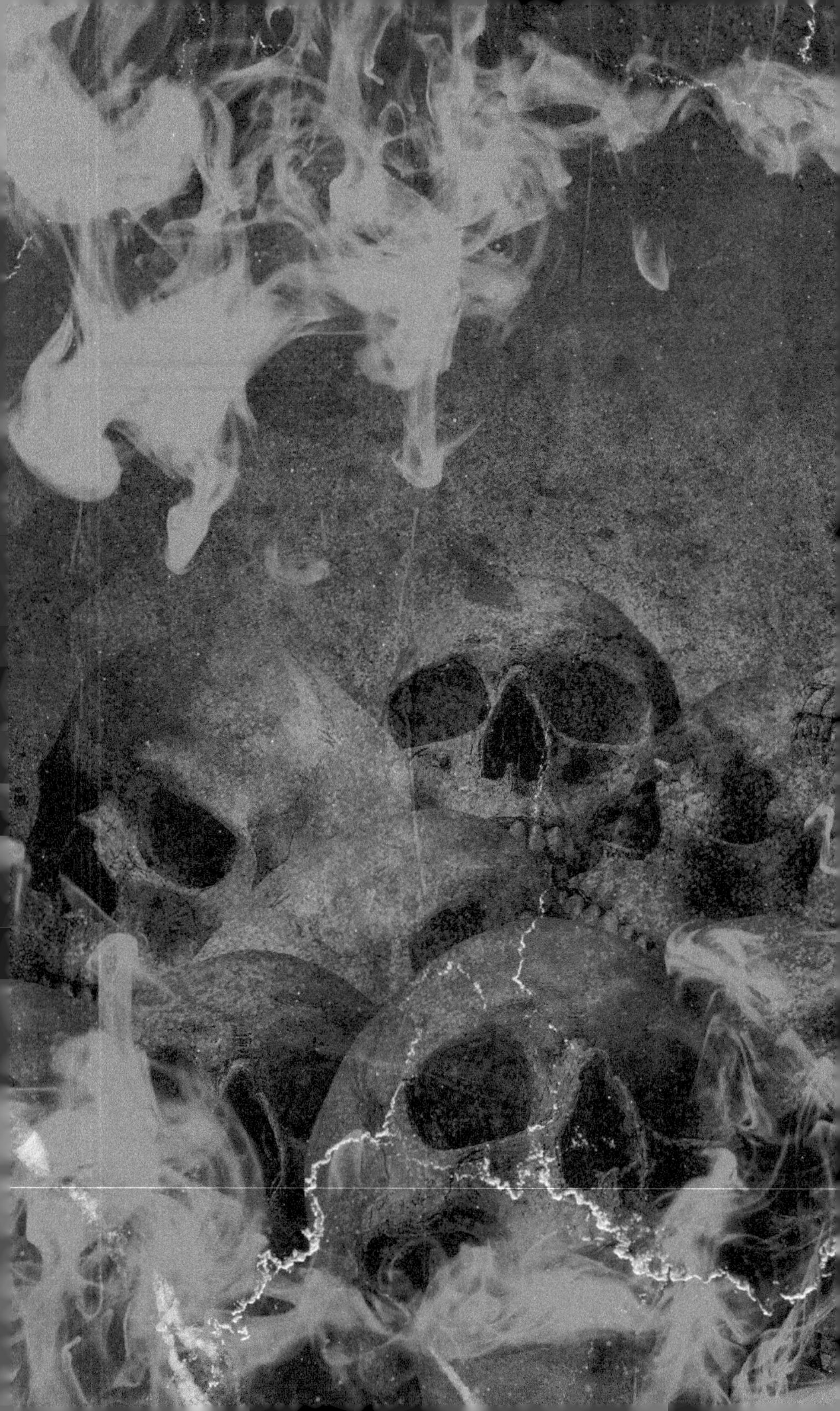

Together we can heal these wounds.
Together we can create something anew.
There is more to love this go around.
Our hearts, big enough to fill others.

I will always find you.
You are mine to love and hold.
I carry you with me in my spirit.
I will continue to carry you.

We shall meet very soon.
This I know to be true.
All this love that I have for you.
I'm coming for you.

— E.G. Poa

CHAPTER 36
"WE HAVE TO MAKE IT OUT ALIVE"

ATTICUS

It all began when my uncle died, and I worked to settle his affairs. In my mourning, Ansel showed up, pretending to know where Anabel was.

He mentioned how he'd been trying to find her for years when he discovered she wasn't dead. *They're twins, or triplets rather.*

I could see her in his eyes, that same beauty, only it was more masculine. He fooled me so easily.

Due to my grief, I believed everything he said. Ansel was so poised and respectful; I never received any *off* vibes. The guy was too good.

Once he secured a car, we drove for two days until arriving at his Gothic-styled home with macabre decorations in the foyer. *Then, the energy shifted.*

The minute I walked into the place, I was knocked over the head with something hard, blacking out immediately.

When I awoke again, I was tied to a fucking chair. That's when I began to learn the truth about him and their family.

"I can see the appeal of you, Atticus. You and I are both beautiful. Of course, she'd take to your looks."

I was lost and confused until he began his spiel. My head tilted to the side, and I noticed the coffins in the corner of the basement with corpses in them. I squeezed my eyes shut and Ansel laughed.

"Ah, yes, let me introduce you to the family. Don't look away now. It's rude."

I made a noise in the gag, daring to listen. What kind of morbid person had their family corpses in viewable coffins?

Ansel gestures to the first of five. "This is my sister. A shame we weren't meant to be, but only two of us could live, so that's why the rope marks. I did what I had to. She's strangely well preserved." He tapped on the glass fondly before moving to a woman.

"This is dear-old Mother, quite the cunt if you ask me. Dad is next to her, along with my aunt and uncle. There was a murder-suicide; that's why Uncle is missing part of his face. It happened not long after Anabel's accident."

Accident? Truly?

I wasn't entirely sure I believed it. I couldn't look at the corpses anymore either way. I found myself looking at the opposite corner, closest to me. There was a shelf with objects in jars. I dared not even think about questioning what was in them as it looked gross.

Ansel leaned against the stone wall, nonchalantly.

Did the guy not have any morals?

All I knew was that the nice-guy thing was all an act. There was something sinister underneath.

"You see, Atticus, our family dynamic is complex. We keep our family line, well, within the family. That's why you will never see the light of day again. You are here for blackmail. If Anabel doesn't show up or give me what I want, then you're my leverage. I saw your letters while she was at college. That's how I found you. Then, I started to pretend to be you as

*I got to know you. It was so easy, really. People nowadays are so gullible.”
He laughed more to himself, because I certainly didn't find that shit
funny.*

*"Anyway, Anabel was always meant to be mine. From the womb
until death. It's as it was always meant to be. What our parents groomed
us to be. Anabel was more resistant, of course. It's why I pushed her. A
moment of weakness.”*

Bastard! Of course, it was him.

*"I know, I know. I'm so cruel and heartless, but you don't know
what it was like to grow up in this fucked up family and in this fucking
house.”*

Then, why do you still live in it?

*"I've had to fix it up, just to cover old blood stains and cleanse the
negativity.”*

*He sounded angry, huffing a sigh before turning his head to look at
the coffin-corpse displays.*

*Thank goodness I didn't eat recently, because I would've thrown up.
The smells down here certainly didn't help.*

*"Perhaps, I've kept them down here as a reminder, so I could mock
them like this. Cruelty returns cruelty.”*

Cruel or not, Ansel is fucked.

*"Anyway, I tire of looking at them. I'll feed you once a day and let
you use the bathroom. Can't have you dying on me just yet. I'll see you in
the morning.”*

*With that, he simply climbed the stairs and left me in total
darkness.*

With only corpses for company.

I'm not sure how long I'm in the basement, but the day that
Anabel comes down here by accident, I want to sob in relief. I
can't believe she came to this place. It's debatable how I

should feel. She's risking a lot being here, and she's already been through enough.

I can't imagine what Ansel's done to her or the lies spewed. The minute she pulls the string for the lights, and I see her for the first time in years, I hang my head to cry, but I'm dehydrated, so not many tears spill. My throat is scratchy, and I can't remember the last time I ate or drank anything. My legs have gone numb from sitting there tied for days. I can't move or speak.

Ansel has been slacking with food and water to keep me alive. *I'm barely fucking hanging on.*

Yet, seeing Anabel's beautiful face again gives me light where there was none before. She's grown more beautiful, if that's even possible. God, I missed her to death.

All I've had were her family's corpses as company for weeks. Months? Who knows?

I'm questioning my sanity and things I've seen in the shadows or the voices. I'm not sure what is real anymore.

My own horror show.

When Annie shrieks upon noticing her family in glass coffins, she races to me, while gathering the strength to calm down, I'd assume. I mumble something in the gag, and she finally takes me in, removing it.

All I can do is say her name. That one word that means so much, my lifeline. She's always been my lifeline, ever since I saw her reading in that courtyard alone. I will never forget her, nor have I.

I can't deny the discouragement when we fall to the floor. *New plan!*

I continue to remain down here under the guise of still being tied up. Annie will leave food at the top of the steps if she can, but I don't want to risk anything more. Before she disappears, and after feeding me and giving me much-needed water, I make sure to tell her I love her, as I'm sure she's forgotten.

Her eyes hold so much sadness that it pains me. She's gotten her memories back, and I wish I could be there for her. I know it's been something she's worried about for years.

Seeing her again gives me hope and strength to continue. When Ansel doesn't come the next day, I carefully crawl along the floor like a toddler. It fucking hurts, but I need to build my strength. Time is running out. I can feel it.

The next day, Ansel brings me breakfast. He boasts about how happy he and Anabel are and that he'll still keep me down there until the timing is right. I say nothing as he spoon feeds me oatmeal and makes me down a full glass of water. My stomach expands, aching from not eating. After I shake my head that I don't have to use the bathroom, he puts the gag over my mouth.

"I'm going to find Anabel a dress this week, then I'm going to marry her. Maybe I'll let you live long enough to watch." He smiles, before leaving me in the blackness once more.

I sit there for a while fuming. Ana and I will both need therapy after this. If we make it out.

Fuck.

We have to make it out alive.

CHAPTER 37

"DESTINY"

ANA

A week goes by, and in that time, I listen to Ansel's every move. I figure out when he goes into the basement, and I make it my personal mission to sneak downstairs to prepare food on the days he doesn't. I'll leave sandwiches at the top of the steps with water.

It takes everything within my being not to go down there, which becomes harder and harder every time I deliver food. I hate that I can't put it on a plate and risk being found out.

The following week since discovering Atticus, I wait by the door and hear a slight creak beyond it. Placing my hand on the door gently, my eyes fill up with tears. *I'm so sorry.*

If we make it out of here alive, I will do anything and everything to make sure we heal from the monsters within these walls.

There's been no word from Ardella or the others. No newspaper updates or anything. Ansel doesn't tell me anything either.

One day, Ansel snuck out while I napped, and it pissed me off. *I couldn't see Atticus or check on his strength progress.*

Please, be okay.

At the end of week two, I begin to feel restless. During breakfast, Ansel looks across the table at me. "I think it's time, Ann."

I tilt my head, confused, swallowing the bread and eggs I ate.

"For our destiny," he continues.

My heartbeat grows faster and faster, thundering loud in my ears. He stands and walks over to me, then cups my chin.

"I have a dress laid out for you. But before we begin, I need to prepare. How about I call someone to come do your makeup and hair?"

All I do is stare into a pair of hazel eyes.

"What's the occasion?"

"Our marriage."

Oh…

"We'll schedule it for tonight, so go into your room and bathe yourself. Soon enough, the necessary people will arrive. I think you'll appreciate what I have in store for you. Consider it a special gift to show how much I love you."

I give him an awkward smile as he leans down to kiss me.

"You don't have to go through all this trouble. We can get it over with," I manage to say in a hurry before he begins to walk away.

He turns back to me. "You deserve more than that, Bel. I'm going to give you everything."

Ansel leaves the room after that, and I stare at my food, unable to eat.

I'm so fucked right now.

How do I get Atticus out of here?

No matter what, it has to happen tonight. I can suffer the ceremony, or whatever Ansel has planned, and get Atti out at least. Whether I'm with Atticus in the end or not, doesn't matter, as long as he's alive. *Away from this wretched place.*

It takes me thirty minutes of spiraling to finally get up the courage to go upstairs and shower. I take a nearly, hour-long shower, going over and over in my head various scenarios and possibilities.

Yes, I will sneak out after he's asleep. Maybe I'll set this whole fucking place ablaze. I know where Ansel keeps his gun in the library desk. It's probably the same gun he uses to threaten Atticus with.

Atticus, please hang on.

After my shower, I hesitantly walk into my room and hear an insistent knock.

"Come in," I say, making sure my towel is wrapped tight around me.

In walks two women dressed in stark, crisp black.

"Are you ready for hair and makeup?" The taller one on the left asks, and I agree to let them have at it with a sigh of defeat.

They make quick work of bringing in their supplies and diving right in. It ends up being a whole process. My hair is cut and styled before being curled and put into a half-updo.

The makeup is dark and glamorous.

They quickly leave and one of them brings in the dress and shoes.

"Congrats! We'll be leaving now, Miss."

I nod, thanking them before looking at the soft, lacey material.

The sleeves are long and see-through. The bodice dips low in an alluring cut at the front and has an open back but flows out into a semi-poofy bottom.

It's gorgeous, but none of this feels right.

I put on my black heels and look in the mirror. While I should feel beautiful, *I feel anything but.*

This is not a happy moment. It's chaos and insanity. I don't even want to imagine what will happen once I make it down those stairs.

Slowly, I hold my breath and leave the room. I ignore the family portraits in the hallway; it's almost as if they're mocking me, following me with their eyes. I make it to the stairs, which have been decorated with black lace.

Fiddling with my nervousness, I make it to the bottom. Ansel appears like a proposed, dark daydream. He extends his hand, kissing the top of mine once I bring it forward.

"You look like a goddess of the underworld."

Trapped, my smile is fake as he tucks my arm with his and leads me toward the grand dining room. There are candles giving a false sense of romantic ambiance as they appear more sinister. While it's eerie, I can't help but wait with bated breath. He said necessary people will arrive. *Whatever that means.*

There are no tables, and I see someone standing off near the window. Another is at the front of the room by the lit fireplace. Then, I notice the coffins. *No wonder it's threatening here.*

Ansel notices my eyes widen, and whispers in my ear, "I had to make sure the whole family was here for today, Bel. *Fitting,* isn't it?"

I swallow down my fear.

Who is standing by the window?

As we walk past the coffins that would serve as places for pews if this were a church, I notice it's Atticus by the window, hands bound behind his back.

"I had to make sure Atticus was bathed and cleaned for the occasion. How nice of him to join us on this momentous evening."

I think I'm going to be sick.

Atticus is dressed in black too, and his hair is short and his face is bleeding from cuts. It could be a barber error, but he simply stares, not looking at me.

What the fuck is going on?

We get to the fireplace and an old man stares at us. I can't tell if he's alive or not because he doesn't move. He looks like he's half dead, or in the grave already, with how corpse-like he appears.

"I broke him out of the nursing home to help with today, turns out it's our grandfather. He's happy to be here."

Ansel releases my hand while I stare at the old man giving me a creepy, toothy smile.

I'm in a living nightmare. All my ghosts are surrounding me, crawling up my chest to take up space until I'm smothered in the chaos.

"Atticus's lips are glued shut, so he can't interrupt."

Daring to look, I mouth, *I'm sorry* to him. Due to the low lighting, I'm not sure if he can see me. There's no light coming from outside, so I know it's already evening. There's still a strange ambiance with the floor-to-ceiling windows, and not a good one.

"Begin, grandfather."

Ansel grabs my hands as *grandfather* speaks. Even his voice sounds like it's from the grave. I hear a creaking, and I swear my eyes are playing tricks on me. The coffins *turn around toward the front.*

My ears begin to buzz, low whispers echoing.

Anabel Lee.

Ansel Lee.

I think I'm going to pass out. The room feels like it's closing in, and I'm losing my breath. *Or rather, it feels like life is being sucked out of my lungs.*

I remember the weapon I hid in my breast. *A switchblade.*

Maybe it's the desperation taking hold of me, or something else. Once Ansel turns toward Grandfather to grab the rings, I reach in, flip the blade open, and stab Ansel in his side.

Ansel clutches his side and falls to the floor. I lift my dress, and kick Grandfather right into the fireplace, which is big enough to engulf him.

I back away, turning around to see the coffins facing him.

Running over to Atticus, I kick off my heels, grab his arm, and lead him away. *Thank fuck he can walk now.*

"Let's leave and never look back," I say, once we make it to the front door.

Pulling it open, we're almost free when I hear a gunshot reverberate in my eardrums.

Atticus's hand leaves mine as he falls to the floor, groaning.

"Did you think you were leaving?" I hear Ansel's voice echo.

Crying out with worry, I make the mistake of checking on Atticus. He was shot in the leg. He's still breathing; *still alive.*

For now.

Before I know it, my hair is being gripped, and I'm dragged out the front door.

I scream when I'm shoved down into the yard.

A gun meets my forehead.

"Get up, Anabel. We're going to visit your favorite place. This is the last time you fuck things up," Ansel spits. The evilness within him never left.

Shaking my head and pleading, he half yanks and drags me across the yard, gun in his other hand.

I struggle, begging, "Ansel, please, don't do this again."

His words come out choked while dragging me up the hill. "This is the last time you will make a fool of me. I told you what was going to happen. Did you think there wouldn't be consequences? Did you think I'd ever let you live freely with him while I still breathed?"

All I can do is sob in my infinite misery.

"You are mine, you always were. *If I can't have you, no one can.* Only this time, you won't be alone in death."

The fated edge of the cliff comes closer and closer.

"What a perfect night to die with you, Anabel," he says before thunder crashes and lightning zips across the sky above.

The rain begins to fall, and it's somehow fitting to my end.

Of course, I end up back here; I was always meant to die

in this place. The sea is calling me back home. Years ago, it wasn't my time, but now it appears it's coming to pass.

Ansel's arms go around me as he holds me tight.

"Look at that perfect view, Anabel. Do you think we'll end up in heaven or hell together?"

The wind and rain lap at my face. One step more and we'll be free-falling.

"How can I trust you're not just going to push me this time?" I grit my teeth.

He places his face next to mine and breathes me in.

"I'm holding you," he laces his fingers with mine and wraps his arms around me tighter. "Are you ready, now?"

Tears stream down my face, and I say nothing.

This is the last view I'll ever see; his voice, the last I'll ever hear.

I know I won't survive, and I'm willing to accept that, as long as Atticus lives.

It's time to die and end this fucked up family tree.

Once my friend and lover, now he's my end.

My Anabel Lee,
Whose heart's in a glass by the sea.
Your fate is no longer condemning me.
The further you reach, you'll never be free.

Family ties,
Blood, secrets, and lies.
Flames become our demise,
The truth is sure to be a surprise.

My Anabel Lee,
Can you see me?
Reflections can no longer be,
Shattered, you'll never be free.

Death is coming for you.
No memories can make it not be true.
Only my touch can renew.
You'll lose your breath until you're blue.

My Anabel Lee,
Whose heart's dead, floating in the sea.
In the end, it can only be me.
Forever, we'll cease to be.

CHAPTER 38

"BEFORE ANYTHING ELSE FUCKED UP HAPPENS"

ROMAN

We leave Morella for good and take the hours-long journey to the address Anabel gave to Jackson and me.

"There's only one person we need with us now," Ardella says quietly.

Jackson and I agreed, of course. Anabel is everything to Ardella, and what makes our girl happy, makes us happy. I can't deny that I enjoy Ana's company. I'm sure Jackson feels the same.

We love her in our own way.

With the dynamic of her first love, Atticus, none of us know how it will go. We also weren't sure what to expect after we received her letter from an address hours away.

It's late afternoon by the time we arrive. Two women are leaving with bags. Ardella asks them who they are and what they're doing.

One of the women answers simply, "We were hired to do hair and makeup for Miss Anabel's wedding to Ansel. It'll be starting soon, you don't want to miss it!"

They give us a smile before driving off. The three of us look at each other, confused.

With the sky turning dark quickly, thunder rumbles in the distance and the wind picks up.

"I don't have a good feeling about this," Jacky whispers.

I quickly glance around, "Let's go hide the car. We can leave our bags in it and look around to see what's going on inside the house."

"Who is Ansel?" Ardella whispers in wonder.

"I don't know, Yellow Eyes. Let's go," I say, grabbing both of their hands and running around the side of the creepy house.

We see candlelight flickering and look at each other with worry.

"Do you have your gun on you, Jacky?" I lean in and ask.

"Yes."

"Good, hand it to me. I have a feeling something's not right."

As he does, a wailing sound distracts me.

We tiptoe around to a back garden of some sort to a window. It's hard to see exactly what's going on, but from my view, I can see a rough outline of a man on fire and another on the floor, clutching their side.

"What the fuck?" Ardella whispers.

Someone runs towards the window where someone else is standing with their back turned. It takes me a minute to notice Anabel is the one running toward the person at the window, because I'm distracted by the fucking *coffins*.

Ana runs off down a hallway in the distance where I can no longer see. Then, the man on the floor, gets up and follows after Ana. The guy is burnt to a crisp in the fireplace, long past dead.

Trying to ignore the coffins and how fucking weird it is, I turn beside me. "Okay, Arde, go with Jacky around the other side. I'll go back the way we came."

A gunshot echoes. We drop swiftly, unsure where it came from.

"Check on whoever that was," I take the lead. "I'll see what's happening."

They nod and disappear into the shadows of the house.

Lightning stretches across the sky, and raindrops begin to fall. As I'm running around the side, I hear a scream.

Once I make it to the corner of the front of the house, the sight in the yard makes me halt.

"Ansel, please."

This Ansel guy is dragging Anabel up towards a hill; he's being rough with *our* girl.

A sense of protectiveness courses through me. I follow behind them at a safe distance, and the Ansel-guy doesn't seem to be concerned enough to turn around.

As thunder crashes, I hear Anabel's wails over the wind and rain.

I turn to see Jackson and Ardella. Gesturing toward the door, they creep inside. My attention snaps back to the hill, and I make my way up there.

Ansel and Anabel are standing at the edge of a cliff I realize once I get there.

Fuck.

I think quickly, trying to figure out the best way to get a clear shot without killing Ana in the process.

I have no choice but to sneak behind him.

It's my only chance of not hurting her in the process.

The closer I get, the more I can hear his words. "Look at that perfect view, Anabel. Do you think we'll end up in heaven or hell together?"

Well, this guy is fucked in the head.

"How can I trust you're not just going to push me this time?" Ana asks him.

This time? Is this how she lost her memories?

He drops the gun behind him, mere feet away from me, and my breath stills.

"I'm holding you," he wraps his arms around Anabel. "Are you ready, now?"

Over my dead body will you do this!

After a moment, I hear Anabel say, *"Do it."*

They don't know I'm here, but I take it as a sign to move in on them.

Quickly, I swipe the second gun from Ansel. In my next breath, I'm standing at their side, aiming one gun at his temple and the other at his heart.

I pull the triggers.

Anabel screams and ducks away, but I quickly grab her before she falls. She releases his hands and moves backwards, tripping over Ansel.

The guy doesn't have much of a face left and certainly not a heart after that. She shrieks in horror as I set down the guns and kick Ansel off the side of the cliff.

Bye, motherfucker!

Ana has blood on her; I do, too. I sit beside her and wrap her in my arms as she sobs uncontrollably.

"He won't hurt you again, Ana. I made sure of it."

Shaking, she leans into my chest. I hear someone breathing heavily and turn to see Jackson.

"She's safe. How is everything down by the house?"

"The guy by the door inside is still alive; there's a slow fire building up from the dining room. There are coffins on fire, too."

Anabel sits up immediately.

"Let's get Atticus to safety."

"Ardella patched him up with a tourniquet his leg to help with the wound while I looked for supplies."

That's why he's out of breath.

I assist Anabel in standing. When we make it down the hill, something explodes from the back of the house. I yell for Ardella and see her peek her head out the front door.

"We're fine!"

Anabel races over, hugging Ardella before helping to move Atticus outside.

"Whose blood is that?" Arde asks.

"Not mine," Ana says, as Jackson and I take over pulling Atticus near the road. Jackson quickly runs to get the car that we hid behind the large trees across the street.

"Get Atticus to safety and come back. I need to take care of something. Deli can wait here with me," Ana demands.

All of us exchange looks once Jackson steps out of the car to assist me.

"It's okay, I'll stay with her," Arde says.

I sigh with impatient uncertainty. There's not enough room in the car for all of us.

"We'll be back soon. Stay safe and alive," Jack says, and I agree aloud as we get inside the car.

As we pull away, I see the Ardella and Anabel standing in the front looking at the creepy house.

I can't even begin to process any of this shit.

I hold Atticus the whole way to the nearest hospital, making sure he's still alive and breathing. Even with Jackson speeding, it takes an hour to get there.

Now, to make it back to the women before anything else fucked up happens.

CHAPTER 39

"ALL MY GHOSTS COULD FUCKING BURN WITH IT"

ANA

All I feel is numbness. Now that the back of the house is ablaze, I decide to make sure the whole place fucking burns.

All my ghosts can fucking burn with it.

"Will you help me make sure this place stays gone?" I turn and ask Ardella, wondering if she's truly there with me after the events of tonight.

With all the events for weeks and months, I begin to wonder if I'm even real. I'm so disconnected from myself; reality has blurred those lines.

She grabs my hand, "Of course. Anything for you. Besides, I have experience with this…."

My hand tightens on hers, the warmth from her confirming to me that *this is real; she's here.*

Together we venture back inside.

In the den is our first stop, where the matches and flammables are.

"I'll go upstairs first," I say while leaving the room.

"I'm not leaving you alone for a second, Anabel. Where you go, *I go.*"

For the first time in a while, I give her a genuine smile while we make our way hastily up the staircase. We start in the back rooms, setting the curtains and the bedding ablaze. The fire downstairs hadn't made its way past the large dining room yet.

This corpse of a house doesn't want to fucking go down and stay there.

The house is fighting for its life as it makes obnoxious noises, faint wails in the distance and whispers.

Once we make it downstairs, I dare to go back into the large dining room.

The flames are spreading towards the kitchen, and I look reluctantly at the standing coffins of my family staring back at me.

"Ardella, start in the other rooms, please. I know you have more respect than I do for the dead and you don't need to see this…"

She takes a deep breath. "I can make exceptions…"

I shoot her an obvious look.

"The room outside of here is still close by. I'll be done shortly," I reassure her.

Ardella reluctantly agrees, leaving me alone with my family.

I gather the sense that I'm not alone.

My eye is drawn toward a window where I see a shadow zip by.

Great. I'm losing it for real this time.

I close my eyes for a few moments before opening them and see Ansel standing next to our family.

Fuck!

I ignore the rising panic that we're back at the cliff's edge and going over it.

He looks like himself, *but not.* I *saw* him go over the edge. *There's no way he could've survived.*

Sibling blood be damned.

"Great," I begin, grabbing the match and fluid, "now that the family is all together again…"

I move closer, dowsing the coffins in fluid.

"It's sick that you kept our family in the fucking basement."

Ansel says nothing, the closer I get; it takes me longer than I care to admit that his form isn't fully there. An apparition of him is. His face is ghostly and upset, but he almost looks real. With the flames climbing up the tall walls and spreading toward the ceiling, I know I don't have much time left to finish the job.

I'm questioning my own sanity as I toss the fluid on him, too, and it goes right through him.

Okay, he's a full ghost now. Great.

Ansel even looks down and then at me, watching and waiting.

Let's get this over with.

I glance at the corpses in the coffins.

"This time, all of you are going to stay gone. You will not torment me in my dreams or reality. This ends right here, right now!" I say with all of my might, swiping the match.

I shoot Ansel a quick look as he starts toward me the minute I flick the match toward mom and dad.

A weird screech echoes and rattles my bones. *"No!"*

It's his voice, I can hear it as clear as day.

Ansel rushes me, the force knocks me back, but I feel him *go through me.* The sensation takes my breath away.

I must've screamed, because soon the flames are going wild on the coffins, and my vision blurs. My ears become muffled to my surroundings.

I swear I see Ardella standing over me, but then I see shadows screaming until it all goes dark and empty.

E.G.POA

CHAPTER 40

"YOU WILL NOT HAVE HER"

ARDELLA

I can hear muffled sounds from the next room over. I didn't want to leave her alone with those creepy family coffins. I know *I'm* morbid, but even that's a bit too deranged for me.

I quickly light the curtains on fire like in the other rooms.

Then, god-awful screams erupt, and I drop everything to run back into the dining room.

The coffins are on fire, and there are shadows surrounding Anabel on the floor.

I scream and rush to her side as her eyes flutter closed.

What the fuck just happened?

I don't give myself much time to think, only act. Whatever happened, the fire is now spreading faster toward the ceiling and time is limited.

Fuck, fuck!

"Anabel, don't you fucking die on me, bitch!" I plead with her to wake up, while pulling her out of the room and down the long hallway. She's a complete deadweight, but I'm desperate to get her to safety.

"You know I can't do this shit without you! It's you and me!"

The flames seem to *follow* us. The house is alive and rebelling. From one haunted being to another, a spooky lady knows when a place is *off.*

My panic intensifies at the knowledge that the house is after my Ana as adrenaline pumps through me.

The flames and shadows intertwine, reaching for Ana and me.

I scream at them. "You will not have her!"

Crack!

The sounds echo around and above in the foundation. Whispered voices travel with me as I'm nearly to the front door.

"Come on, come on!" I cry out, frantically checking on Anabel. The bitch isn't even awake, and I'm panicking.

"If you die on me now, I'll never forgive you!"

Crying and dragging her by her arms, I find myself so grateful we left the door open. The minute I have her out on the lawn, the house explodes with loud wail that rattles my bones, as if the house cries out one final time.

I hover over Ana to protect her after the explosion, and I wait for the dust to settle before I check on her. With her lack of movement, I'm already shattering at her side.

"I knew I shouldn't have left you," I lean my head on her chest and hug her tight, weeping.

"I can't do this without you," I repeat quietly through my tears.

I listen to the remaining groans of the house dying for who knows how long.

Just when I've nearly given up, Ana jolts and coughs.

"Thank god!" I cry out, hugging her tight the minute I see her eyes open.

She hugs me back weakly.

"It's over," she reassures me once her coughing ceases.

I can feel the heat from the flames engulfing the house; the wails from within cease.

"Come on, let's back up more. I don't trust this place," I urge as we both crawl further away, closer to the road than the house.

I sit behind Ana, holding her tight, afraid to let her go.

"I was so fucking scared, Beli."

She holds my arms as we watch the house burn. As someone who recently burned down my own childhood home, I have experience and satisfaction from the catharsis of it, starting anew. The past doesn't define us, no matter what those paint-peeled walls of history have to say.

I had lost *everything*.

Now, here I am watching Ana go through the same shit.

"Me too, Deli. I never thought I'd see all of you here, even if I hoped and wondered. I thought I'd die in that house. *Again.*"

She shudders, and I hold her tighter. I'm so grateful we made it in the nick of time, too.

We remain like that for a while, holding each other while afraid to take our eyes off the house. Until the roof collapses. Not long after that, a car pulls up behind us. I jump when I hear two doors slam.

Looking to either side of me, I see Roman and Jackson. *What a relief.*

"What the fuck happened?" Roman says while he checks on Anabel and Jackson checks me. Then, the two men trade places to repeat the action.

It softens me to see how they care for Ana, almost as much as I do; they just don't know how to approach a new dynamic.

Ana and I would both eventually have to show them, but first things first. *Getting the fuck away from this place.*

The top floor of the house appears to cave in on itself then.

"I'm assuming you two had something to do with this?" Roman asks, and I nod.

All of us stare at the house, completely engulfed in flames and half sunken.

"Let's leave this place behind willingly," I whisper in Ana's ear.

"Yes, let's," she agrees.

The guys help us both into the car.

I sit in the back with Ana while they ride up front. I hold her to me after we turn around in the seat. She continues looking at the burning house out the back window—for confirmation, I would assume. Once it leaves eyesight, I continue to hold her as she weeps into my neck.

I catch Jackson's eyes in the rearview mirror. Roman even turns to look, the two men exchanging various glances after.

"We aren't leaving you, Ana. You have us. *We* are your family," I say aloud.

She cries harder, clinging to me, and I cry along with her. It hurts me to see her like this. She always wanted her memories back, but at what cost?

I didn't know the full story, but I wouldn't pressure it out of her either. All of us need healing after that ordeal.

There's the matter of Atticus; we needed to make sure he was still stable. Both Ana and I have torn clothes with blood and dirt on them. Our world is in chaos. I don't know what happens after this, aside from a hospital visit, but I don't care. I'm with the people I love. As long as all of us stick together, then all will work out as it should.

Roman and Jackson understand who Ana is to me, and they welcome it as long as she's comfortable.

I love her more than I did myself. While I love Ro and Jack, they are different in ways. Ana and I have history and a past, and we've always been committed to each other. Lovers and friends, not that titles dictate the love given to another person.

We came to each other at a weird time in our lives. We were young and traumatized by our own ghosts. The paths paved weren't completely our doing when we were so inexperienced and trying to find ourselves in our youth and in college.

Either way, I wouldn't want to be anywhere else. I was blinded by my grief for a while after my father passed, and Morella was only dragging me down into the grave.

Ana will always have a place in my life. *My heart, too.*

Who knows what the future holds? Either way, we don't have to go through it alone anymore.

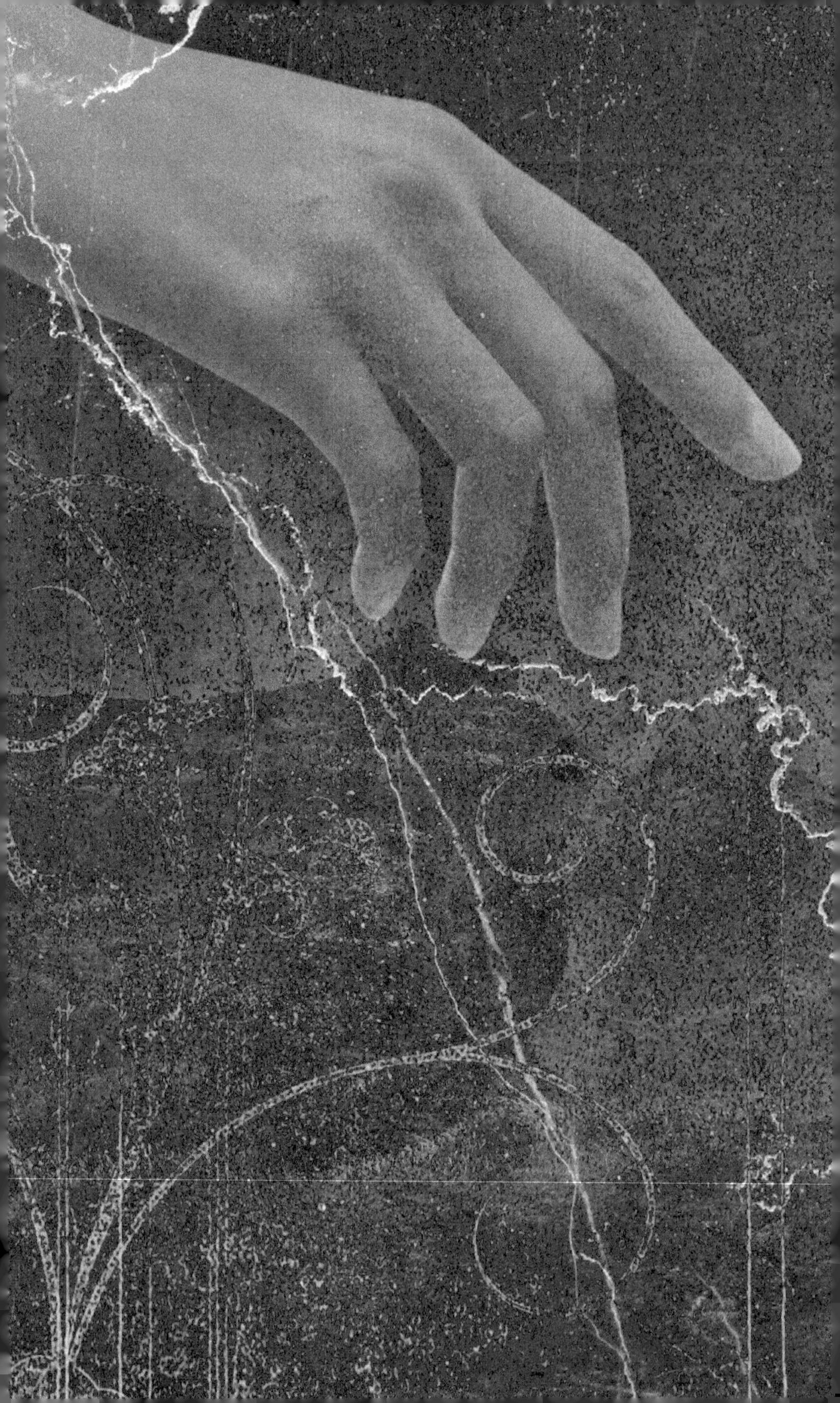

FOREVER AT BEST

City lights and dark sunrises,
While the past gave room for surprises,
This time we're under no guises.

Love is dark and light.
So colorful, not always black or white.
You have to be careful not to hold too tight.

Moments can be too rough.
Pulling and pushing,
reasoning is not enough.
No need to call a bluff.

Freedom is not unattainable.
We go as far as we're able.
Everything is now on the table.

Our souls are entwined,
Destined for greatness down the line.
This love will change in time.

In a fluid way.
So as not to sway,
Come what may.

I am here.
While you are near,
You are free to shed your fears.

All that I am and will always be,
Yours,
Until you'll have me no more.

—E.G. Poa

CHAPTER 41
"I BEGIN ANEW"

Time is a funny thing.

It causes grief and anguish, yet other times it's full of love and honesty. The heart of me is a tidal wave, like the sea from where I came from. Who I was, is no more.

Memories or not, I begin anew.

After being treated at the hospital for smoke inhalation, Atticus had a long recovery period. At first, he didn't say much to me. He needed time to heal, just as I did.

It's my fault he's in this mess. He suffered because of me. Because of my family tree.

Although *they* are no longer, I'm the last remaining member of the House of Lee. I caused the fall and I have no regrets.

It still amazes me that Ardella, Roman, and Jackson arrived in the nick of time. As grateful as I am, I wasn't meant to die on that cliff or in the sea.

Everything happens for a reason, I suppose.

The three of them take turns keeping me company and

giving me space, while we temporarily stay outside of Blackwood until Atticus gets better.

He's been recently transferred to an inpatient facility to help heal his mind. Like me, he has nothing left. No home or family. It feels as if we're back at square one. I don't even know how to start the process of healing when it comes to him. Before he went inpatient, he did mention not hating me because of my traumatizing family, but that he needed time.

The least I can do is respect his space, even if my chest tightens in guilt. The trauma runs blood deep, and we almost didn't make it out of there alive.

Jackson and Roman found a temporary place to live while Atticus worked through his treatment. They graciously let me stay with them and are helping me get back on my feet.

I can't even begin to think about how to repay them both for everything, Ardella, too.

Ardella has hardly left my side these past few months.

There is a rift between all of us, one of my own making, because of my own inner turmoil and guilt. I still carry so much shame, and I couldn't just jump back into bed with the people I carried about most.

We heal in various ways, but I can tell the two men want to do more.

I won't let them—not yet.

I've been dealing with my own wallowing pit of misery. A lot of reflection has gone into these past six months. Even though Ardella is my silent support, and I get that she's trying in her own way, but I know it hurts her to see me so withdrawn like this.

Time is also a fickle thing.

It speeds up and slows down as it pleases. I've been a walking shell for the past six months, though worse off in the beginning due to flashbacks and the nightmares. The nightmares of being back in that haunted place.

Ardella held me close on those nights, if only to drive them away for a little while…

Without telling the others, I slip away to the sea—to the reason I'm here.

The house is barely standing, mere ruins of what it once was. Ansel's body was found days after the fire. *Death by storm, they ruled. Accidental.*

I didn't want anything to do with the ruins of this place nor burials. Ansel was cremated.

How funny life is.

As part of my healing, I find myself walking up that hill willingly. The cliff's edge is a reminder of so much pain, but I need to process and move on. The house fire aided only so much in patching up my memories.

Healing my mind is another story.

Having my memories back is a curse in disguise.

I cannot run anymore or pretend I didn't wash myself in the blood of my family's sins.

You can't run from yourself.

The waves crash below. The moment changes when the sun peeks from behind the clouds. Rays of light trickle in, giving it a heaven-is-coming-down effect.

Looking up, I close my eyes and breathe it all in.

I may not be okay today, or even tomorrow. But that's alright. I will learn to let others in, and together we can work toward a better tomorrow. Whenever Atticus is ready to talk to me, it will be an even better day. But for now, I'll keep at it. I can't give up and let everyone go.

I find my resolve.

So, I vow here on the cliff to myself. *We'll make tomorrow better.*

And live.

CHAPTER 42

"THERE'S NOTHING TO BE SORRY FOR"

JACKSON

The past few months have been uneventful. Ro and I are doing our best to give space to Ana and be supportive, but we can see how Ana's withdrawal is affecting Ardella. Neither of us want to put any pressure, it's clear that awful things happened in that burned down mansion.

Ro and I have been mostly keeping each other company. Tonight, the two of us are cuddling close in bed.

"What are we going to do, Jacky?"

Rubbing his back, I sigh as words fail me. "I'm not sure. You and I both know we can't rush grief and healing. They've been through a lot."

He exhales, nodding. "I know, you're right. I just wish there was something we could do."

The sound of the front door has us both sitting up fast.

After a single glance, the two of us get up to investigate. It takes me two seconds to read the clock on the stand that reads 1:00 AM.

Did Ardella or Anabel leave?

Once we make it to the foyer, I see Anabel in wet clothes, shivering. Thick tears cascade down her cheeks.

Before Ro or I make any moves or say anything, she steps closer to us.

"I'm sorry."

Tilting my head in confusion, I see Ardella standing just out of my periphery, leaning on the doorframe. I'm assuming she was waiting for Ana.

"What are you apologizing for?" It's all I can think to ask at the moment.

"For everything," she replies, stepping toward me first.

Reaching for her cheeks, I wipe her tears. "There's nothing to be sorry for. It's not your fault, Ana." I meant every word.

Her arms tightly wrap around me, and I breathe out in relief. Roman hugs her from behind while she sobs into my chest. For the first time in months, she's allowing all of us in— just when we thought we were losing her.

"It's okay, Ana, we've always been here," I hear Ro whisper at her back.

"We're not going anywhere," I add.

Ardella moves closer, standing at my side and leaning her head on me with silent tears of her own.

All of us stand there until Anabel's tears dry up. I don't care about my wet shirt—only about the crying women.

Ana wipes her eyes, hesitantly meeting my gaze.

"We love you," I say to her, cupping her cheeks and kissing her forehead.

"Had you said those words before, I'm not sure I would've believed you. But I do now," she whispers.

Roman runs his fingers through her hair.

"We'll spend the rest of our lives proving it. We're in this together," Ro speaks so softly and tenderly, I'm reminded of the loveable asshole he is.

Ever since meeting Ardella, we've both grown so much,

from foster brothers to friends, then from friends to lovers. It's why we understand Ardella and Anabel. We know what it's like; only the women didn't hesitate for years to admit feelings for one another or wait to fuck like Ro and me.

Roman takes a step back, kissing Ardella's cheek before coming to the other side of me.

Ana and Ardella gaze intensely at each other with teary eyes, a moment of acceptance passing over them both before hugging each other. I feel Ro's hand settle on my hip as he lays his head on my shoulder. None of us were expecting this moment, but we're so glad it's happening.

Leaning my head against Roman's, we watch the women kiss and hold each other, whispering words of forgiveness. Ana apologized for leaving Ardella abruptly and added her own reassurance.

"Are you both open to coming to bed with us? No funny business, just let us hold you both and sleep." I speak first, and Roman nods in agreement.

They slowly look at us, accepting our proposal. Ana's hair is dark while Ardella's is light, a fun combination every time I look upon them both. They both exude light and dark, even if their personas show otherwise when they stand next to each other.

I reach for their hands and lead them into the primary bedroom with a bed big enough for all of us and then some.

Ardella grabs a night slip for Ana from the closet. Roman and I strip out of our wet shirts. We keep our pajama bottoms on while Ardella crawls into bed. Roman crawls in behind her, but not before giving her a long kiss.

Moving to the other side of the bed, I hold open the covers for Ana. She glances at them before looking at me.

"You're shivering and cold, let us warm you up. You never have to do things you don't want to but know you're ours to protect and love."

Ana nods simply before climbing in. I catch Roman

smiling at me while Ardella's golden eyes water in appreciation.

I slide in behind Ana once she scoots closer to Ardella. All of us adjust and settle in more comfortably.

Roman whispers, "We missed you both."

My arm wraps around Ana, as she curls into both Ardella and me.

Eventually, we fall asleep, and everything begins to feel alright. And even if it wasn't, I know it will be someday.

CHAPTER 43
"AND SO IT SHALL BE"

ANA

When I wake up, I'm surrounded by warmth. After that night down memory lane from my childhood home, I haven't left their side.

Each night, we'd take turns sleeping in various positions. Sometimes Ardella and I would be in the middle or on the outside. It varied. All three of them work so hard to make me feel loved and valued.

This morning during breakfast, I look up from my clean plate. "Can I ask something?"

This feels weird to ask.

They glance up from their plates to look at me and then each other.

"What is it?" Ardella asks first.

I awkwardly run my fingers through my hair.

Jack adds, "Whatever it is, we're here. You should know you can ask us anything."

It takes a moment to gather my thoughts and words. "I know you three are together, and I've joked before about whether you needed a fourth... Yet, so much has happened since. I know things are improving as of late, but what does that mean for the future?"

There. I said it.

Ardella and Ro exchange a secret smile. Jack moves his chair next to mine.

His pretty eyes distract me as he leans closer. "What do you want it to mean?"

"Well…" I can't form the right words again.

Jackson tilts my chin up. "Say the words."

I swallow, my mouth suddenly feeling parched. Warmth travels down my spine, settling in my belly. I haven't wanted to play for some time now, but here, in this moment, I find it's changing. Parts of myself are slowly molding together—all the little, broken pieces I thought I lost. I can put those pieces together how I see fit. No one can take that from me again.

"If there's room for me," I begin, hearing the other two get up, but not daring to look away from Jackson. I can't remember how his or Roman's lips feel.

"Keep going," I hear Roman say from behind me.

Breathing in and out slowly, I say what I mean and mean what I say. "If there's *still* room for me, there's no one else I'd rather be with for the rest of my life. Whether Atticus decides to have a future with me or not, I'll always love him… I want to call you all *mine.*"

Jack smiles and rubs my back. "Good girl. And so it shall be," he says before claiming my lips in a needy kiss—one that speaks to how much he missed me and how much he held back for my sake.

I want to cry at their feet.

There were times I doubted deserving them, but that came from a place of grief. Now, I'm realizing they are the ones I needed all along.

I moan into Jack's mouth, as he cups the back of my head and deepens the lovely kiss.

"The answer is," I hear Ardella say from beside us,

causing me to pull away from Jack to gaze into her bright yellow eyes. "All of us always agreed that when and if you were ready, we'd welcome you with open arms. You should know you'll always be my girl."

My eyes water over her words before she claims my lips next.

"Don't forget about me," Roman pipes up.

We break away, giggling his words.

I twist around to meet Ro's waiting, luscious lips. He takes my hand after we part and tugs me away from the group.

"Let's show her," he suggests before leading me into the bedroom.

I'm flush and warm, feeling more exposed than ever.

When all of us had our fun before, I wasn't fully *me*, but now I am after all is said and done.

Standing at the foot of the bed, Ro pulls the slip over my head.

Pairs of lips begin to find their way across my skin.

I look down briefly, seeing Ardella kiss her way up my thigh while Jack kisses my shoulder.

They're both naked as I watch; Roman strips, too. His cock springs from his clothes, and a core memory of it being in my mouth reminds me of who or what I've missed.

Roman and I are similar in temperament, while Jackson complements other parts of me. Ardella, well, she's the full package as well, especially with our long-standing history. Together we bring new and old things to the table, and together we continue to be loved and cherished.

I lick my lips, rejoicing in the soft lips roaming my skin. Roman steps forward, claiming my lips more hungrily this time around, while cupping the back of my head.

A slender, helping hand makes her way toward my pussy. All sensation comes rushing back. The sensations of what I love about sex. The touches, the feeling of heat, and *the orgasms.*

Roman's cock is poking me, and Jackson's hand moves to stroke him. Ro's hands are in my hair, devouring my mouth as if it'll be the last thing he does. Ardella's hand teases my clit.

Ro and I share a moan and make room between us without letting go.

Ardella tells me to lift my leg, and I put it over her and Jack's shoulders.

Her devilish tongue is almost too much.

Jackson is sucking Roman off, and I'm so turned on by the sounds of my favorite people offering all their pleasures.

Roman's arm settles behind me to keep me afloat, and I find my gaze drifting onto all three of them.

"Come for us," Deli whispers as I swell, knowing what's heading for me.

Ro pulls his lips away to curse, and I see Jackson's mouth full of him.

"I'm about to cum, Jack! *Fuck, just like that.*"

Seeing Ro cup his head only makes me come faster with how adorable they are together.

I hold Ardella's head to my pussy as she licks up all I've given her. I tilt my head back, crying out, and my legs shake.

Just when I think I'm done, I fall back onto the bed. Opening my eyes and heavily breathing, Jackson lines his cock up, teasing where I'm already soaked. Ardella drops beside me, kissing me briefly, and I taste myself. *Fuck me.*

Then she spreads her legs, moaning at Roman licking up where she's waiting. I open myself up more, using my legs to pull him closer.

He gives me this to-die-for, sexy smile.

"Come here, so we can make up for lost time," I say in a sultry tone I don't recognize.

Jackson slides in, stretching me good. His cock hits me deep, and I arch upward with a moan of delirious pleasure.

I've missed dick. I definitely missed Ardella's sweet pussy, too.

I look toward the woman herself, whose eyes are on mine.

"After he gets some, then I want you on my face," I tell her.

She nods before moaning and claiming my lips. Jack's face hovers until we finish kissing. He flips me over, hitting me deeper inside. My head spins and my sex drive is back in full force.

He tugs my hair, and I'm gone after that.

"Come all over this cock," he says to me, my face contorting into another rising sensation.

Ardella cries out, shaking next to me as my pussy obeys Jack's command.

"Fuck. Keep squeezing me, and I'll be filling you up soon, baby."

I melt over his words, and he soon has me on my back once more. I'm so sensitive from coming and find Ardella moving towards my face.

She gives me a sweet smile before kissing me upside-down. Then, I tell her to bring her pussy over. Roman watches us as she does. I groan at how deliciously wet she is. I'm in heaven. My hands cup her ass as she rides my face. I'm full of cock and pussy. It tastes so fucking sweet.

Glancing up, I see Ardella with her head tossed back with her mouth agape, in constant moans. I tease around her clit, licking up her labia until I begin my assault by sucking.

Roman crawls into bed, claiming our girl's lips.

His dick is hard again, and I can't help but tease him with my other hand. Deli assists me in teasing him, and once I get her off, I'm going to tease Roman.

To my delight, it doesn't take her long as I suck and lick in a constant rhythm.

"Oh my God, Ana," she grips my head, and we let Ro's cock hang there for a minute while she rides my face, wetting it with her cum.

Jack is still fucking me in slow strides, but part of me

thinks he's enjoying the show and doesn't want this to be a quick ordeal. *Which I'm fine with.*

I bring her through her twitching, until she falls beside me with heavy breaths.

"Got her warmed up for me, Jacky?"

I see him nod while I lick Ardella's juices off my face.

God, I love this. What better way to celebrate than all of us making love to each other?

Ro's dark eyes are on me as Jack pulls out, and I gasp, feeling empty without him.

"How's she taste, Ardella?" Jack asks her.

She sucks on him for a moment before pulling away. "Tastes like my favorite meal," she says with a grin, and my pussy is throbbing.

I sit up partially watching Roman move closer, teasing my nipples with his tongue.

Biting my lip, his cock is soon within me, and I don't feel so empty now. He pulls me up, my breast falling out of his mouth with a pop. I wrap my legs and arms around him and let him pick me up.

Staking my claim on his lips that taste like Ardella, I moan into his mouth. He sits us down on the bed, so that I can straddle him.

Ardella is getting fucked on the other side of the bed, and I love how pleasurable all of this is. *I've missed being like this with them.*

Roman's arms are around me tight as our tongues lick and tease. My skin is clammy and sweaty, and I'm so swollen and needy. I hold him to me in turn, and it all clicks within me.

I'm supposed to be here with them. My destiny is with *them.*

I move my hips in sync with Ro's, a rhythm of our own. While we fucked before plenty of times, this time is different. All of us have declared where we stand.

My heart and cunt are so full, I love every second.

For I have a home in them, no matter what happens.

If that isn't love, then I don't know what is.

CHAPTER 44

"YOU SHOULD ALWAYS LIVE FOR YOU"

ANA

"Miss Lee, this is what you are owed as the last remaining member of your family. Your inheritance."

The lawyer hands me a check with an absurd amount of money that makes my head spin.

I just want to be done with this shit already.

"I don't want this," I say without thinking.

Ardella tugs my hand, giving me a look and shaking her head.

I grumble. "Fine. Is that all?"

The lawyer shakes his head, digging into a folder.

"There are two more things. The first being a check for the damage to your home and to start anew."

What? That house isn't mine.

I nearly fell out of my chair, at the amount for the *house*. I've never seen so many zeros before.

Are they fucking kidding?

"The last thing?" I dare to ask.

I'm so glad Ardella is with me for this today.

"There's a deed to a house some ways away. Valerie left it

in her last will and testament. She recently passed away from leukemia."

My eyes water, and I look at the deed.

"Why would she give this to me?" I squeak.

Ardella rubs my hand for comfort.

The guy put on his glasses to read something on a sheet of paper.

"Please give the house deed to Anabel Lee, a dear friend of mine from my youth. Then, she left an unopened letter with your name on it. The second property is lovely, Miss."

I take the letter, tucking it to my chest and letting my tears fall, not understanding why or what one my first loves from my youth was thinking.

Val is too young to go like this.

Ardella hugs me as she whispers consoling words.

"Thank you," I say aloud.

The lawyer nods, "That is all I have, Miss Lee. Good luck."

I say nothing and grab the letter and deed paperwork before leaving.

Ardella falls in line beside me as we walk down the steps of his office.

I'm in shock and utterly speechless.

"Can I have a minute to read the letter?" I ask Ardella as Jack and Ro pull up with the car.

She rubs my back. "Take your time, we'll wait as long as you need."

With a quick peck on the cheek, she meets with them and informs them on what's going on.

I take the envelope out of the folder with shaky hands.

My Dearest Ana,

I hate that this is the last thing you receive from

me, but if you somehow get this letter, wherever you ended up, it means I am gone.

Please, do not grieve me. Remember the good times, and know I am not suffering with this sickness any longer. You'll be pleased to know life did improve.

After leaving Arnheim, I completed school and met an agreeable man. I told him all about you, and how cherished you will always be, even if I am to never gaze upon your lovely face again. I accepted that when I left Arnheim. We were on other continents, so it was unlikely I would.

We got married and had two children. We have two estates, so they are not without a home, and he has family to help take care of them when I'm gone. When our vacation home was purchased, I told my husband my intent. I know with how our lives started out and how we came to Arnheim wasn't good. Atticus and I were your only family for a time. It may seem odd, but I wanted to give you a home, even at Arnheim, I felt that way.

I'm not sure if you ever regained your memories, but I hope, either way, that you are happy now. I always felt you deserved more in life. You were never an empty, blank slate, but a girl who needed more love and care than what she was given. Even though we haven't seen each other in some years, my feelings for you never went away. That's how much I love you.

I hope with all my might you are happy and healthy now. That when you continue forward in life, you can do so in this home I've bestowing you. My final gift to you.

When you roam these halls and this beautiful lush greenery, I want you to feel me in spirit and all the love I poured into this home. Yes, I made it my own home, too, but once I was diagnosed, I made necessary changes with you in mind.

You deserve a home, too, Ana, and whether you have one or not, I hope you can make good use of this place just as I did. Just like people, buildings are full of energy. We feed into these environments and places. Home doesn't have to be a place of pain and sorrow, but of beauty and love.

Even though we had a short amount of time together in our youth, you made a lifetime impression. I'm sure you already know you were my first love. This is a gift of that.

I had great years with my husband. For a while, I regretted not being able to see you again, which is why I started scheming, as you know I like to do, and I came up with this plan instead.

I know Atticus and I meant a lot to you, and I give you full permission to make space here for him. I expect no matter where he is, you are on his mind, equally so. I hope you get married and make a life, or whoever else, of course. Maybe my hopes are too big? You could be different people now. How would I ever know?

Either way, the home is yours to do with what you will. I do hope you keep it and make a life for yourself here even if it is far away.

As I always told you, we are in charge of our destinies. You should always live for you.

I'll see you on the other side someday.

I love you,
Val

I'm not sure how long I've been crying, yet I continue to reread Val's letter again and again. I have no words to express my love and gratitude. If it weren't for Val, I wouldn't know the capabilities of human emotion, and how big my heart is for people. I owe a lot to her.

I'm glad she made her way in the world after Arnheim and lived with all her might.

Still, I can't stop my heart from breaking over how sad this shit is. At such a shitty realization, I sob harder and hear doors close before warm bodies sit beside me. I let them comfort me and wonder what I did in this life to deserve the care I'm receiving. I'm not this sad, empty vessel that I thought I was. My memories didn't make me less of a person, just a person who had to get up again and again. I'll keep doing so as often as I need to, so I can be who I'm meant to be. The location doesn't matter as long as I have my partners.

CHAPTER 45

"ATTICUS"

The facility stands in front of me. I can't deny my nervousness about the possibility of going in and being rejected. I'm not sure if the boy I love is still there. I spent the past week preparing myself for whatever he decides.

He's been away from me for so fucking long. A week ago, Roman and Jackson got a call that Atticus is being released. They asked various questions, I'm sure, but I didn't have it in me to ask *what*. The place had asked that I come alone to pick him up. I haven't been able to make out why, but it scares me endlessly. Who knows what's in his mind now or if he wants anything to do with me. Is he ashamed or regretful like I was for so long about my fucked up family?

The last time I saw him, Atticus was nearly murdered by my psychotic brother, and I can't even fathom the trauma he endured before then while locked in the basement with *corpses for company*. The image of him in the basement is engrained in me forever, along with the sorrow of knowing it was all my fault.

Go inside, Anabel. No matter what, you have to respect his decision.

I take a few deep breaths and slowly make my way inside the building. After signing in, I'm pointed to the waiting room, while Atticus signs discharge paperwork and gathers his belongings.

As I wait, I chew on my lip and stare out of a window. I can't sit still and I'm full of buzzing, nervous energy. The anticipation is almost too much.

Jackson had let me borrow the car and said to call the landline if I needed anything. It took some convincing to get Ardella on board, as she is old fashioned with technology.

In the time Atticus was here, all four of us have grown so close; we are nearly inseparable.

I know I'll have to explain it all to Atticus; but first things first, *seeing him again.* Maybe then I'll find out what he wants to do with the rest of his life or if he wants me in it at all.

A door clicks and opens, and I wait with bated breath before turning to see if it's him. I'm in the lobby alone, so I can only assume.

My eyes water when I confirm it is. Atticus stands there taking me in, while I do the same. He only has a small bag in his hand.

His blue eyes are clearer than I've ever seen them. He looks healthy and similar to what I remember; Only, he's a few years older, refined, and dare I say, more beautiful than ever before.

He inches closer until he's a couple of feet away from me.

"Can we go somewhere private and talk?"

I nod, trying to ignore the sinking sensation in my abdomen. Whatever is about to be said, it probably won't be what I want to hear. Regardless, I need to be ready to listen no matter what the outcome is.

Holding the door open for him, we leave for the car.

"Are you hungry or anything?"

"I'm fine, Ana. Is there a park nearby or something?"

I swallow hard. "Yes."

Reeling my tears back inside me, we get in the car. I drive us for ten minutes, in suffocating silence, to a quiet, nature park that I often find myself roaming around for a fresh perspective.

The day is surprisingly nice. Atticus looks freshly groomed in pants and a button up shirt. I tried to put in effort with a forest green dress and simple, low-effort makeup. Ardella helped me get ready hours ago, and the three of them kissed me goodbye and wished me luck. Roman and Jackson tried to encourage me the best they could, but my guilt was eating me alive.

The ride over was silent and uncomfortable for me. I wanted to say how sorry I was for how he suffered at my expense and that I'll regret it for the rest of my life.

That he almost died because of me.

That's been my hardest pill to swallow.

I park the car, and he gets out before me. I'm unsure if he's upset by how quickly he leaves the car.

My heart sinks.

Only after two deep breaths do I get out, too.

He's standing there with his eyes closed, face turned toward the sunlight.

I'm afraid to get too close to him, in the event he's done with me after this walk in the park.

"It feels nice to be out in the open air again. In complete freedom."

Unsure on what to say, I don't speak.

I let him have his continued moments of silence in the sunlight, trying my best to remain as calm as possible.

"I can feel your tension all the way over here; breathe," he says calmly, opening his handsome eyes and looking at me from the side.

"I can't help it," I say while he sighs heavily.

"Before you get ahead of yourself, I want you to know first that I don't blame you for anything."

"You should!" I choke out, and the emotions I held back rise to the surface.

He runs a hand through his freshly cut hair.

"You almost died because of me. Because of *my* family drama. It had nothing to do with you, but you got dragged in because I loved you. Because I hung on."

Tears flow down my face.

"Not you. *Him.* Did you tie me in the basement with corpses for company? Did you kidnap me against my will? Did you try to kill me?"

I wipe my eyes. "No, but—"

"It's not your fault. Blaming yourself doesn't help anything. *You are not your brother.*"

"How can you look at me and say that? We were siblings."

He's gazing at me now, and with the look on his face, I can't tell if he hates me or not. I wish I knew what was on his mind.

"Walk with me, Ana." He inclines his head away from the car toward a walking trail.

I follow him down the path and into silence, until he stops at a large tree by a creek and leans against it. I cross my arms, holding myself. There's some distance between us, but it's only by a few feet.

"You know, in the beginning I worked through it in my mind, but never once did I blame you. I blamed myself for being so gullible. Your brother was very persuasive."

Tell me about it.

"He took advantage of my grief from my uncle's death. He knew how to lure me with the promise of you. The psychopath won."

While choking on my tears, I hear him shuffle, but he doesn't comfort me. Instead, he exhales and stares into the water near his feet.

"Until you came down into the dark with me."

Wiping my eyes and more than likely smearing my

makeup, I wondered what the fucking point was for the effort in my appearance just for me to cry it down my face.

Blue gems observe me, his hands casually in his pockets.

"I've never been more scared in my life than when you left. He was so deranged, I wondered how you could possibly be related and share DNA."

He doesn't know how often I saw Ansel in the mirror for the first couple of months after the night I thought I lost Atticus.

"Then, he scrubs me down, cuts my hair, and shaves my face. I thought he was going to kill me the entire time. He wanted me to see that he won, so he glued my lips shut and tried to make me watch you marry him."

I kneel down, sobbing and pulling at my hair before placing my head in my hands. I feel like I'm reliving that dreadful night, about to lose him all over again.

"I've never been prouder of you than when you kicked your grandfather into the fire and stabbed your brother."

He walks over toward me, gazing down as I glance up at him through blurred vision.

"You and your friends saved my life. I thought I lost you, too." He kneels down in front of me, cupping my cheek.

"I thought I was going to die, Atti. The same cliff that brought you to me was almost my finality. I owe everything to the three of them," I whisper.

"As do I," he says softly, rubbing my tears away with his thumb. "Once I was told you were fine, I sunk into myself after I recovered. I wasn't at my best, and I needed to heal and grieve. I still never grieved my family's loss, and then it all added up, so I had to go away for a while."

My eyes don't stop leaking, and I'm so broken up over his revelations.

"I don't know if you know this, but over the past month, I was able to chat with Jackson and Roman. They are nice gentlemen. I can tell they care about you. Ardella, too."

They talked to him more in depth and didn't tell me?

I frown and his other hand cups my other cheek, making me meet his eyes.

"I told them not to tell you anything."

"I'm confused. Why did you speak to them?"

He chuckles, and I'm thrown off.

"To thank them for one, but to also check in on you."

I huff, and he stands, offering his hand to me. I take it, rising and dusting myself off.

"I still don't understand, Atticus. You didn't want to speak to me? Are you...*done* with me forever?" My throat feels like it's closing.

I hear him take a deep breath, but he's still holding my hands in his. My heart can't take it anymore.

"I could have been, but then I wouldn't be here talking to you. I needed time to figure out the right words and say my peace before I leave."

Oh, no.

"L-leave?"

He nods. "Leave *with you*. If you'll still have me."

I smack his arm, and he startles.

"I thought you were going to say it was over, you ass!"

Beginning again, I cry, only this time it's pent up emotional release and happiness.

"Did you forget my promise, Annie?"

He takes both of my hands and tucks them into his chest, standing close and leaning his forehead to mine.

"Promise?"

"That I'd always come back for you, even if we had to part for a while."

I hiccup and throw my arms around him, sobbing. Holding me back tightly, he continues. "I never stopped loving you. I'll keep loving you until our time is up. Ardella mentioned your relationships last month, so I had time to prepare myself, and I told her my intentions and how I look forward to meeting them again."

That damn, Ardella. I'm going to get her back for this! With a kiss or two.

"And what are your intentions?"

"To marry you and love you until our time is up."

"Until our time is up?"

He grabs my face and kisses me hard.

"Yes, silly woman. You're stuck with me for the rest of your life. So, yes, until death. *Until our time is up.*"

I smile, kissing him. *Finally.*

"Until our time is up," I say with confidence.

EPILOGUE
ONE

ANA

It's not awkward at all when Atticus and I return home. I give them the stink eye under my mess of makeup to which they hug me for, and I pinch Ardella for plotting against me.

"Ouch!"

"Don't hide things from me again, you whore!"

The men giggle over my choice of words as Arde hugs me.

"You love me, slut."

"You're lucky I do, baby," I say before kissing her deeply.

Roman clears the air for Atticus.

"We have the rooms packed up and ready to move."

"Move?" Atticus asks while we walk into the kitchen.

"We're not staying here in Blackwood. We're going far away, starting anew with all five of us—if you're open to it," I mention to him while handing over Val's letter to me.

He opens it, confused at first, before realizing the context.

I see his eyes water, pulling me into his hold once he finishes.

"I'm so sorry, Annie. I know how much she meant to you, and she was a good friend to me, too."

I sniff, hugging him tight, overjoyed by the fact that he's still here with me.

"Well, I can't wait to start over," he says, and I agree.

"Blackwood has taken enough from me and most certainly, enough fucking time," I mention bitterly.

"Cheers to that," Ardella says, handing everyone shots of liquor.

"Before we leave, can I request something from you, Annie?"

I see the others exchange glances, and I look around to see Jackson pass Roman something to Atticus.

We take our shots of liquor first, and when I make a face, I blink, finding Attius kneeling in front of me.

"Marry me, Annie." My mouth falls open, the sight of him unreal in front of me.

I glance from him to the others until my eyes finally land on Ardella.

"Tell him, *yes*, bitch!"

"Yes, bitch!" I shake my head, remembering who I should be addressing before turning to Atticus abruptly with an apologetic awkward smile.

"Yes, Atti."

He slides the blue gem on my finger, one that looks like his eyes.

Atticus stands, picking me up and claiming my mouth with his.

"Bedroom is that way," Ro jokes, and Atticus grins.

"Let's consummate early," Atticus says, carrying me off.

"Can we watch?" Ro shouts back as we disappear.

"Not this time!" He echoes back, kicking the door closed behind him.

"I look terrible, you sure you want to do this now?" I question as he drops me on the bed, slowly unbuttoning his shirt.

"No more stalling, I need you like I need air to breathe and blood in my veins to survive."

My mouth falls open as he lifts my dress, kissing up my thighs.

"Oh," I say, half-leaning on my arms, and watching his head disappear before he pushes the dress to my waist.

"Fuck, I've missed this," he says, licking up and down my slit.

"O-oh."

I lay completely flat on my back, pulling my dress over my head.

"You're as perfect as ever, Annie."

"I've missed hearing that from you," I say, running my fingers through his hair.

"You don't have to miss it anymore. I'll say it every day for the rest of my life, and until we're old and gray."

"I'll take it," I say, right before I moan when he starts devouring my clit.

He does this thing where he'll suck it between his teeth and lick at the same time with the tip of his tongue. *It drives me wild every time.*

It doesn't take me long to shake under him as he plays with my breasts.

I hear a groan as I come, arching my back off the bed like I've resurrected. Atticus has a knack for it, after all.

"That sound is *my* favorite," he says, licking his lips before unbuttoning his pants and taking them off.

"You know I'm a needy sex addict, so I plan to wear you and the others out."

"I look forward to it," he says, pushing inside me slowly until reaching the hilt.

"I'm going to put a baby into you first. However many you want after that is your choice. *First one is mine.*"

Feeling him deep, finally after so many years without him, I pull him down with me, claiming him with my legs wrapped around him and my breasts pressed tight into his chest.

"Anything for you, Atti," I say before a moan escapes, and

I kiss him hard and desperately. The missing piece to my heart. No longer gone from me. *He's finally here.*

His pace increases, as we make love like rabbits. First, on my back, then bent over the bed, nice and deep, before riding him to the finish line.

When I come, I come *hard*. I see stars speckling my vision, and I can't help but cry.

Atticus sits up and hugs me.

"Shh, it's okay. I'm not going anywhere. I'm here with you."

"Until our time is up?" I ask as he holds my face with a nod; all the love shines through those blue pools of his soul.

"Of course. Until our time is up."

FIVE MONTHS LATER

Val was right, the house is beautiful, and so is the property it's on. Large green trees adorn the area, with a small forest located beyond the house. There's a manmade lake in the forest, and the home is large and open. It's lightly colored, Victorian while being cozy and elegant.

It's not dark and depressing, and there's a positivity exuding from the walls within.

I feel you here, Val.

Part of me wonders if she died here or in the hospital. Either way, I wouldn't mind. It's one ghost I wouldn't mind haunting me.

I rub my slightly swollen belly. It took longer to move than we originally planned.

We made it, after all, Val.

My mind remembers her as I knew her, and the precious gift she passed on to me.

Atticus stands beside me, kissing my cheek.

"Ready to live the rest of our lives here, wife of mine?"

I grin, gushing over his flattery.

"Always."

Ardella walks between Roman and Jackson. She just found out she's pregnant, too, so we'll be raising our kids together in one home, surrounded by so much love.

I didn't think it was possible to be so happy, but they continue to surprise me.

EPILOGUE

TWO

ATTICUS — TWO YEARS LATER

Our house is growing by the numbers.

After baby one with Ana, Roman and Jackson fought over who was next. I've never seen them so excited to be dads, but it was a good look for them. Roman won the battle, impregnating Ana afterwards.

I was third in line for Ardella, and we worked hard together to love one another and raise our kids in a home better than what we experienced and lost.

Our healing took time, but each of our relationships is made better because of it.

Loving them is easy and fulfilling. Ana and I may be married, but I don't love the others any less.

Ardella and I are similar to how Roman and Ana act around each other, and Jackson is, well, *Jackson.* A league of his own that meshes and molds well with the rest of us. The icing on the layers of the cake.

So Ardella felt included, all of us bought her a ring to wear, a black sapphire that suited her morbid and beautiful writer mind.

She still picked up her pen every now and then.

Once the kids are tucked in bed, we all collapse on ours, in our large master bedroom. We recently remodeled the bathroom to hold all of us in one tub, a good investment if you ask me.

"Shall we work on more baby-making?" Roman asks, and the rest of us chuckle.

"Such a family man," I comment as Ana reaches up to caress his face.

"You're a good daddy, but let Jackson take care of this one," she says with a sly smirk, cupping and rubbing him.

Ro groans before dipping his face down to claim Ana's lips.

"Come here, Daddy Jack," Ana coos, and I point my finger to Ro once he looks at me. Ardella is lying on the edge, looking up with me.

Jack and Ro switch places.

"Want to compete for kid three?" I tease him as he stalks around the bed and steals a kiss from Ardella first before moving onto me.

Ardella recently found out she's pregnant with number three, *and he's mine.*

"You two are ridiculous. This body can only birth so many kids."

Ro and I chuckle as I sink to my knees and tease him.

"This is a good place for you," he says to me, and I tug his pants down and take him into my mouth.

I never thought I'd like dick so much, but when I observed Roman and Jackson together, that changed. Ardella and Ana worked on making me comfortable, too. I can't deny how sexy the men are, in such that it made me want to be a part of it. I could see their love for each other, and it didn't take me long to become involved.

I hum and fondle his balls before sucking on one, then I hold my finger for Ardella to suck on. I've done this to him before, and it's one of his favorite things.

She grins, making sure my finger is nice and soaked. Then, I sink it into his ass, teasing him before I do.

"Oh, fuck." His hand goes into my hair, scrunching it as I finger his ass and suck his cock.

I can tell I'm driving him crazy as he tries to fuck my face, but he gets distracted by *my* fucking. When he comes, he comes in cute spurts, spilling down my throat. *Goddamn, he tastes sinful.*

"Come here, Daddy Atticus," Ardella beckons, her legs opening for me as I stand up.

"My ass is yours," I tell Ro as she goes over to Ana and Jackson.

Jackson is standing while he fucks my wife from behind.

I can't deny how much I love watching her get fucked from this angle, with her mouth open and crying out. Roman stands behind Jack, teasing him and kissing him. Getting distracted, I meet Ardella's gold eyes.

"Sorry, momma bear," I say, spitting on my dick and enjoying how she scoots closer to the edge of the bed for me.

"I love it when you call me that. *Daddy bear.*"

"You're so horny when you're pregnant, I love it," I praise her, sliding home and leaning down to kiss her.

"I'm so happy to birth all of these kids and have you all," she says, her eyes watering.

"I agree with her," Ana barely gets out, and I can't help but chuckle before she begins moaning more unsteadily, meaning she's close to coming.

My strokes slow, and I gaze upon her.

"You are beautiful, darling. It's *we* who are lucky to have *you.* You and Annie deserve all the best things. Just as Jack and Ro do. All of us deserve the happiness we bring to each other."

"You make me hard when you say sweet shit," Ro pipes up, and I catch Jack and Ana smiling at me right before she comes.

"Come here and fuck me then," I taunt.

When he returns to my side, I get his dick wet quickly before sliding back inside Ardella.

"Lean forward, baby," he says to me and I do, opening myself to him. He prepares my rear to receive him.

"I love you," Ardella whispers to me.

"I love you, darling," I say sweetly, kissing her before looking up and winking at my sexy wife, who smiles back at me.

"And I love this ass," Ro says before I chuckle, and it's cut off by his dick easing in my ass.

"Fuck, right where I want to be."

I groan at the bliss of his stretch, and we find an easy rhythm.

Jackson is soon coming into my wife, and her face is blissful when he does.

I smile down at Ardella. "Want to taste them?" I ask her.

"Fuck, yes."

After a quick kiss. I stand tall and pump slowly while Roman tortures me further with his love and gentleness.

He sucks on my neck, and I see my wife facing me while sitting on Ardella's face.

Jackson strolls over to tease the two of us, taking turns kissing me and Ro.

My soul is beyond overjoyed and happy. A sense of elation falls over me every time we have sex and express our affections.

Once Jackson and Roman kiss, I look at my pregnant wife. Her bump is small, but she's as beautiful as she always is.

"Come here, lovely," I whisper to her, leaning forward and groaning as Roman continues to fuck me.

She does, her glassy bedroom eyes sorting out my heartbeats.

"I love you," I say to her before I steal a precious kiss.

She meets my gaze, repeating our words, "Until our time is up."

I smile at her before she comes.

"Come here, beautiful, I'm not done with you," Jackson says before fucking her again.

"My poor pussy," she complains briefly before a pleasured noise escapes her.

"What was that?" He asks, leaning down to kiss her.

I find Ardella staring up at me.

"I'm about to come, Atticus," I hear Ro say, and I wink at Arde.

"One sec, lovely," I say to her as he fills me up with a blushing moan.

He pulls out and kisses me hard.

"Alright, go on and fuck her senselessly. She's waited patiently," he teases, crawling into bed to kiss her before he goes and showers.

"Let me taste those lips first," I say to her, doing so.

She moans into my mouth, as I increase my pacing.

Anabel and Jackson are on her lips, and it drives me wild.

I love tasting all of us on one another's tongues.

My hand slides down to toy with her clit, and because I had edged her for so long, she comes within seconds, shattering in my arms.

Then, I stuff her full of me, joining in our shared delights. I hold her to me, letting us both catch our breaths.

"Wanna shower?" I offer, and she nods, stealing my lips.

"Then sleep?" She asks, and I agree immediately.

I help her up, and we join Ro in the shower, enjoying another round with each other before finishing and crawling into bed. Ana and Jackson finish as we do and take a shower, too.

Once all of us are tucked in, I drift into a cozy sleep along-side the people I love. Just where we belong, surrounding ourselves with warmth and the love we share toward one another.

THE END

Acknowledgments

Firstly, thank you to my beta readers and ARC readers for reading and reviewing, and my two partners for listening to me babble on.

It's because of you that I keep going, and my undying gratitude doesn't feel like it's enough.

Thank you to Colby, for your cover skills and formatting skills and my last minute changes even though I'm pretty sure you want to strangle me over it. I have undying love for you, and I'm grateful you put up with me for all these years!

To Amy, for putting up with me and my freakouts when something implodes or if I need to pick her brain.

To E.M. Lee for being my last minute editor on demand (LOL), I couldn't have done this without you and I have millions of kisses to give you

To Adam, listening to complain about deadlines and school intertwining with this release, and for loving this human disaster.

And last, but certainly not least, thank you to YOU, the reader, who picked up this book and made it to this point. Edgar Allan Poe isn't for everyone, and Anabel Lee deserved to have her story told separately from Poa even though both books intertwine.

Until next time, Preylings ♡

ALSO BY R. N. ARCADIA

The Para-Series

Parasite

Para-Psych

Triad Bite Series

Into the Black

Into the Red

Into the Blue

Into the Fire

Standalones

Pod

Lee

The Misfortunes of Tommelise

Granite & Sugar

Horns Trilogy

Horns & Heat

Horns & Flames

About the Author

R.N. Arcadia is a neurodivergent, day-dreaming Pisces. They live in New Jersey with her family. When R.N. isn't writing or working, they enjoy traveling, going to the beach, binge-watching/binge-reading whatever series they find themselves engrossed in, and listening to all sorts of music to stay sane.

https://linktr.ee/r.n.arcadia